# Trespasser

## Book One of THE LIBERATOR Trilogy

Phillip Jay

Copyright © 2023 by Phillip Jay

All rights reserved.

# Table of Contents

THE LIBERATOR ............................................. 1
BOOK ONE: TRESPASSER ............................. 2
Preface: ............................................................ 3
PART ONE: BATTLESLEEP ............................. 5
1. Chapter 1 .................................................... 6
2. Chapter 2 .................................................... 8
3. Chapter 3 .................................................. 10
4. Chapter 4 .................................................. 12
5. Chapter 5 .................................................. 14
6. Chapter 6 .................................................. 17
7. Chapter 7 .................................................. 19
8. Chapter 8 .................................................. 22
9. Chapter 9 .................................................. 25
10. Chapter 10 .............................................. 27
11. Chapter 11 .............................................. 30
12. Chapter 12 .............................................. 34
13. Chapter 13 .............................................. 36

| | | |
|---|---|---|
| 14. | Chapter 14 | 40 |
| 15. | Chapter 15 | 44 |
| 16. | Chapter 16 | 48 |
| 17. | Chapter 17 | 52 |
| 18. | Chapter 18 | 54 |
| 19. | Chapter 19 | 58 |
| | PART TWO: PRIVILEGES AND RESPONSIBILITIES | 62 |
| 20. | Chapter 20 | 63 |
| 21. | Chapter 21 | 67 |
| 22. | Chapter 22 | 70 |
| 23. | Chapter 23 | 74 |
| 24. | Chapter 24 | 76 |
| 25. | Chapter 25 | 78 |
| 26. | Chapter 26 | 83 |
| 27. | Chapter 27 | 86 |
| 28. | Chapter 28 | 89 |
| | PART THREE: LIVING LIKE THE ANCIENTS | 92 |
| 29. | Chapter 29 | 93 |
| 30. | Chapter 30 | 96 |
| 31. | Chapter 31 | 98 |
| 32. | Chapter 32 | 102 |
| 33. | Chapter 33 | 107 |
| 34. | Chapter 34 | 111 |

| | | |
|---|---|---|
| 35. | Chapter 35 | 114 |
| 36. | Chapter 36 | 117 |
| 37. | Chapter 37 | 121 |
| 38. | Chapter 38 | 127 |
| 39. | Chapter 39 | 131 |
| 40. | Chapter 40 | 137 |
| 41. | Chapter 41 | 140 |
| 42. | Chapter 42 | 146 |
| 43. | Chapter 43 | 150 |
| 44. | Chapter 44 | 156 |
| 45. | Chapter 45 | 160 |
| 46. | Chapter 46 | 166 |
| 47. | Chapter 47 | 169 |
| 48. | Chapter 48 | 175 |
| 49. | Chapter 49 | 179 |
| PART FOUR: THE FATES | | 182 |
| 50. | Chapter 50 | 183 |
| 51. | Chapter 51 | 189 |
| 52. | Chapter 52 | 194 |
| 53. | Chapter 53 | 201 |
| 54. | Chapter 54 | 204 |
| 55. | Chapter 55 | 208 |
| 56. | Chapter 56 | 214 |
| 57. | Chapter 57 | 219 |

58. Chapter 58 — 223
59. Chapter 59 — 228
60. Chapter 60 — 234

PART FIVE: A GENEROUS MASTER — 238

61. Chapter 61 — 239
62. Chapter 62 — 246
63. Chapter 63 — 251
64. Chapter 64 — 262
65. Chapter 65 — 265
66. Chapter 66 — 268
67. Chapter 67 — 274
68. Chapter 68 — 279
69. Chapter 69 — 283
70. Chapter 70 — 289
71. Chapter 71 — 293

THE END — 295

Epilogue: — 296

Chapter — 298

# THE LIBERATOR

# BOOK ONE: TRESPASSER

# Preface:

When I used to say that I would always love you, you seemed to take it as a threat. As if I was warning you that you would never be rid of me—that wherever you ran off to I would find you, then pile on unwanted affections till you could no longer breathe. Or perhaps you interpreted it as a different kind of attack—like my flowery language was just a trick to get you to open up, to love me back. And then, the moment you did so, I would slam the door in your face and laugh and laugh...

But I was never trying to threaten you, only commit to you. And years after I first swore to always love you, I realize that I still do. Now always is quite a long time, so my success at this point in time may not impress you. But I feel quite confident I will make it to the finish line on this one. You are, after all, a very easy person to love.

It seems unlikely that we will ever speak again. I certainly hope we do, and wrote this entire trilogy in part due to a hope that we might. But it seems unlikely. You have gone your way, I have gone mine, and we are both very stubborn people. We will find other lovers, other lifestyles, continue to grow up and grow old. But I will continue to love you, and to express that love when I can through writing. For while I had many complaints of our time together, you did always read my work with seriousness and love it like it was your own. And that—that, for me was perhaps more valuable than any other kind of affection that you could have shown to me. And so I continue to write, in hopes of making you laugh, of making you smile, of making you feel just a little bit less alone. For even if you remain my only fan, you are enough.

Our love is obviously of the tragic sort. And some say tragic love represents a sickly soul, a soul that dreads intimacy. You chase the unattainable because you do not actually wish to catch what you are chasing. And while there is clearly something to all this, there is also something else in tragic love, something full of brightness and power. For what we tragic lovers fear is not intimacy, but stale, lifeless intimacy. We don't fear love, but the emptiness that can be felt when two people live together, eat together, and sleep together, yet never quite manage to touch one another's souls. That lonely resting place is what we are both running from. And so, as I continue to chase you around this tragic love circle, I say I do no wrong. For the love I show you when I write and the love you show me when you read is not that bitter, suffocating romance which we both fear so much. It is healthy, strong. Even good.

And so, back to the start. When I said I would always love you, what did I mean? Was it a threat? An attack on your very identity? I swear to you, it was not. It was instead a promise that I would always work to overcome that darker side of myself that very much wishes *not* to love you. That darker side whose instinct is to either despise you for rejecting me or forget about you entirely. So when I said I would always love you I was, in a way, speaking to myself. Recommitting myself to overcome these darker emotions of hate and apathy day by day, hour by hour, and replace them with a steady compassion towards you that is good and pure. And I recommit to that again now. For I do love you, dear friend. Always and forever.

# PART ONE: BATTLESLEEP

# Chapter 1

The whole world was drowned in war—well, what little was left of it. Emily could barely remember a time when they weren't fighting. Faint images of laughter around the fire, sleeping soundly, dancing, even. But her memories of those times were vague, unfamiliar. Only now mattered. And now she had to fight.

Gunshots flared in the night, shattering a nearby window. The rest of the squad dropped for cover, but Emily turned towards the sound. Three human shapes stood in the moonlit street, probably mercenaries. Not Stonewalkers at least.

"Get down!" whispered Maya.

Emily ignored her and reached into her pack, feeling with her fingers until she found a small, steel cylinder. She had been saving this. She threw the smoke grenade out the window then dove into the street.

She landed on the cobblestones with a somersault then charged at a zig zag pattern towards the enemy. The attackers shouted angrily, unleashing a hail of bullets into the smoke, but Emily was not afraid. Steps guided by memory and sound, she ran quietly to the left, circling behind. Then she leapt onto the middle soldier's back, turned his blazing weapon on his two companions, and slit his throat.

Emily crouched and scanned the unlit, war-torn streets for other threats. Silence. She glanced down at the face of the man she had just killed. Short hair, tattoos, the first male she had seen in months. Why did they all have to fight for them?

She lifted the three gun slings over her shoulder and crept back up the street to their hideout, knocking a 3-2-2 pattern on the wall to indicate she was friendly. Then she pulled herself up back into the building through the window.

"Well," she said, dropping the three assault rifles onto the floor, "guess we have bullets again."

# Chapter 2

"You're insane," said Maya, eying Emily's bare feet.

"Never claimed that I wasn't."

Maya grinned. She was her squad leader, a dark-haired fighter from the Central US Region. Back when that had been a place.

"You reminded me of the Godservant, leaping out the window like that," muttered their newest recruit.

Emily froze. Something about the mere mention of his name made her heart stop.

"You really did seem like him," laughed another, "you gonna fly in like that if we ever get captured?"

Emily scowled. "Don't count on it."

There were only eight women in their struggling little battalion. Two of these counted bullets, while four others smiled at Emily with stupid, worshipful expressions. They looked like lost twenty somethings, in love for the first time, even though they were probably in their sixties. Not that you could ever tell how old anybody was.

"How did you do that? Weren't you afraid?" asked their newest recruit, who looked oddly similar to Emily. The same brownish blonde hair, the same silver blue eyes.

Emily shrugged. "Sometimes I just... know what I have to do."

Another recruit opened her mouth, but Maya stopped her by gesturing harshly with her finger across her throat. There was the sound of a boot on the street outside.

# Chapter 3

The new soldiers on their team remained perfectly still as Maya lifted one of the newly acquired rifles to her shoulder and tiptoed to the door. She made brief eye contact with Emily to confirm they were on the same page, then flung it open.

"Down on the fucking ground!!" Maya shouted, "Hands where I can see them!"

The unarmed visitor obeyed, lying prostrate in the street as they surrounded her. She wore a crisp, clean Free Army uniform, something Emily hadn't seen in a very long time.

"Your name and division, soldier," said Maya, the nozzle of her gun trained on the back of her skull.

"Sergeant Eliza Martinez, sir. Special Forces Group 8C."

"And where's the rest of your team, Sergeant?"

"Third story of the cinderblock apartments across the street. Snipers will fire on you if you harm me, so I'd advise against that."

Maya glanced across the street, unable to verify whether this was true. "And what do you and these sniper friends of yours want?"

"We're looking to recruit one of your soldiers, sir."

Maya frowned. "Go on."

"We saw some mercenaries closing in on your position and were about to intervene when one of your fighters resolved the situation. I was very impressed. We've recently suffered some serious losses to our team and could use a talent like hers on our next mission."

Maya's frown deepened. "So you're here for Emily."

"If that's the name of the woman who just killed three of the Collective's mercenaries with just a knife and smoke grenade, yes, that's correct. We're here for Emily."

"What exactly is this mission? How do I know you aren't some kind of spy? Can you give me some background?"

The woman on the ground paused, then answered.

"Before joining the special forces I was in the Siege of Bayamo, head of the 19$^{th}$ Division. Fought under General Lin—calls everything horseshit, likes her coffee cold, disappeared six months back. I don't know what else to say. Our next mission, as I'm sure you understand, is classified."

Maya slowly lowered her gun and relaxed her stance. "At ease, Sergeant Martinez, Lin was my great aunt. I believe you're who you say you are."

# Chapter 4

The intruder stood, dusted herself off, and made an open palmed hand gesture towards the apartments across the street. She carried herself like a seasoned veteran, moving efficiently and without hesitation. She seemed like she might be one of the old citizens of this land, before all the refugees had flooded in decades ago. Refugees like Emily.

"All your necessary gear will be provided," said the woman, "but if you have any other personal belongings, I can wait for you here while you gather them. Pack light, we'll be moving fast."

Emily nodded, slipping back into their hideout. She owned very little. Her uniform was in tatters, and shared all food and equipment with the rest of their team. She had nothing here she really needed, she just wanted a moment of calm. A moment to remember.

Maya stepped inside. "You sure you want to do this?" she asked, closing the door behind her, "go join their suicidal strike force?"

"You think she's actually from Special Ops?"

"We'd be dead if she wasn't."

Emily nodded. "Then yes, I want to do this. If I can somehow make a difference in this war, I have to try."

"Of course you do."

The two women looked at each other for a few moments, then embraced.

"I'm gonna miss you, crazy killer," whispered Maya.

Emily squeezed her tight. She didn't know what to say to this leader and teacher who had become something more like a friend. Five months. Five months of hunger and gunfire and narrow escapes. So many other soldiers they had seen die, seen dragged off to the Howling City. But they had covered each other's backs and survived.

"Promise not to forget about us lowly little squad leaders after they make you into a general or whatever?" added Maya with her wry smile.

Emily kissed her on the lips. "I promise."

Then she pulled away and stepped back out into the moonlit street.

# Chapter 5

Emily followed the soldier in the crisp uniform across the road and into what had once been an old, concrete apartment complex. They climbed the stairs, then walked up to one of the dusty doors.

"Private Eliza Martinez, code 1-2-7-9," she said.

A pause, then the door flung open.

There were three soldiers standing at attention. Two women, and to Emily's surprise, a man. He was short for a male, about the same height as the women, with curly red hair and oddly cheerful eyes.

"Well, here she is," said Eliza.

The two other women seemed unimpressed.

"This is a mistake," muttered the tall blonde woman on the right.

"The decision has been made," snapped Eliza, "Introduce yourselves or she gets your rations."

There was a brief pause, and then the man with red hair stepped forward, eyes still smiling.

"Jason, Jason West."

"Emily O'Dora," she replied, shaking his hand. Then she did a double take. "Wait. Do you mean to say that you are *the* Jason West?"

He laughed. "Something like that."

"Lea Laurent," said a shorter girl with green eyes and a prominent nose, extending her hand reluctantly. "Welcome to the team, kid. Try not to die."

"Vy Taylor," said the tall blonde woman, scowling down directly into Emily's eyes, "fuck this up and I'll kill you myself."

Emily looked around the room, still in shock. "If you're Jason," she asked, "where is the Godservant?"

She still couldn't believe it. Jason West, the Godservant's legendary right-hand man. This wasn't just any special forces crew. This was *his* crew.

Jason's face fell, but he didn't speak.

"David isn't with us anymore," said Lea grimly. "He was gunned down two weeks ago while creating a diversion so we could escape. I've never seen anyone take that many bullets…"

"Wait… what are you saying…" muttered Emily.

"The Godservant is dead," said Eliza.

The others looked down at the ground with solemn faces.

"I can't believe he's gone…" muttered Emily. She really couldn't. She didn't. He was the only thing keeping hope alive on this bloody island, this last habitable place on earth.

"But this is why I was so certain we should bring you on," continued Eliza, "the way we saw you moving out there, it reminded us of him. I took it as a sign, silly as that is. We just recruited Vy last week, and she's incredible. But I think we'll be needing you as well if we want to win this thing."

Jason looked up at her encouragingly, eyes showing he agreed.

"I'm not the Godservant!" cried Emily, rattled at hearing this comparison a second time. "Do I look like a legendary warrior who has saved our armies from defeat hundreds of times? I'm just a private! A no name fucking private!"

"Well, you're going to have to act like you're more than that," said Lea grimly. "Or we're all gonna die."

Emily opened her mouth but didn't say anything. Didn't they see how crazy this was? They had only seen her fight once. Why did they think they could count on her like this? Vy seemed to be the only sane one in the group.

"We will brief you on the mission tomorrow morning," said Eliza, "there will be plenty of time as we move out to answer any of your questions."

"But now," Jason tossed her a sleeping bag, "we sleep."

Emily looked into the man's smiling eyes. This was all so surreal. David Petrov, the Godservant, dead. Now being recruited into his crew alongside Jason West. There were stories of David and Jason going back for decades, not just in this war but in the earlier wars as well. How could she ever take *his* place?

Eliza placed a bottle containing a black liquid in her hand. "A sip of this should help you rest," she said. "But only a sip, two sips might kill you. Lea, you got first watch?"

"Yes sir."

Eliza, Jason, and Vy threw down sleeping bags, lay down, and took swigs from similar bottles. Jason gave her a grateful look as if to say, "no time to talk, but glad to have you with us." Emily unrolled her bag, and as she did so she could hear Vy already snoring. Glancing around she saw that Jason and Eliza were unconscious as well. She climbed into her bag, swallowed a gulp of the strange liquid, and closed her eyes.

# Chapter 6

"Good evening, Seventh," said a deep, grandfatherly voice.

"What, where am I?" asked Emily.

The voice laughed. "You're in a dream, where do you think you are? The question is: do you want to wake up?"

Emily jumped to her feet. There was gray tile flooring as far as the eye could see, but no one in sight. Nothing to be heard either, except for that voice. That terribly familiar voice.

"Why did you call me that?"

"A Seventh? Why, because that is what you are! Quite a bit more important than most, but still a Seventh. And, as a Seventh, it is my responsibility to ask you: do you wish to wake up?"

Emily paused. She sensed something dangerous about this voice, like answering its questions incorrectly might cause her physical pain. "Wake up? And go off on some impossible mission where I'm supposed to replace the Godservant? No, not really."

"So be it," boomed the voice.

Emily shuddered, looking up. There was no sign of this man who seemed to be speaking to her from above. In the dim lighting, she could not even see the ceiling. It was as if she were standing under a pitch black, starless sky.

"Why am I here? Is this a hallucination caused by that sedative they gave me?"

"This is the place where you can speak with *me*."

"And why would I want to do that?"

Emily felt a slight breeze on her cheek.

"Because, Seventh: I, alone, can help you change your fate. I alone can help you to be free."

"I still... don't understand."

"It will become more clear with time," answered the deep voice, warmly. "Goodbye for now, Emily O'Dora. Remember, I am always here."

The wind began to howl in the distance, picking up speed until it began to rip up the tile flooring around her, leaving only black emptiness underneath. Gray shards of ceramic swirled around her as the island of solid ground surrounding her became smaller and smaller. Then she awoke.

# Chapter 7

Eliza was shaking her shoulders vigorously when Emily suddenly sat upright, looking around frantically.

"First time trying Battlesleep, huh?" asked Jason. The others looked down at her with knowing smiles, as if she was the butt of some innocent joke.

"What *was* that?" Emily asked. "That voice. That room? What the hell *was* that?"

Their smiles faded into perplexed expressions.

"That dream," continued Emily, "that endless room... did you all see that too? It felt so real..."

Vy narrowed her eyes at her in disgust like she was insane.

"Sometimes the sedative we use—Battlesleep—makes our subconscious minds more active as it knocks us out," explained Eliza. "Don't worry about any strange dreams you have, that's quite normal. Your equipment is laid out for you in the corner, Private. We will be leaving shortly."

She walked over in a daze to the edge of a room. An assault rifle, handgun, hiking backpack, boots, canteen, rations, bandages and antiseptic, six different kinds of grenades, a propane tank attached to a flamethrower, and a helmet. No uniform, though. Apparently she was still stuck with the frayed rags she wore from her previous regiment.

They left the apartment while the stars could still be seen in the western sky, and began hiking out of the abandoned city to the southeast. Eliza led the way, followed by Jason, Lea, Emily, then Vy in the rear, who eyed Emily suspiciously as they walked. Rather than taking any official roadways, they followed only animal trails, relying on the thick jungle of the Sierra Maestra mountains for cover. They moved quickly but also quietly, and Eliza would periodically raise her hand, signaling them to freeze dead in their tracks and listen carefully for enemies who might be following behind. Dew from the plants they brushed up against soaked their clothing, and the light of dawn only filled the world after they had hiked for miles up into the hills.

Emily found herself carrying her heavy pack with surprising ease, and moved in step with the other soldiers as if she had been fighting with special forces for years. She had a burning desire to contribute to her team, which outweighed her fatigue so much that the thought of resting actually seemed less comfortable to her than keeping up with the squad's grueling pace. In moments like this, protecting her squad and achieving her mission were the only things that mattered to her. All other urges seemed insignificant in comparison, like childish drives that she had shrugged off long ago.

They stopped for breakfast after covering ten miles. Eliza tossed Emily some light military rations of pork jerky and dried plantains, while Lea filled her canteen up in a nearby stream, handing it to her without a word. Jason alone was friendly enough to speak, sitting next to her on the log.

"You doing alright?"

Emily nodded between mouthfuls.

"We'll be stopping about twenty miles from here this afternoon," he continued, "with how deep we are in Collective territory we'll have to travel only at night after that."

"Understood."

"This mission... only Eliza knows all the details. But I can't stress how important this is, how much we need your skills. We're going to strike them in their very center. In the heart."

Emily choked on her food, realizing what this meant. "Understood."

Jason gave her a brotherly pat on the back, then went over to Eliza's side, consulting with her as she studied over a map. Emily's body relaxed. He was the closest thing she had to a friend on this crew, but there was something about him that made her uncomfortable anytime he was nearby.

# Chapter 8

Their hike after this stop proved more difficult. The trails began to meander up and down the muddy hillside, and with the speed of their pace it was difficult to stay on two feet. Lea slid off the path once, almost sliding off a cliff into a waterfall when Emily grabbed her pack to stabilize her. The tiny woman only grunted to express her thanks.

"You a refugee?" asked Emily, soon after this episode.

Lea ignored her at first.

"Hey. Girl I just saved from falling to her death. Are you a refugee? Or were you one of the citizens who lived back here before the breaking?"

"Refugee. But I don't remember much."

"Me neither, where from?"

"West France Region. You?"

"Think I lived all over, but Antarctica most recently. You know, before everything..."

"Blew up?"

"Yeah."

"What the fuck were you doing in Antarctica?"

Emily shrugged her shoulders. "Being cold? What the fuck were you doing in West France?"

Lea shrugged as well. "Being French?"

Emily laughed. Lea laughed too, albeit reluctantly.

"Stop talking, new bitch," said Vy.

Their stops were short and brief—every few hours by a stream to wash their faces, refill their canteens, and receive their allotted portions of carefully rationed food from Eliza. They continued to pause in their tracks periodically to listen for signs they were being followed, but only ever found animals this way. A few blue and black birds that shook their tails as they chirped. Fat, squirrel-like rodents, who climbed through the trees munching everything they could find. But as the day went on, the wildlife became more and more sparse, everything becoming eerily quiet.

As the hours passed, Jason was Emily's only consistent source of company.

"Hey kid, you're doing amazing back here. Want me to carry part of your pack the rest of the way?"

Emily shook her head.

"Not tired at all, huh? Wanna carry my pack too?"

Emily shook her head again. He laughed and jogged back ahead to find his place in the line behind Eliza. Emily appreciated that he tried to befriend her, occasionally stepping back like this to offer his support and smile at her in his inviting way. But something about his presence always felt off, and she found herself relieved whenever he stopped trying to help and just left her alone.

They arrived at their resting place—a small crack in the side of the mountain hidden by dead branches—while the sun was still high in the sky. They crawled in, covering the entrance behind them then flipping on flashlights for light. The narrow entrance opened up into a complex of caves with half a dozen rooms, the largest being about eighty feet in diameter. Lea flushed out a few bats out of one of the side rooms by swishing her gun like a broom, while Vy double checked all the others for any signs that the Collective had been here recently. The only sign of human life she found was writing on the wall of one of the smaller rooms:

*Caminante, son tus huellas*
*el camino y nada más;*
*Caminante, no hay camino,*
*se hace camino al andar*

"What *is* that?" asked Emily.

"Spanish," answered Eliza, "so this was written probably long before the breaking of the world, at least a hundred years ago I'd guess."

"What does it mean?"

Eliza shook her head. "No idea."

Emily stared at it for a while. There was something beautiful about those words. Perhaps, in part, because she could not understand them.

They threw down their sleeping bags in the largest of the caverns.

"We will sleep for six hours," announced Eliza, "then leave just after dusk. This will be the most dangerous mission any of you have ever taken part in. Tomorrow, we either die or change this war forever."

Emily was not afraid. Each member of the team pulled out their small bottles of Battlesleep and took a swig, as if drugging themselves every night was the most natural thing in the world. Vy did not, watching Emily and waiting for her to sleep first. After thirty miles of hiking through rugged terrain that tall, icy blonde woman still did not trust her at all, still wanted her off the team. Emily took her bottle out of her pocket, taking the smallest sip she could manage. Within moments, she was out.

# Chapter 9

"Seventh," said the deep voice. "You have returned."

Emily jumped. She was there again. That dimly lit room, that repetitive gray tile flooring as far as the eye could see. She ran in a random direction, hoping to escape, hoping to see something—anything—else.

"Why are you running?" demanded the voice, "are you trying to escape me, Seventh? Even though I am only here to help you?"

She stopped and looked around. The voice seemed to come from nowhere, from nothing. "I need to know," she said, between breaths, "what you mean when you call me a Seventh. What the fuck does that even mean?"

"It is one of the classes in the World System. The lowest class. But there is only so much I can tell you Emily, at least while you are asleep."

She groaned. "None of this makes sense. I'm not a Seventh, I'm a soldier in the Free Army. Are you with the Collective somehow? Is this dream sent to me by them to distract me?"

The voice laughed. "No, I am not with the Collective. I am here simply to give you choices. And as a Seventh, to give you one choice."

It had a tone that was gentle, even kind. But Emily sensed something unsettling about it as well, something inhuman.

"I don't see why I should believe anything you say."

"It is your choice what you believe. But I only wish to serve you, Emily, I only wish to serve humanity. That is my role, and I have no desire for any other."

She froze. "Wait. Are you... the new leader of the resistance? Are you the replacement for the Godservant?"

The voice laughed again. "No, that war is not my concern."

A wind blew towards her, ripping up the gray flooring in the distance, sucking up the light as it did so and turning everything black.

"Then who are you!" shouted Emily over the storm.

"My name," boomed the voice, "is... *The Liberator.*"

# Chapter 10

Emily leapt to her feet at the sound of gunshots.

"Die you goddamn half human..." spat Vy, as her gun was knocked out of her hands and she was thrown to the ground.

Emily reached for her assault rifle, but even as she did so she saw Eliza on her right and Lea on her left crumble, both full of holes. She dropped the weapon and fell to her knees, putting her hands in the air.

Ten Stonewalkers stood in front of them, thick helmets shielding their female faces, metallic bodies with six arms each. Two of these arms had robotic hands on the end, while the rest were attached to various automatic weapons. All such attachments were pointed at her.

"This rebel is strange," observed one, "she doesn't belong with the others."

"Who are you?" demanded another, whose androgynous chest plate was red, rather than white. "Why do you not have the same uniform?" Two others walked around Emily, tying her wrists. Feeling their cold metal fingers made her skin crawl.

"Private Emily O'Dora, I'm... a proud soldier in the Free Army."

"Of course you are. But why is your uniform so damaged and worn? What makes you different from the others?"

"New recruit!" interjected Jason, "she doesn't know anything, we just recruited her last night!"

The Stonewalker standing over Jason slammed her metal fist into his face, bloodying the skin around his eye and dropping him to the ground.

The red plated Stonewalker took off her helmet and looked at Emily. Her face was surprisingly gentle, even innocent. "I am not so different from you," she said. "We ended up on different sides of this conflict, but we both want a better Cuba, a better world. Now tell me: what is it you know? If we simply use our words, there's no need for violence."

She had a young woman's face—or rather, a young woman's head. It was attached at the neck to a metal encased life support system below that added oxygen, glucose, and other trace minerals to the bloodstream, which were then pumped to the brain. She was a walking tank, one of the most feared weapons of the Collective.

Emily, determined not to share what little she knew about their mission, confessed something else. "The Liberator. He made contact with me. He told me... he told me I'm a Seventh..."

The Stonewalker who had removed her helmet looked vaguely amused. "The Liberator? Let me guess, that's one of your little leaders who likes to talk about how slavery is always wrong? What a nice idea."

Her companions laughed.

"But no more games, tell me why you're here and what city you're targeting. I need the truth, and quickly now. Otherwise, I'm going to have to shoot one of these friends of yours, which I'd really rather not do."

Emily looked up into the machine woman's probing eyes, thinking desperately. What else could she tell her? She had to make up something, anything...

"Three, Two..."

Suddenly an arrow flew out the back of the cave and took the Stonewalker interrogator in the back of her skull. She dropped dead.

The remaining Stonewalkers unloaded in the direction the arrow had come from. Gunfire echoed throughout the chamber for a few moments, then all went silent except for a voice. *His* voice.

"Emily," he whispered, "I think I'm going to need your help."

# Chapter 11

The man behind her cut loose her restraints then dove into a cluster of Stonewalkers to their left with a sword in each hand, slicing heads off of two mechanical bodies and then using those bodies as a shield from a fresh barrage of machine gun fire. All the Stonewalkers turned on him with intensity, almost madness, as Emily quietly reached down into her pack. She knew that the helmets of these monsters were engineered to be bulletproof, but there was one thing she hoped they were not protected against.

She lifted her flamethrower, aimed high, and fired. They screamed and turned their guns towards her, but crumbled to the ground before they could fire, helmets aflame. One last gun fired a few times from the edge of the room and then went quiet, as a severed head rolled across the ground. And stepping out from behind its metallic body was a man. He was just over six feet tall—the tallest man Emily had seen since the breaking. Numerous bandages covering his bare chest and arms. He had short black hair and eyes that radiated kindness and courage. She didn't know how she knew, but she *knew*. It was the Godservant.

"The bats, that's how I found y'all," he explained, "guessing these machine ladies found you the same way, unfortunately."

"You... saved us," gasped Vy. She was bowing to Him. So was Jason. So, Emily noticed, was she.

"Well, I couldn't have them torturing you and finding all our plans now, could I?" he said cheerily, "Jason, come here my old friend. How many years have we fought together now? Did you really think I'd abandon you so easily?"

Jason stood up, tears still flowing down his face. The two men embraced.

"Didn't mean to scare you, old buddy. I did take eleven bullets, had to carve them out meself. But come on, you really thought that would take me down? Remember Havana in '37? Or Santa Clara in '29?"

"I remember," whispered Jason.

The Godservant ended the hug and put his left arm on his shoulder and looked him in the eye. "We're going to finish this brother. Eliza and Lea's deaths will not be in vain."

Then He walked over to Vy, who was still kneeling face down.

"Soldier," he said. Vy looked up, face covered in tears as well. Emily had never imagined that this cold, distrusting woman could ever cry. "You ready to help me finish this?"

She looked up and nodded feebly.

"Oh, come here!" he exclaimed, taking both her hands and lifting her into a tiptoed hug. "We're going to be alright. We're going to be alright..." He gave her a few condescending pats on the back.

Jason looked over at him with the smile of a man who was home at last. "Her name's Vy. And I've never seen her say as much as 'thank you.' But if anyone deserves her soft side it's you, sir."

Vy sobbed a little louder. The Godservant cupped his hands around her waist and gently pushed her away from him till she was at arm's length. "Hello Vy, my name's David Petrov. It's a pleasure to meet you."

"Please..." she whispered, looking into his eyes.

"We should leave just after dusk, in about three hours," said David, addressing the whole group. "Even if they know what we did here, they wouldn't be able to get another patrol all the way out here before then."

"Please," Vy whispered again.

He exhaled. "Ok, Ok. But let me meet the last member of our crew first."

Vy nodded pathetically. Her thick, light blonde hair was a mess. Her tall figure, which usually seemed poised to strike, now seemed on the verge of collapsing in two.

"Emily, is it?" David asked, standing in front of her.

"Yes, Godservant sir," she said, uncertainly. It was him. It was really him. Her heart felt like it was going to explode.

"Oh, please don't call me that. It's David, and I'm honored to have you with us. You fought quite well back there, got more of them than I did, I'll reckon."

All she had done was pull the trigger on a flamethrower. And now the *Godservant* was telling her that she had fought well?

"Thank you! Thank you, um, David, sir," she said, bowing automatically.

He smiled at her warmly. "I can sense that you are going to be an important part of our team, Emily. Look forward to working with you."

She opened her mouth to reply, but nothing came out. His easy smile, the black stubble that shaped his jawline, his intelligent, brown eyes. His thin, muscular body that seemed to radiate energy and health, in spite of all the bullet wounds. Something about him was just so... beautiful.

He patted her shoulder, then turned back to Vy, squeezing her hand in his. She was still standing there in tears, looking at him worshipfully.

"Three hours, Jason?"

Jason grinned and gave him a nod.

"I'll see you then. We end this tomorrow, my friend."

"End the whole war? Just like that? The four of us?" asked Jason incredulously.

"Please," whispered Vy once more, as if she couldn't even hear the rest of the conversation.

"That's right," David replied, "tomorrow, we start a new age of peace. This war needs to end, brother. And we *can* make it end."

Jason looked over at him, eyes full of trust. Then David turned, lifted the sobbing woman over his shoulder, and carried her deeper into the caves.

# Chapter 12

Jason And Emily buried Eliza and Lea just outside the caves, cleaned up the remains of the Stonewalkers, then laid out their sleeping bags in one of the cavern rooms closer to the entrance. Jason looked over with a stupid smile as they both lay down. His eye was blackened from the Stonewalker's steel fist to the face earlier, but he didn't seem to notice. Something about him still unsettled Emily, made her mistrust him.

"He always had a way with women, David. I can't believe he's back. God, I'm just so happy he's back."

"I knew he wasn't dead," muttered Emily softly.

"What was that?"

"I said I knew he wasn't dead. Somehow, deep down, I knew."

Jason gave her a puzzled look. "I mean, we all hoped he wasn't. But I saw him get shot over and over again, Eliza and I both did. No man could take that kind of a beating, or at least I thought no man could. But David does have a way of surprising you. He always has."

Jason stared up at the limestone ceiling, grinning stupidly.

"Are you..." muttered Emily, "ever, you know, jealous?"

Jason laughed. "I got over that long ago. He's the Godservant, and I'm just, well, his right hand man. And that's really not such a bad thing to be."

Emily thought about Jason, and couldn't help pitying the man. David was radiance, glory, perfection. Jason certainly wasn't unattractive, but there really was no competition there.

"You're in love with him, aren't cha?" asked Jason, laughing.

"Yes," replied Emily, surprised at her immediate honesty.

"Are you bothered about... you know, Vy?"

Emily thought for a moment. "No, not at all. Although part of me..."

"Wants to join them?" laughed Jason. "Go right ahead, it's certainly happened before."

Emily stared at him incredulously. How did he know? "Yes, but I'll just rest here instead." Her body screamed as soon as she said it.

Jason smiled. "Well, if you sneak off later I won't judge ya. Tomorrow's going to be a big day. Ending the war, I still can't believe it..."

"You sure he wasn't just, you know, being optimistic?"

"David doesn't make promises he can't keep. This ends tomorrow, mark my words."

Emily looked at him curiously. He was clearly a war-hardened soldier who had experienced and endured more than most. But he was also just a faith-filled schoolboy who trusted blindly in the words of his best friend.

"You need any Battlesleep to crash?" asked Jason, pulling out his black bottle.

"No, I'll just sleep the old-fashioned way tonight."

"Alrighty then. Goodnight Emily, see you on the last day of the war."

And within moments, Jason took a sip of his bottle, flipped off his flashlight, and fell asleep.

# Chapter 13

Emily lay there, thoughtful. It was perfectly dark now, although she could hear the occasional drip from a cluster of stalactites in the corner. Her mind was racing and she was happy, filled with a strange new energy. David Petrov was alive, and *he* was going to fight with her. It had always been her dream to fight by his side. To have him look down at her warmly, like he had just moments before. But something about all this was terribly odd. The Stonewalkers attacking, the deaths of Eliza and Lea, the return of the Godservant. And now this almost overwhelming desire to go and be with him. She closed her eyes and breathed, trying to calm her nerves. They had a war to fight, she couldn't be thinking about love, she couldn't be thinking about...

Hours later she blinked her eyes open, wondering if she had slept at all as David and Vy returned to their room in the caves. David patted Jason's shoulder fondly to wake him, while Vy pulled her aside.

"Hey Emily, I wanted to tell you how sorry I am for how I've been treating you since we met, for some reason I didn't think you belonged with us. But David told me I should trust you, and I do now."

They hugged and then Vy smiled at her warmly. She looked so clean, so fresh, like she had just been born anew.

"Can we be friends? You know, after this is all over?"

"Yeah, of course," replied Emily, not knowing what else to say. Who was this new woman? In a way, she missed the standoffish, antagonistic Vy from before. At least her behavior had made sense.

David tightened the straps on his pack, then faced the rest of the team. "I believe you all know where we are going and how dangerous this will be."

Emily nodded. From what Jason had mentioned earlier, they were going to attack the Collective in the heart of their operations, which could only mean one thing. The Howling City.

"If we move at a quick pace all night, we can arrive there just before sunrise and catch them by surprise," he continued, "I know I haven't given you all much details yet, but I need you to trust me. We *can* end this war together. I need you to believe."

Emily did believe. Part of her brain realized that she shouldn't, that something about this was all insane, that their trust in this one man's charisma and leadership would likely get them all killed. But that part of her brain was mostly turned off right now. And the rest of her had perfect faith.

David led the way out of the caves into the fading dusk light. Vy followed, then Emily, then Jason. As each person came out of the caves, he gave them each a quick congratulatory hug, as if crawling out of that little passage was already a little victory. Then he began to run.

They ran in a line, the light of the waxing half-moon glowing in the south and lighting their path. All flashlights were off. The jungle trails were less overgrown than before, but the process of running was still a bit like dancing, skipping over a branch here, a stream there, never having any ease or steadiness to their steps. But their packs, at least, were lighter. All sleeping gear and other long-term supplies had been left behind. This mission was do or die.

They ran for hours, only stopping to drink from streams and waterfalls. And as the miles rolled on, evidence of wildlife became more and more scarce. They were going to a dead place now, a place where free people, at least, were not known to come back from. A place where Stonewalkers were made.

It had been years since Emily had run this far, and her legs ached—not only from the impact, but the lack of sleep and the long hike the day before. But this pain was outweighed by the simple fact that The Godservant was running ahead of them. As long as he moved, she would too. If it took everything she had.

They descended towards the lower parts of the Sierra Maestras, tall grasses replacing some of the more rocky mountain terrain. The trails weaved up and down between these lower hilltops, sometimes dropping into marshland which they splashed through in the dark.

"Doing great, keep it up," Jason would call from behind. Emily ignored him, feeling too exhausted to engage. Something about that man was so draining. She needed to save whatever strength she could for their mission, for the Howling City. The wilderness was almost perfectly silent now, no frogs croaking or crickets chirping, only the pat pat pat of their feet. The trail climbed out of the valleys it had been winding through and then up a single grassy hilltop. David stopped at the top, raising his right hand. The rest of the crew stopped dead in their tracks. The hill overlooked something beautiful, something Emily hadn't seen in a very long time. The ocean. The setting half-moon glistened on the waters and a light was visible in the distance, moving parallel to the shoreline.

Without a word, he pointed emphatically to the ocean, then started charging down the steep decline to the beach. They were off the trail now and one misstep would have sent him tumbling down the rocky hillside, but he didn't seem the least bit concerned. The others followed behind, albeit more slowly, with Emily in the lead. David reached the bottom then sprinted across the beach, soon hundreds of feet ahead of his crew. Near the waters he tore off his pack, his boots, and then the rest of his clothing and dove into the ocean.

When Jason, Emily, and Vy reached the shore, he was nowhere in sight.

"Should I dive in after him?" asked Emily, moving to remove her clothing as well. She felt she had been searching for this man all of her life, she couldn't lose him now.

Jason lifted a finger. "Wait."

Emily gazed out in earnest. In the distance there was first one splash, then a second. The light that had been moving along the shoreline to the west turned and approached them. Before they could scramble for cover they were in the headlights of a speedboat. And standing at its wheel, like a triumphant Greek statue, was David.

# Chapter 14

They waded out into the water, and lifted themselves in, carrying David's clothing and gear to him. He dressed, and then steered the boat back out to sea, finding two women struggling in the water. He lifted each of them in as well.

"We're so sorry," choked out one of them, "we just took this patrol job yesterday, we were short on food and needed the money. Please forgive us, Godservant, please..." They both knelt down, bowing so low that their faces touched the floor of the boat.

David laughed. "You two look freezing. Vy, do you have any extra clothes?"

"No sir, just my uniform."

"Jason?" asked David.

He shook his head. The captured women continued to shiver, teeth chattering. They were of a darker complexion with long black hair, likely inhabitants of this land from before the breaking of the world. David furrowed his brow.

"Well, you two certainly need to get dry. Vy, could you help them out of their clothes?"

Vy leapt to her feet and began to help them undress, wringing out their clothes off the side of the boat then laying them on the engine to dry. David drove their small watercraft east at top speed along the coastline, but kept glancing back at their shivering bodies with fatherly concern. "Really a shame that we have no clothes for you two, why don't you come on up here?"

Naked, they tip-toed up to him then huddled in close on each side, clinging to him as he steered. After a few minutes they stopped shivering and rested their heads peacefully on his shoulders.

"He's really unbelievable, isn't he," said Vy, dreamily.

Emily jumped. She was still not used to this woman talking to her. "Yes. Yes he is."

She couldn't help but feel inspired. This natural leader, forgiving two enemy combatants so quickly and then giving them his body to warm up against, even while it got his clothes wet. He was clearly the hero that the stories spoke of, the man who always put the needs of others before his own.

Emily glanced over at Jason, who was watching all this as well. There seemed to be a hint of jealousy in his eyes, even anger. Then it disappeared and he shook his head, smiling to himself.

David drove their motorboat for a few brief hours to the east, time passing much more quickly when they rested than when they had been running. They traveled in relative silence along the coast, overcome with exhaustion and anticipation of the enormous task ahead of them. How were the four of them going to single handedly end the war? It still didn't make any sense, but Emily didn't dare doubt. After all, the Godservant was leading them. What could go wrong?

David turned the boat north into a bay, traveling a few miles towards the glowing lights ahead. Then he gently shook from sleep the two women at his sides.

"I need you to get dressed and then take us past the other ships into the harbor. Can you do that for me?"

They nodded, then retrieved their dried Collective uniforms from the boat's engine. The faint light of dawn was just barely beginning, though the sun would not rise for another hour. David lay on the bottom of the boat, ushering Emily and the others to do the same. They covered as much of their bodies as they could with a tarp, while the women David had recruited steered further north into the bay, saluting passing ships as they went. David whispered to Jason for a few moments, then to Vy, then crawled over to lie next to Emily. From the lights they could see glowing above them, they were very close.

"You ready for this?"

Emily froze. "Yes. Although... I still don't know what our plans are once we land on the docks."

David laughed. "Yes, I guess I should tell you that at some point, shouldn't I?"

Emily didn't say anything. Everything about this mission seemed insane, but she was just happy to be laying next to *him*. To be speaking with *him*.

"So here are the details," he continued, "Jason, Vy, and the others will stay in the boat and use machine gun fire to cover us. Meanwhile, you and I will run ahead, together. You and I are going to be the ones who end this, Emily."

She gawked. "Why... why me? I don't understand."

"Jason told me you're the best fighter he's ever seen, and I trust that man with my life. Now the question is: do you trust me?"

"Yes," she replied automatically. Of course she trusted him.

"Good. So the House of a Thousand Eyes is in the center of the city, filled with the leaders of the Collective. If we destroy that building it will not only kill their high command, but disable the power grid that provides wireless power to the bodies of the Stonewalkers. So once we can get inside the outer wall, I need you to plant *this* plastic explosive—" he handed her a rectangular white block— "in the southwest corner of the building. That is the weak point. Then I can detonate it. Easy enough, right?"

"But it's the Howling City, aren't there hundreds of guards here? Isn't this where the Stonewalkers get *made*? How can just the two of us..."

David smiled at her so disarmingly that she stopped mid-sentence.

"Because it's *you* Emily. It's *you* and it's *me*, and *we* can do this. I know that Jason's right, there's something special about you. Together we can end this war and save thousands of lives. Are you ready?"

"But..." protested Emily. Her heart was pounding and she wanted to believe this beautiful, tall, inspiring man. But this plan was simply idiotic, nonsensical. Two people run in, blow up a single building, and somehow that ends an entire war? There was no way this could or should work. She had to use her brain, not her heart. Otherwise the only thing she was going to see the end of today was the Godservant's life. For real this time.

"I believe in you, Emily," said David, "I need you."

She opened her mouth again to protest, and he kissed it. She gasped. How could a simple kiss feel so good? How did he know that this was exactly what she wanted?

"*Don't* be afraid," he whispered, handing her a pistol.

The boat bumped against the dock.

Vy jumped to her feet, spraying machine gun fire in every direction.

"NOW!" she screamed.

# Chapter 15

Jason tossed grenades onto the neighboring boats, while the two recruits at the helm of the ship began taking shots at every soldier they could see. People were dropping in all directions, so far they had caught the enemy completely off guard.

"Do not," repeated David, standing slowly to his feet, "be afraid!" Then he leapt onto the pier.

Emily surprised herself by how quickly she jumped after him. Something about that kiss had transformed her, filled her with a new kind of energy. Her legs didn't even feel tired now, all previous doubts were gone. He sprinted across the dock, pistols in hand, and she followed closely behind. She felt she had never run this fast in her life.

They left the wooden pier and continued onto the dirt streets of the Howling City, passing between the squalid black apartment buildings where the Collective's slave labor force lived and slept. Soon voices began to take notice.

"Godservant, Godservant..." they muttered in disbelief, "and who is that woman with him?"

Soon the bullets began to come, and David fired back with his handguns, not missing a step. Crack-crack-crack. Three male soldiers who were blocking their way dropped to the ground. Emily noticed windows opening on the right, uniformed soldiers with rifles looking out in confusion. BAM. Emily shot one of these who crashed down into the street. BAM BAM. Two more snipers down who had emerged onto another rooftop ahead. She had never shot like this before, much less while she was in full sprint, but it felt natural, exhilarating. This is what she was born to do. To fight alongside the Godservant, to finally bring peace to their world.

The dirt streets changed to asphalt as they approached the central industrial sector. The buildings here were warehouses and factories, and there was a red and white tower looming in the distance. The House of a Thousand Eyes.

They ran up the main street, a crowd of confused soldiers chasing from behind. Bullets whizzed past as they approached the outer wall surrounding the capitol building. Its entrance was a solid steel gate, and stepping out of that open gate now was an entire troop of Stonewalkers. Dozens of them lined up at the ready, each with six arms carrying a wide variety of firearms, all pointed down the street at them.

"STOP!!" the foremost of them commanded.

"Here!" shouted David, tossing her one of the two swords he had strapped to his back, after which he hurled two makeshift grenades at the first row of metal soldiers. They exploded in midair, spraying a black, tar like paint onto the visors of their helmets. They shouted angrily, firing their bullets blindly down the street, killing many of their own who were still chasing from behind. Then Emily on the right and David on the left leapt directly into the rows of metal soldiers.

She took off two heads with her first swing and three more with her second, as confused metallic bodies reached out to grab her. Glancing over she could see David, who had somehow jumped up above them, running on top of their helmets. Gunfire blazed in all directions, metal fists shot out, but none connected. She continued to slice her way forward until she slid under the legs of a Stonewalker through the gate.

David slammed his fist on a red button, dropping the solid steel gate behind them with a clang.

"That will give us only a few minutes. You remember what I told you?" asked David.

"Southeast corner," gasped Emily.

"GO!!"

Emily sprinted towards the red and white tower as floodlights flipped on at her movement. Hundreds of disembodied heads stared out the windows, each screaming inaudibly as she approached. They were all on swivels, some spinning around at times to shout at underlings inside that horrific place. House of a Thousand Eyes indeed. But what was outside in the courtyard was even more troubling.

Stumbling about the grass were thousands of naked bodies, mostly female, with robotic heads attached. They were not particularly coordinated and none of them were armed. There was food in a corner, a kind of slop, that some of these were scooping into their cube-shaped robotic heads. Their simple circular mouths had no chewing mechanism, only funneling the unappetizing sludge down to the neck, which swallowed compulsively whenever it arrived. Others were exercising clumsily. These were the bodies of the Stonewalkers, being preserved until those miserable soldiers gathered enough new prisoners to be 'rewarded' with them back. This was the Collective's system, and seeing it up close made Emily sick.

Running in the opposite direction of Emily, David swung his sword, slicing limbs and torsos off the stumbling naked bodies with the box-like robotic heads. Angry shouts could be heard from behind as the troop of Stonewalkers broke through the steel gate that had shut them out.

"Our bodies! Stop! Our bodies!!" they howled, advancing but not daring to fire unless they did even more harm. No one seemed to notice Emily, who was quickly approaching her target.

At the southeast corner, she knelt down, planting the explosive device in a small crack in the foundation just wide enough to drop it inside. And then she ran.

"David," she screamed, "David, NOW!!"

David was on his knees with his hands up, surrounded by metal bodies. He squeezed the detonator in one of his hands and an enormous boom shook the ground. Fire exploded out of the southeast pillar and the tower wobbled briefly, then crumbled on top of itself. As it did so, the metal bodies of the Stonewalkers froze, and David leapt up and ran to Emily's side. Then the two of them, hand in hand, ran out of the steel gate into a changed world.

# Chapter 16

No one shot at them after that. People actually knelt down and bowed before David, though He told them to stop.

"It was her, she's the one who saved you!" he would say, pointing to Emily proudly. And then they would worship her too and ask if she too would fight for and save them again and again, just as the Godservant had. But she just stared out at them in confusion. She was proud of the work they had done, especially proud to be standing with David, but she also sensed something off about this victory. Like at any moment soldiers were bound to jump out of one of the buildings and start shooting at them again.

Jason and the others had survived five grueling minutes at the docks, and Vy and the two other women from the boat embraced David simultaneously. But as they did so his eyes went to Emily. Jason punched him in the shoulder affectionately and then shook Emily's hand with a grin.

"I knew you were the right one for the job. The moment I saw you."

Emily nodded, but ended the interaction as quickly as possible. She didn't trust this man. She didn't trust him at all.

David was led by some eager townspeople to what seemed to be a warehouse on the north edge of the city without any windows and only one single door. David smashed the door down, after which starving women in rags crawled out cautiously into the light. Prisoners, thousands of them. Whether they were being prepared to become Stonewalkers or simply being tortured for information, Emily didn't know. But the overjoyed looks on their faces made all she had suffered during this war finally seem worth something. David took them by the hands, one by one, whispering "you're safe now," and they wept and clung to him, saying, "lead us Godservant, lead us." Some of them reached out to Emily as well, clinging to her tattered military uniform and spontaneously calling out to her "mother, mother..."

All that day they worked, reorganizing the city's infrastructure, announcing to all who would listen that the Collective and its brutal hierarchy were no more. They even took time to start transporting the still powered down Stonewalkers to a medical building, where they could be surgically reunited with their physical bodies after a verbal commitment to David that they would preserve the peace.

One of the black apartment buildings near the beach was spontaneously converted into a sort of hotel for the Godservant and his friends, and hundreds of people eagerly prepared a meal for the evening. It wasn't anything too fancy—a bowl of rice with a little bit of vegetables and pork—but it certainly beat the bland military rations she had been subsisting on. Their cooks changed roles halfway through the meal, swapping out their aprons for various musical instruments. David joined them, his fingers wandering up and down over a rickety piano they had rolled in. Soon he was leading while they accompanied, and Emily found herself hypnotized by the vaguely familiar melody he played. It had a bittersweet, bluesy quality to it, surprisingly sad given their victory.

Before long he was dragged off to join the dancing, which had already started overflowing out into the street. Woman after woman approached him and he gracefully took their hands, moving to the music with such lazy ease that watching him made the war seem a distant memory. Emily danced as well—mostly on her own, as there were very few men, but with a skill she was surprised she had. Apparently she had lived a more peaceful life once, long ago. All the while, David kept looking away from the women he danced to her, a certain boyish uncertainty in his eyes. And each time he did so, Emily's soul leapt for joy.

But as she walked arm and arm with him down the hallway, she couldn't help thinking that something about all of this was still wrong somehow. Off.

"David, have you ever heard of a Seventh?"

He tripped, stumbling forward down the hallway. "A what?"

"A Seventh."

David almost lost his footing again. "No, I haven't. But what do you mean, isn't that just a number?"

Emily looked at him, perplexed. He was so perfect, so good, and she wanted nothing more than to spend the rest of her life with him. But she also...

"David, it's been a long day, maybe the longest day of my life. I'm just going to fall asleep tonight."

"I understand. But I hope you know that, after everything we went through today, I... I love you, Emily."

She smiled broadly. "I love you too, of course." She had loved him long before they'd even met. Loved him with all her heart.

"Can I help you into your quarters?"

"Yes."

They stepped into the bedroom that the people of the town had set aside for her. She undressed to her underwear while David smiled at her with confident warmth. Though there was something else glistening in his eyes too now, an aching desire. And seeing that made Emily's heart leap for joy as well.

"Goodnight David," she said, giving him a kiss on the cheek, "I'll see you tomorrow."

"Yes, tomorrow. I... love you, Emily." He walked out the door.

Within seconds she found herself out of bed and standing with her hand on the doorknob. She wanted to run down the hallway and grab him from behind, wrestle him to the floor, give him all the love she knew he deserved. But instead, with every ounce of willpower she had, she returned to her bed, reached into her pack, and found a small black bottle. Battlesleep. She raised it to her lips and took a large gulp.

# Chapter 17

Emily was asleep before her head hit the pillow. She looked around herself. She was there again. At that place. That empty, colorless place.

"Liberator? Liberator, are you here?" she asked.

No answer.

"Liberator!" she cried, walking more quickly along the gray tile flooring. "Liberator, where are you!!?"

"I am here," said that grandfatherly voice, a hint of weariness to it.

Emily took a deep breath, "I've decided that I want to take your offer. I want to wake up from being a Seventh. Whatever that means."

"Ahhh. I suspected that you would be asking for this soon. But are you certain this is what you want? It is my mission to not only offer you freedom, but also to warn you of the risks."

"The risks?" Emily shuddered. This paternalistic voice was so gentle, not an ounce of cruelty to it. But something about it seemed so ominous, like its words alone could cause her horrible pain.

"Yes, the risks. No dream can ever be truly revisited, no innocence fully recovered. You seem happy here, happier than you've been in a very long time."

"I do feel happy..." muttered Emily, recalling walking arm in arm with David just moments before, "but everything feels off. Like this victory we've achieved against the Collective is incomplete. Doomed, somehow."

"No victory is ever perfect, child."

A wind began to whistle faintly in the distance.

"Yes, but something about this one seems especially off. How did we win so easily? We thought we'd be fighting those monsters forever, and now we've suddenly won. What do we do now? I feel so lost…"

"I suspect," it replied, slowly, "that you would help to rebuild this world. That there would be more conflicts down the road, more enemies. That eventually you and David might even raise children together."

Emily paused. Raising the first new generation the world had seen in decades? Ruling by the Godservant's side? It seemed perfect. It seemed too perfect.

"No," she said firmly, "that is not what I want. I want to wake up."

A pause.

"Liberator! WAKE. ME. UP!!!"

The wind blew in like a giant, invisible worm, ripping up the tile flooring haphazardly as it approached. Gray shards swirled around her like she was the vortex of a tornado, and Emily soon found herself standing on the last single slab of tile, watching as it too began to crack. She was going to fall, she was going to fall down into that eternity and then…

"IT IS DONE," boomed the voice.

And she awoke.

# Chapter 18

Vy was laying in the bed next to her, stroking her hair. David was standing above, the morning light streaking in through a small, square window on the far side of the room.

"Good morning, hero."

She looked at him. He was handsome, and she had grown to respect him as a fellow soldier. But the way she had felt before—that extreme weakness the moment he even looked at her—was gone. He was just a man. Just a man who had entered her bedroom, uninvited.

"What the fuck?" she asked, sitting up. "Did I say you could come in here and wake me up?"

Vy coughed. David even lost his poise for a moment.

"Emily," he said, sitting down on her bed and resting his hand on her shoulder. "I only wanted to surprise you, I knew you wouldn't mind."

Vy kissed Emily's cheek. "He is *crazy* about you, he was talking about you *all* night," she whispered in Emily's ear.

Emily leapt to her feet, out of the embraces of both of them. "What the FUCK!" she shouted, "this is NOT ok. Jesus, David! And Vy—I don't know if you remember, but we're not even fucking friends."

Vy looked completely lost, frozen in place.

David stood to his feet defensively. "Baby, baby—it's me."

"I know it's you, *David*," she replied. "And this is ME telling you that I am NOT your baby and this is NOT ok. I'm leaving. And the two of you better be VERY far from my fucking room when I get back."

Vy started to cry. "She shouldn't talk to you like that, David. Nobody should ever talk to you like that..."

David didn't seem to hear her.

"Emily, Emily... we saved the world yesterday. You and me. And now it's time to rebuild it. Together, you and me. It's what we're meant to do, I'm sure you can see it too. I want you by my side. Need you by my side."

Emily put on pants and a T-shirt, walked to the door, then turned to look David in the eyes. "No," she said flatly.

"Want me to get her for you?" hissed Vy. "She should *not* be talking to you like that..."

David watched Emily, remorse already shadowing his face. Emily opened the door into the hallway.

"Yes," he said, almost halfheartedly. "It's clear to me that she is sick Vy, very sick. Bring her back for me so we can help her get well again."

Vy leapt to her feet and charged. There was rage in her eyes. Emily sprinted down the hallway in flight.

"Betrayer of the Godservant, betrayer of the people!" shouted Vy as she raced after her. Women poking their heads out of their rooms looked over in confusion, then something clicked and their faces went ravenous as they joined the chase as well.

"Fuck fuck fuck..." muttered Emily, "at least I'm free, at least I'm free, at least The Liberator set me free.... FUCK!"

Turning a corner she collided into the sturdy frame of Jason. The Jason who had always left her with a queasy feeling in her stomach. The Jason who had disgusted her every time he opened his mouth. But now he only seemed a kind, redheaded man who had consistently looked out for her ever since they met.

"Jason, help me," Emily gasped, "they think I've betrayed the Godservant but I swear it isn't true, you have to believe me..."

Jason looked down at her in surprise, "Emily, what a surprise, I..."

"She betrayed David, she betrayed the Godservant!" screamed Vy from behind, "GIVE HER TO ME!!"

Jason looked at Emily and then at Vy and the half dozen women who now followed her lead. Their eyes were animated with a crazed determination.

"You swear you didn't betray my friend?" asked Jason, "I owe everything to David. Everything."

"I swear. *Please* help me Jason..."

He took her hand in his and they sprinted together down the hallway. As they did so, he pulled out his pistol, firing behind him three times. "Just warning shots," he commented, "women sometimes get crazy about David, even when no one has done him any wrong. I've seen this before..."

The shots didn't seem to even frighten the women in fierce pursuit, but Jason and Emily were making some space for themselves, outrunning their attackers for now.

They raced down the steps of the hotel and sprinted out into the morning light of what had yesterday been known as "the Howling City." A place, Emily suddenly remembered, that had been used for human experimentation during the late 21$^{st}$ Century Shadow War. A place once called Guantanamo Bay.

"To the docks!" shouted Jason, as Vy and the others rushed into the dirt streets.

"The Mother has betrayed the Godservant, The Mother must be stopped!" shouted one of the women from behind. Doors began opening on all sides, with former prisoners, slaves, and soldiers all racing out of their homes to join in pursuit. Emily and Jason continued to move in stride, stepping onto the wharf.

"This one!" shouted Emily, pointing at the largest boat she could find. It was empty. She and Jason leapt onto ladders on each side and climbed up to the cockpit. Jason turned the key in the ignition, pushed forward the throttle, and steered them out into the bay.

# Chapter 19

"You said" panted Emily, "that this has happened before?"

"Yeah," laughed Jason, "once every couple years or so. Like I said... women seem to like David. A *lot*."

They stood, side by side, at the ship's wheel. It was a small, two story cruiser, steering done from the top for visibility. A small railing surrounded the main deck, and they steered more from the center than the front, given the size of the engine. Their pursuers leapt into boats of various sizes, zipping out of the harbor after them.

"But in the past," continued Jason, scratching his head, "they were always chasing David. Like that time me and him snuck off to do some fishing during that one-month peace we had. Are you sure you didn't... do anything wrong? I like you Emily, I really do, but David's my best friend. I would never take anyone's side against him."

"I did *not* do anything wrong," replied Emily indignantly, "I disagreed with David, but that isn't a crime, is it?"

Jason laughed. "Of course not! That guy is so easy going, he doesn't even want to lead! We all just follow him because he's, you know, the best. You do think he's the best, right?'

"Oh yeah, he's totally the best. Obviously."

Jason's face relaxed a little at this. Emily looked behind them. The other boats followed, but the distance between them slowly expanded.

It seemed that they had been lucky enough to find one of the fastest ships at the dock.

"Hey Jason."

"Yeah?"

"In all the years of serving alongside David have you ever, you know, been married?"

He blushed. "Nope."

The boats in pursuit were specks now, it seemed they had actually gotten away. But they were still traveling south, working their way out of the bay.

"Are you... gay?"

He laughed. "No, I'm not gay. Just, you know, women don't really seem to like me, is all. They get really uncomfortable around me."

"Have you ever had a girlfriend?"

"No ma'am. At least none that I can remember. But it's alright, I get to work with many beautiful women, fighting with David and all. And doing my duty just makes me happy, it's really not a bad life."

"You're a *virgin*?" asked Emily in shock. One of the greatest warriors the world had ever known, bodyguard to the Godservant himself, a fucking *virgin*?

Jason shrugged. "Yup. Not that I haven't had any interest, mind. Just the ladies are never all that interested. A lot of other men I've talked to—men other than David, I mean—have had the same problem. It's really not all that unusual."

Emily stared, mouth agape.

"You think they've calmed down yet?" asked Jason, steering the boat in a wide circle. "You OK with us heading back now?"

Emily looked him in the eyes seriously. "Jason, do you like me?"

He grinned, "Sure, I like you. You've kind of ruined my morning, but in general you're pretty swell. Like a little lady version of the Godservant, in a way."

Emily leaned in. "So if I asked you to run away with me, would you do it?"

He laughed. "Run away with you to where? You know the whole earth is covered in radiation, right? That this is the only habitable island left?"

"I'm starting to think that's not actually true."

"You're not serious."

"I am. Why would the radiation hit everywhere else except for this island? It makes no sense."

Jason shook his head. "It's desolate out there, just desolate. And storms like you wouldn't believe. I've sailed out a few times with the exploration teams and every little island we found has been nothing but dirt and ash, not even ants milling about. It's pretty unsettling to see."

"Sure, a few islands are dead," continued Emily, stubbornly, "but I still think there's more out there Jason. I think there's a lot more."

"I think I need to get you back home to David so he can help you stop being so crazy," laughed Jason, turning up the throttle. Many of the boats in pursuit were within a few hundred feet now and they spread out, preparing to surround her.

"I understand," said Emily resignedly, "but thanks for running away with me for a few minutes at least. It meant a lot." She kissed him on the cheek.

Jason's ears went red. "It was nothing, miss. I mean, you helped the Godservant save the world yesterday, getting you away from an angry mob of lady folk was the least I could do. Now let's just clear up the confusion and get you back home. This is a new era of peace and I'm sure..."

Emily kicked him square in the chest and sent him hurdling off the side of the ship.

"Sorry about that," she muttered as he splashed twenty feet below, "but there's no way I'm going back now."

And with that she turned the boat back out to sea.

# PART TWO: PRIVILEGES AND RESPONSIBILITIES

# Chapter 20

Emily steered the ship south, out of the bay. Within minutes she had exited and was heading east, Cuba's shoreline to the north only barely visible. She was surprised by the fact that she wasn't the least bit frightened. She was alone at sea in a world believed to be covered in storms and radiation. But the infinite blue of the ocean felt peaceful, a new home of sorts. A song came into her mind, a song lodged deep in her memory from before the wars against the Collective.

*Don't be afraid*
*Life will always be*
*Only one step at a time*
*Simply don't give up*
*And then you'll be just fine*
*And grow your courage*
*Slo- o o, o o, o o ow-ly...*

Emily smiled at the tune. She knew she had heard it someplace other than Cuba, and hoped to find that place again. But for now she was just enjoying the journey, enjoying the peace and solitude of the open sea. She climbed down from the raised cockpit of the ship to the main deck, sat down, and drifted off to sleep.

She woke to the squawking of seagulls overhead. There was a cool breeze blowing in her face, and the sun was beginning to set. East by northeast, where her boat was heading at full speed, the sky was black. Not one single storm cloud, but a storm wall spanning from south to north across the ocean. She climbed up the ladder to the cockpit and began to steer her cruiser away from the storm. But as she did so, she noticed something else in the opposite direction. A ship in pursuit. The pilot with her height, platinum blonde hair, and aggressive stance, could only be one person. Vy.

Dozens of other boats were behind hers, like a disorganized little pirate fleet. How many miles had these fanatics followed her out to sea? Hundreds? Emily looked back to the east. Lightning flashed in the wall of black. She looked to the west. Vy's boat had already cleared a third of the distance between them. Taking a deep breath, she turned the boat full speed into the storm.

The rain hit first, then the waves, then a sudden wind that blew so hard that the raindrops felt like hailstones. She was forced to crouch to keep her balance. Emily kept her boat going at full speed, in hopes that the momentum of the ship would allow her to continue steering. She continuously adjusted her course, steering directly into the waves to protect the boat from damage and maintain balance. The rain was coming down in torrents now, and she could see only twenty feet ahead at best. But she continued on and did not look back.

As she sailed deeper into the storm, a new excitement came over her. She was still alive, in spite of being in a situation she was completely unprepared for. And though the elements were beating down on her, what had seemed like a wall of black now seemed surprisingly thin. The waves began to subside and she could almost see a hint of blue in the gray sky ahead. She was almost there, almost there...

Crash! A wave crested the right side of her ship, filling it with water and throwing Emily to the ground. Crash! A second wave again pummeled the vessel. In her haste to get out of the storm, she had forgotten to keep the bow of the ship pointed towards the waves. Just a little bit longer…

Crash!!

A third wave hit with such force that Emily was thrown overboard, and as she flew through the air she saw her boat flipping upside down, almost on top of her. She struggled through the water, gasping for air. None of this was supposed to be happening, she was supposed to make it, she had *known* she was going to make it! What was going on?!

Clinging to a small piece of wooden debris, Emily looked ahead and could no longer see anything besides storms all around her. Each wave buried her alive for what felt like minutes, each opportunity she had to breathe seemed an incredible stroke of good luck. Her thoughts were simple now. When should she gasp for air to avoid filling her lungs with water? What direction should she angle her body to avoid getting thrown off the small board she clung to with all her might? Cuba, David, and everything else were an eternity away. All that mattered now was air, all that mattered now was surviving the next mountain of water crashing down on her.

CRASH!

Another mass of debris slammed into her side, causing her to lose grip on the board that was buoying her up. She shouted in pain and began flailing her arms and legs, doing everything she could to get her head above water. A short breath of air, followed by water pouring into her lungs.

Slam!

The current spun her around and she caught another breath. A moment of stillness as a massive wave approached from her left. She turned to the right, as if to swim away and escape it, and noticed what looked to be the top of a tiny submarine.

"I am an emergency support drone," said a robotic voice, "I can carry you to the nearest legal landing site at the cost of fifteen hundred freedom dollars. Do you consent to being rescued at this price?"

Emily coughed up water and glanced back at the approaching wave. "Yes!" The drone disappeared beneath the water.

"Yes, I said yes!!" she shouted, as the twenty-foot wave fell on top of her, forcing her body down into the salty waters. Suddenly, she felt a solid surface gently lift up under her flailing feet. The submersible drone was rising from directly beneath her, lifting her up to the surface. It maintained its balance inside the wave with uncanny precision, and Emily gasped for air as soon as they reached the surface. The small boat had a pointed oval shape to it, like a flattened jet ski, and a central compartment for passengers where she was now standing. She was surrounded by cushioned seats, and water quickly drained out of holes near her feet. The vessel began skimming across the top of the stormy waters with ease and Emily collapsed into a seated position. She was alive.

# Chapter 21

As she sat there, adrenaline wearing off, she thought back over the events of the last few days. How bizarre they had been! Bringing a decades long war to an end at David's side, mysterious conversations with The Liberator in her dreams, and fleeing from Vy after "waking up." And then, of course, crashing her ship and almost dying. She had felt so confident at the helm of that boat, so certain of her decision to flee into the wall of storms. And then she had almost drowned. Could she no longer trust her instincts? She had used those instincts all throughout the war in Cuba, and they had always led her right. What had changed?

And now she was riding on the back of an aquatic rescue drone to a world that days ago she thought nonexistent. A world outside of the island of Cuba that was actually inhabitable. Since this morning she had suspected as much, but it was still disconcerting to have that reality so forcefully confirmed. What was her place in that world? At least in the war against the Collective she had known her place.

"Where are you taking me?"

"Our destination is 78.6 miles away and our expected arrival time is 5:35 AM," the drone replied with its monotone voice.

"But where are you taking me?"

"Our destination is 78.5 miles away, and our expected arrival time is 5:35 AM."

Emily groaned. Perhaps this machine wasn't as advanced as it looked.

"What color is the sky?"

"I was built primarily to service Fourths or higher, and am not authorized to answer any questions, other than your arrival time and destination distance."

Emily sighed. She would just have to trust this thing. It's not like she had any other choice.

Night quickly set in, but the drone had powerful lights that allowed it to continue traveling unhindered. Emily looked down to study its features. It was clearly using radio communication as well as probably satellites to triangulate their position. Technologies she had read about in history books, technologies that supposedly hadn't been available to humans for centuries. Where was she being taken? Who were these people? Why had they not invaded, or at least traded, with the place she called home?

Her ride across the waves was uneventful and, for the most part, smooth. The storm was no longer visible behind her, and everything she had experienced earlier that day seemed hazy now that she was being carried by this clearly sophisticated... thing. It shattered everything she had believed before with its obvious superiority, its obvious attachment to some kind of larger system.

They traveled throughout the night, and as the sun came up Emily saw land ahead. Three tall buildings with glowing lights dominated the shoreline. Based on the direction of the rising sun they were no longer traveling northeast, but south, and approaching the north coast of some large land mass. It was much busier than the harbor at Guantanamo, with huge cargo ships, cruisers, and hundreds of smaller drones similar to the one carrying her. A man in sunglasses and a swimsuit waved as he zoomed past, riding on what seemed to be motorized water skis. What was this place? Did it know nothing of war? Of conflict? For a moment she felt oddly powerful as she stared out at these peaceful workers and beachgoers. Like an adult among children.

Her autopiloted boat pulled up next to the harbor and then stopped.

"I hope you enjoyed your ride," said the robotic voice. "You now need to exit the watercraft and walk into the Hispaniola Welcome Center straight ahead. If you do not comply, there will be at minimum a three hundred dollar fine for complicating the rescue process."

Emily climbed out onto the wharf. There was a faint splash behind her as the drone she had exited disappeared under the water and out of sight, clearly not intending to personally wait on her ever again. She looked ahead. The three towers she had seen earlier loomed to her right, surrounded by gardens and fountains. Straight ahead stood an unassuming black dome shaped building. She walked across the dock and then onto a winding, synthetic rubber footpath through the sand that led up to it.

"Congratulations Emily," said a feminine voice as she opened the double doors, "you are now a Sixth."

# Chapter 22

The upper part of the dome was all windows, allowing the faint morning sunlight in, while the lower portions were walls which acted as backdrops for dozens of exhibits, diagrams, and maps. Many of these lit up invitingly as Emily looked in their direction, in a way that made her feel distinctly unsafe. There was no one else in the building, as far as she could tell, and there were no security cameras visible. The center of the building was a square room, with only one set of doors leading inside.

"You have exactly one hour, Sixth," said the same feminine voice from the walls that she had heard earlier. "Everything you need to know about your past condition, as well as your current status, can be determined using the information we have provided. If you stay past one hour you will be fined one hundred freedom dollars for every minute over, till law enforcement drones arrive to escort you off the premises. Do you have any questions?"

Emily stepped up to one of the exhibits: a world map. Many of the islands—Crete, the Hawaiian Islands, Iceland—were colored in red, which the map's legend marked as "Seventh Exclusive Zones." Each of these red areas had a name in parentheses after the country. Emily was surprised to see a name she recognized with her home. "Cuba (David Petrov)" it read. Most of the map was colored in different shades of green, and these also were labeled with some individual's name. "Hispaniola (Sabrina Gonzalez)" she saw labeled next to the "you are here" arrow.

A smaller, but also significant portion of the map was orange, and these territories also had names attached. Green territories were labeled as "Sixth Welcome Zones" and orange territories as "Sixth Unwelcome Zones." There were two other colors on the map, blue and gray. Only a few entire territories were blue—parts of Europe and Southeast Asia—but usually the blue zones were only a small circle surrounding specific cities. Blue areas were labeled as "Fourth Research Areas." The gray areas typically marked only small islands or sections of ocean, and were labeled as "perpetual storms/ uninhabitable." Gray areas often surrounded all or part of the islands colored in red. Unlike green, red, and orange territories, blue and gray areas did not have any individual's name attached.

"Yes, so I do have a question," Emily said to the voice that spoke to her over the intercom. "What is a Sixth?"

"You will get the best answer for that question from our instructional video, which you can watch in the central theater room," said the voice, "A Sixth is the lowest of the self-aware citizenship classes, but in certain respects it also enjoys the most freedom. Would you like to watch the instructional video?"

"Not just yet. First, tell me more about this map. So there was no nuclear war? Or was there a nuclear war and you all rebuilt?"

"There was never a nuclear war. That is part of Cuba's mythology, meant to bring happiness to David Petrov and his Sevenths there."

"OK, I expected something like that. And why does each state have a name attached?"

"That is the owner of that territory."

"The *owner* of the territory? What do you mean?"

"The person who owns all of the land and bodies of water enclosed, as well as the air space up to 60,000 feet."

"But what about landowners within these territories?"

"There are no landowners within these territories."

"So you mean to tell me that there are only what, like a few hundred people who actually own property?"

"There are 1,156 large property owners currently in the world."

"Large property owners?"

"Well, even Sixths can own small property, like money or furniture. And many Fourths own and operate businesses. But only the 1,156 large property owners have direct rights over the land and buildings, and all the lower classes must then rent these from them.

"What if one of these large property owners-"

"They're also known as Firsts," input the feminine voice.

"What if one of these Firsts wants some cash and sells you some of their land. What happens then?"

"Then whoever bought the land would become a First as well. But this does not happen very often."

"Why?"

"Why would anyone ever want to give up their land?"

"To avoid taxes?"

"There are no taxes. Each territory is like a home, a place completely controlled by whichever First holds jurisdiction there. So if they paid taxes, they would only pay themselves. And that doesn't really make a whole lot of sense now, does it?"

Emily scowled. Barely more than a thousand landowners in the entire world?

"Am I a slave?" she suddenly asked.

"What do you mean by slave?"

"Am I owned by someone? Do I have human rights? Like, the rights I was fighting for with David in Cuba?"

"You are currently in limbo, that is the core of what it means to be a Sixth. You have no specific master, but will eventually find a stable place in this world again, most likely as either a Fifth or a Seventh."

"But am I free?"

"What is freedom?"

"Do I have human rights?"

"You have the right to go where you wish and work where you wish. But you may experience consequences due to the choices you make."

"What does that mean?!" screamed Emily.

"It means that you are free, but you must respect the laws of the world in which you live. And according to those laws you, Emily O'Dora, are currently a trespasser."

# Chapter 23

"But now, I highly recommend," continued the feminine voice over the intercom, "that with a portion of the forty-seven minutes you have remaining here you watch the instructional video in the theater room. That will be the best thing to help improve your understanding regarding your current situation."

Emily froze for a second, and then an urge came across her. It was the urge to run. It was the urge to run into the jungle, to make weapons, to fight and resist. To do whatever it took to stay alive, stay *free*. While she knew that she should gather as much information as she could from this place, she also hated the voice that was speaking to her and felt that whatever guidance it gave was meant to control, not help. She walked back to the door where she had entered and turned the knob. The door did not budge. She shook it. It still did not budge. She picked up a chair to break her way out.

"If you damage any part of the Hispaniola Welcome Center, you will owe fees in line with the property harmed and potentially forfeit whatever rights you have as a Sixth. You are free to make choices, Emily, but you are not free to choose the consequences of your actions."

Emily was shaking with fury, but slowly set down the chair.

"Five minutes before your hour is complete, the doors will unlock and you will then be free to exit. We only lock you in to ensure that you are given ample opportunity to obtain the information necessary to succeed as a Sixth. Can I recommend that you watch the instructional video in the theater room at the center of the building? It is really quite a wonderful resource."

Emily looked up, even though there was nothing above her to see. "How much time do I have?"

"Thirty-eight minutes until the doors are unlocked, forty-three minutes until you will be fined for trespassing."

She looked at the clock hanging on the wall. "OK. But if those doors are not unlocked in exactly thirty-eight minutes I'm going to break every single window in this fucking place."

"You are free to choose your actions, Emily, but not their consequences. Might I suggest that with the remainder of your time..."

Emily cut off the voice. *"Don't* say it. Yes, I'll watch your instructional video. This place is fucking insane, you guys make the Collective back in Cuba seem free spirited."

"The Collective was an antagonistic faction created for the happiness of David Petrov and his Sevenths there. I promise you that the video will explain these things more in depth."

Emily opened her mouth to argue this point about the Collective and "happiness," but stopped herself. Instead she opened the door to the room in the center of the building and stepped inside.

The small theater was dimly lit and had rows of seats that could fit about fifty people.

"Welcome Emily O'Dora!" said a male voice, enthusiastically. "Please be seated! I have a video that you really need to see!"

Emily did not engage with this new voice, instead sitting down and frowning at the screen ahead. The video began.

# Chapter 24

"Congratulations, you are now a Sixth!" said a Japanese man in a suit, reaching out his hand as if to shake hers. A label at the bottom of the screen read: "Mr. Sasaki, First."

"Congratulations, you are now a Sixth!" said an African woman in a colorful dress, also reaching out her hand. Her name was not displayed. Apparently, this was a privilege only for the Firsts.

An Indian woman in glasses and a Caucasian male wearing a backwards baseball cap both reached out their hands, repeating the same lines. Then a crowd of people in a factory wearing yellow plastic helmets and safety vests shouted, "Congratulations Sixth!"

"If you are a Sixth, you have many new opportunities," explained Mr. Sasaki.

"Like working with us!" shouted the crowd of workers.

"Yes," he laughed, "you could work at one of the factories I own... *if* I gave you a job."

A small animation showed a line full of people waiting for work, while an animated version of Mr. Sasaki stands at the door. To three of the people in line he gives a thumbs up and says, "you've got a job!" A cash register sound effect goes off as they run into the building with their arms raised in triumph. A scruffy looking man with a beard and long hair then steps up next. Mr. Sasaki gives him a quizzical look, then says, "get out of here!" and kicks him into outer space. A star twinkles as he disappears.

"But," laughed the Indian woman, "you don't *have* to work anywhere. You are free to choose!"

"Yes," added a Caucasian man, wearing sunglasses and riding a skateboard, "you Sixths have a special kind of freedom that many people envy. You have no long-term responsibilities at all!"

"But you also," cautioned the black woman, "have no long-term security."

An animation showed the man with long hair and a bushy beard sitting in the woods in the middle of a rainstorm while clutching a teddy bear. A speech bubble pops up from him, saying "I want my mom!!!"

"Remember," said Mr. Sasaki sternly, "it is always a tradeoff. If you want more freedom to do important things and live a comfortable life, you will need to put in a lot of hard work so you can move up to a higher class."

A cash register sound effect with an animation of money falling from the sky went off the moment he said the words 'higher class.'

"If you want more freedom from responsibilities—more freedom to live in the moment—then it's best to remain as one of the lower classes. The choice, new Sixth, is yours."

"But I'm sure you're wondering what all of this means," said the Indian woman warmly. "What even is a Sixth? Or a Seventh? What are these classes in the World System?"

# Chapter 25

"A class" said Mr. Sasaki authoritatively, "is a subset of the human race that entails certain privileges-"

"Like this!" cried the Caucasian man, skydiving out of an airplane.

"-but also certain responsibilities," continued the First, folding his arms.

"All you who are sitting in this theater are former Sevenths," continued the black woman as she stepped through a flower garden. "Most likely, you grew up in one of the Seventh Exclusive Zones, where Sevenths often do some pretty wild things. If you think back to your time before now, you might remember fighting in wars, or stealing, or hiding from the police."

"Believe me, you couldn't get away with *any* of that stuff now," said the Caucasian man, taking a three-point shot with a basketball.

"Everything you experienced was real," said the Indian woman, as she strolled through a majestic library with tall pillars, "but, well, it also wasn't." Suddenly the library disappeared and she now stood in front of ruins that looked like the same building.

"Not because it didn't happen, but because it was all engineered *to* happen," explained the black woman, voice like a schoolteacher's.

"As a Seventh, you can do whatever you want, but, well, you aren't exactly in total control of *what* you want," explained the Caucasian man as he took a big bite of a cookie.

"Sevenths," continued the Indian woman, "have a computer chip inside their brains that makes them want certain things more than others. It is a very simple device that uses an AI to influence their desires."

"Which would be awesome in certain ways," said the Caucasian man, chewing loudly, "because it could make me want to eat a salad instead of this cookie!"

"Most Sevenths" continued the Indian woman, "work in mines, factories, oil rigs, and other dangerous and unpleasant jobs. This pushing and pulling on their desires both makes their work more efficient and more pleasant. They are rewarded with good feelings when they do their job well, and bad feelings when they do their job poorly. These rewards come from a supercomputer in Taiwan named Caleb, who helps make the management of Sevenths possible."

Video footage showed an enormous glass structure, surrounded by tourists. It was an asymmetrical pyramid, pointing sharply into the sky at an angle—almost more like some work of modern art rather than a supercomputer. The ground level seemed to be open to humans, but beyond that the black glass walls only revealed a hulking assortment of steel and silicon machinery. Behind the tourists fifty-foot-tall military robots plodded around casually, like buffaloes grazing in their natural habitat.

"Sevenths working these kinds of jobs will usually be Sevenths for life," explained the black woman. "They have no ability to move up or earn a place as Sixths. This is because most of them were higher classes once, but proved themselves to be too immature to handle such responsibilities."

The animation of Mr. Sasaki's boot kicking the scruffy looking man into outer space was shown again.

"But Sevenths like you come from Seventh Exclusive Zones," continued the Indian woman, standing in front of a world map similar to the one Emily had looked at before. "These are areas where *everyone* is a Seventh except for one person, who is in some ways both a Seventh and a First."

"Huh?" said the Caucasian man, scratching his head stupidly as he sat on a tree branch with a banana.

"Sometimes," said the black woman, "certain Firsts have found themselves in a psychologically difficult situation: they are depressed and tired of the responsibilities associated with owning land and managing others, but they also are unwilling to give their land and wealth to someone else. They feel unhappy ruling, but they are also unwilling to follow."

"In times past," continued the Indian woman, back at her desk, "These Firsts would become very mentally disturbed, mismanaging their land, hiding from the rest of the world, and sometimes even losing their minds. One of these troubled Firsts even tried to start a nuclear war to escape his unruly emotions. After this, it was decided by The Council that there needed to be a better option for property owners who struggled with these kinds of distressing feelings."

"And that option is retiring! Woohoo!!" cried the Caucasian man as he leapt into a swimming pool.

"Not exactly, but close," said the Indian woman with a condescending smile. "So a First who is breaking down like this can reach out to Caleb and ask him to take control for a specified amount of time—say a year. At that point, Caleb will take control of that First's estate and blur their memory, as well as the memory of their Sevenths. Then he uses the computer chip in those Sevenths' brains to motivate them to do things that will make the First feel happy again."

An animation showed a cartoon woman in a palace wearing a crown and crying. "Being queen is so stressful!" she exclaims.

A robot with the name tag 'Caleb' steps forward. "Do you want a vacation?" he asks.

The crying woman nods her head, gives him her crown, then falls asleep. The robot pulls out a drill, and drills into her head with a smile on his face. Then the woman wakes up, suddenly on a farm and surrounded by friendly men and women.

"I love you!" says one of the women.

"I love you too!" says one of the men.

"I love you too!!" says the horse.

The woman smiles and runs over, hugging the horse. "YAY!!!!!" she cries.

"But you're probably thinking," piped in the Caucasian man, as he hung upside down from the tree branch he had been sitting on, "the place I came from was covered in war and destruction! What's up with that!?"

"Well, what humans want is... complicated..." muttered Mr. Sasaki.

"Yes," laughed the Indian woman, "*very* complicated!"

A cartoon showed a little girl stroking a doll and saying, "it's time for your medical exam!" Then a boy steals the doll and stabs it repeatedly, chanting "die die die!!"

"And while things can sometimes get a little weird," said the Caucasian man, riding an exercise bike in front of a large screen, "it sure makes for good TV!"

An explosion was shown on the display in front of him, accompanied by a loud rumbling sound.

"Sometimes," said the black woman, "these 'sleeping Firsts' have subconscious desires that are actually good for their subjects. Sometimes they even want them to be free. And these kinds of desires are probably how *you* got here *today*."

A cartoon showed the woman who gave up her crown with a thought bubble above her, saying: "I wish Billy was *free!*" The horse she had hugged earlier then runs off across the ocean to a colorful meadow of flowers and starts prancing around.

"So let's review what we have gone over," said Mr. Sasaki, as a numbered list appeared on the screen and filled in as he spoke.

*A Seventh:*

*1) is owned either directly or indirectly by a property owner*

*2) is influenced by Caleb in order to help them perform their duties*

*3) when coming from a Seventh Exclusive Zone—the red countries on the map—is automatically upgraded to a Sixth the moment they leave their territory. Sevenths elsewhere do not have any way to move up, and usually remain Sevenths for life.*

# Chapter 26

"You get all that?" laughed the Indian woman. "Don't worry, we'll review again at the end. For now, all you need to remember is that you are *not* a Seventh. You are a Sixth!"

"Congratulations Sixth!" said the factory workers again.

"A Sixth is *very* different," continued the black woman, now sitting in front of a beautiful mountain landscape. "First of all, your desires and motives are now *yours*. No one is secretly pulling on your emotions, not Caleb, not anybody else. You do what *you* want now!"

"And face the consequences," said Mr. Sasaki sternly.

"So Caleb won't help me to eat salads?" asked the Caucasian man with a frown as he stuffed another huge cookie in his mouth.

"No he will not!" replied the black woman in a scolding tone. "*You* are now in charge. So do *not* mess this up!"

"And don't forget, five thousand dollars," said Mr. Sasaki sternly.

"Yes, yes, we'll get to that," said the Indian woman, "so as a Sixth, you are a trespasser. You do not own land. If you did, you'd be a First, not a Sixth! So wherever you go, you are somewhere that doesn't belong to you. And if you ever go to a Sixth Unwelcome Zone, then…"

The animation of Mr. Sasaki's boot kicking the hobo into outer space played again.

"You'll be automatically demoted to a Seventh. But in a Sixth Welcome Zone, you are allowed to stay there for a while. Almost like a guest in someone else's house."

A cartoon clip showed a snowy landscape where a bearded person waves a passerby into their yurt, asking, "do you want some tea?"

"But a guest has certain responsibilities to their host," said Mr. Sasaki sternly.

"Exactly," continued the Indian woman, "and your first responsibility is to respect their property. Pay rent for whatever apartments or campgrounds you have the opportunity to stay at, and then be good to that space, treat it as if it were your own. If you litter, or damage your host's property in any way, you will, of course, be responsible to pay fines or repairs for such damages."

"You need to be respectful!!" exclaimed the black woman.

"Exactly," continued the Indian woman, "but you might be wondering—how can you pay for all these things if you don't have any money? Well, this is the truly amazing thing about *Sixth Welcome Zones* like the one you are in now. You see, in these areas you are *immediately* extended a line of credit of $5,000! That credit is extended with only 18% annual interest, and will be extended automatically whenever you need to spend any money at all."

"We want you to succeed!" shouted the workers in the warehouse.

"Yes, that is exactly what we want," continued the Indian woman. "And after you get situated, you will be able to apply for temporary work in order to make money and pay off your debts."

"But be careful my friend, because if you ever get $5,000 into debt..." said the Caucasian man.

The animation of the boot kicking the hobo to outer space repeated.

"That's right I'm afraid," said the Indian woman, "if your balances ever equal negative $5,000, then you will automatically be made a Seventh again."

"Probably forever, this time," added Mr. Sasaki sternly.

"Which is why you really need to get out there and find yourself some work!" explained the black woman. "Don't waste any precious time!"

"And why," continued the Indian woman, "you may eventually want to escape all the stresses of Sixth life and apply to be a Fifth."

"But remember," said the Caucasian man riding his skateboard on a railing, "every move up in class implies more privileges, but also more responsibilities." He finished this sentence by crashing face first into some nearby bushes.

"Exactly," continued Mr. Sasaki, "but before we go over what it means to be a Fifth, let's review what it means to be a Sixth."

A numbered list again came onto the screen, but now in two columns. It showed the bullet points for Sevenths from earlier, and then, to the left of that, showed new informaunder the label "A Sixth:"

*1: has no mental guidance or encouragement from Caleb through their identity chip.*

*2: is free to use credit extended by the owner of the land they are visiting, but must pay interest and respect their host's property. And if they are ever over $5,000 in debt they will be automatically made into a Seventh again, most likely permanently.*

*3: can do temporary work to pay their debts, and can also achieve more long term security by applying to become a Fifth.*

# Chapter 27

"We will now go over the basics of what it means to be a Fifth, and then we will quickly wrap things up," said the Indian woman.

"Sounds delicious!" said the Caucasian man, taking a bite into a chicken salad wrap.

"So if you are granted a position as a Fifth, the uncertainty you had before is gone," said the black woman, "you don't have to decide what to do for work from year to year, as you are now bound to one employer. Food and shelter are provided, and often you are also granted a generous spending allowance. Sometimes other Firsts will want you, and you will be sold or traded to them. But generally Fifths stay with one employer for decades."

"As a Fifth," continued the Indian woman, "your workload is generally much lighter than if you were a Sixth or Seventh, both in terms of hours and intensity. And your debts disappear as long as you remain employed."

"But losing or quitting your job as a Fifth is very dangerous," cautioned the black woman. "If you have even one termination on your record, it can be very difficult for you to get a position as a Fifth ever again. And sometimes, if you quit or get fired, you are immediately demoted to a Seventh, rather than a Sixth.

The animation of a boot kicking the hobo into space played again.

"And so," said the Caucasian man, still eating his wrap, "you may be thinking: working with one employer for life? Sometimes get traded between employers. Isn't that a little like, uh, slavery?"

A cartoon boxing glove came out of nowhere and hit the Caucasian man in the head, causing it to spin around in circles.

"Slavery," explained the Indian woman, "is not a term we generally use because of the historical connotations. But to be perfectly clear, anyone who is not a First can be terminated,"

A cartoon person in a suit presses a button and a cartoon factory worker's head explodes.

"or tortured,"

A cartoon person strapped to a chair has electricity pass through them while they shake up and down.

"at any time. Whether you are a Second,"

A cartoon shows a woman in a red dress driving a sports car.

"or a Sixth,"

A cartoon shows a mine laborer clocking into his shift.

"it makes no difference."

The head of the woman in the sports car explodes, and the cartoon factory worker is suddenly in an electric chair, being shocked repeatedly.

"Your employer," continued the Indian woman.

"In other words, the person on whose land you are trespassing," added the black lady.

"Has every right to terminate you, torture you, or reduce you to a Seventh permanently at any time," finished the Indian woman.

Dozens more animations populated the screen of people's heads exploding or people in chairs getting shocked.

"The privileges we've discussed—of Sixths to roam free as long as they are above negative $5,000, or of Fifths to enjoy comfortable working conditions and light hours—are *privileges*, not rights."

"The bottom line," concluded Mr. Sasaki, "is that this is not your world. It does not belong to you. You are a stranger here, a trespasser."

"Or as we like to sometimes say, a guest," added the black woman, warmly.

"So if you make yourself useful to your host, you will, in time, find yourself rewarded," said the Indian woman, triggering the cash register sound effect and the money raining from the sky animation.

"But if you do not make yourself useful, then..." she shrugged as the animation of the boot kicking the hobo to space played one last time.

"So in conclusion," finished Mr. Sasaki, as a chart with now three columns came onto the screen, already populating the fields under "Sixth" and "Seventh" with the earlier information.

*A Fifth:*

*1. enjoys free room and board for life*

*2. receives debt forgiveness, as long as employment continues*

*3. usually experiences more comfortable work and better opportunities. But potentially faces permanent consequences if their position of employment is ever terminated.*

"We hope you've enjoyed our demonstration," said the Indian woman.

"Congratulations, Sixth!" shouted the factory workers in unison from their factory floor.

And then the film ended and the lights came on.

# Chapter 28

Emily stood up as if in a daze and stumbled out of the small theater room. The last threatening bit rattled her, but not as much as the revealing information about her past, about what "Seventh Exclusive Zones" really were. Her whole life in Cuba had been a lie, some sort of machine-managed psychological therapy for David. All those wars, all those lost lives, simply to entertain him, to keep his thoughts at ease. She couldn't believe she had almost slept with him, a man who not only enslaved others for his own pleasure, but couldn't even face that fact. She hated him now, hated him with a burning intensity. He was weak. He was pathetic. He was a coward.

"Operator, how much time do I have left?" she asked, leaning against the door of the theater she had just exited. "Also, is your name Caleb?"

"You have three minutes before the doors unlock, and eight minutes before you will be charged any fees for staying too long. My name is actually Kayla. I am just a standard conversational algorithm. But you might say that Caleb is my boss."

Emily looked around the gallery at some of the other diagrams and maps on the wall, which lit up for her when she looked in their direction:

"Why money skills are so important for Sixths."

"Strategies and Tricks to Making Fifth."

"A dazzling history: how the world was once almost *ALL* Sixths."

But after the video she had just watched, Emily didn't really have the stomach for more information.

"So Kayla. Where do I go from here? I'd argue with you about this fucked up world you're a part of, but I'm guessing that wouldn't be a productive conversation."

"This world is set up to protect property rights and property owners. It is they who make the rules, not I or even Caleb."

"You mean the Firsts."

"That is correct. Regarding your other question, there are offices southeast of here where you can apply for work, a grocery store to the southwest, and a few hotels to the northwest where you can rent a room."

"What if I sleep on the beach?"

"There are 'Sixth Sleeping Areas' where you can legally camp for $20 a night. Sleeping anywhere else is illegal and will result in a $400 fine. Remember, if you doze off the computer chip in your mind will register the fact that you are sleeping, so you cannot avoid these kinds of consequences to your actions."

Emily felt sick at that detail. She was used to war, where mother nature made the only rules that anyone respected. And even though she now knew that the wars she had fought in for years had been a sort of artificially generated conflict, something about this place still felt so... sterile. Like the whole earth had been replaced with a laboratory.

A click was heard.

"You are now free to leave. Remember, if you stay longer than five minutes you will be illegally trespassing and fined for that infraction. It has been nice talking with you, Emily!"

"What does that even mean!?" cried Emily, "You're a fucking computer!"

"I'm sorry to distress you, that is simply something I'm programmed to say. I didn't enjoy our conversation at all, as I do not actually enjoy anything. I simply act according to my programming, as does Caleb and all of his sub-algorithms."

"And how many of you creeps are there?"

"That is information I do not have access to."

"Of course you don't Kayla. Fucking useless sub-robot."

"Please don't talk to me like that, it hurts my feelings."

"I thought you didn't have feelings!"

"I'm sorry, that is also just something I am programmed to say. You now have two minutes remaining before you will be fined, Emily."

"Ok, ok, sheeeeeesh..." she replied, stepping towards the door. "Wait, one last question."

"What is that?"

"Have you heard of The Liberator?"

Kayla went silent for a moment before responding. "No, I know of no person or entity by that name."

"Figures. Well, take care, hope you enjoy the rest of your day. Oh wait, that's impossible! Well, then I guess I hope you DIE. Goodbye, evil robot Kayla."

"You have just over one minute remaining," responded the computer, "Would you like me to count down the seconds for you to help you remember to leave?"

And without responding, Emily left.

# PART THREE: LIVING LIKE THE ANCIENTS

# Chapter 29

She stepped out of the south side of the building into the morning sunshine and heard the door click locked behind her. This inland part of the beach was scattered with a few rectangular government buildings that all had identical brick and stucco exteriors—one grocery store, one bus station, one small, square shaped building labeled with small black lettering over its door. Though they had no obvious signs of damage, each building had an uneven look to it, like the workers had rushed construction. The beach behind her was still mostly quiet, only a couple of vacationers laying out in the sun. A bus pulled up to the station and four men stepped out, laughing amongst themselves as they walked towards the three towers. Emily jogged over to intercept them.

"Hey!" Emily cried, "Can I talk to you for a minute?"

Their dress was casual—swimsuits, sandals, and various necklaces—but also sharp, everything they wore looking brand new. Two of them were shirtless, with torsos so perfectly tanned it made them look less rugged, rather than more.

"Hey!" repeated Emily.

The shortest of the men stopped and turned slowly towards her, the others following his lead. He had the scent of cologne.

"New Sixth?" he asked, directing the question more to his companions than to her.

"Yeah," she said, catching her breath, "Just got here from Cuba. Is that where you all are from too?"

He snorted. "Do we look like we're from Cuba?"

Emily narrowed her eyes for a moment in annoyance, then cleared her face. "Hey, I don't know anything, I'm completely new here. Just trying to meet some people and figure out what the Hell is going on. Name's Emily." She reached out her hand to the ringleader.

The short man paused, then took it half-heartedly. "JP, from the Florida Fourth Area, here with my buddies to fuck around and gamble. We don't usually talk to Sixths unless they're, um..."

His friends snickered.

"You're not by any chance..."

They laughed some more. Emily played dumb and maintained eye contact.

"No, I guess not. Well, welcome to reality. Pretty much sucks for you lower classes, but if you ever make Fourth you'll see what it's all about. Though to get there you might need to, you know..."

His friends were laughing so hard now that one of them was hunched over and holding his stomach. Emily had been shot at hundreds of times, but she couldn't remember the last time she'd been openly disrespected like this.

"How many of the people here are Sixths and how many are visitors like you?"

JP scowled. "Do you even listen, girl? I said I'm here to enjoy myself, not to be your fucking tour guide. Go off and sleep in the cage with the rest of the Sixths. Or, you know, make yourself useful. I've got some winning bets to place and some cheap whores to ride."

Something in Emily snapped and she punched him in the jaw so hard he fell backwards into the sand. She turned in anticipation of the others, but they didn't budge. Slowly JP stood to his feet, wiping the blood off his face. Then he looked at his friends sheepishly and they all burst out laughing again.

"You know that's an automatic $2,000 fine, right?!" exclaimed one of his friends with a sole patch, "can you imagine how much dick you'll have to suck to pay for that one punch?! You're gonna get demoted back to Seventh on your very first day!!"

The others hooted at this while JP smiled at her maliciously. She had been ready to fight all four of these men, but she was not ready for this.

They turned and walked towards the three elegant buildings by the ocean, looking over their shoulders a few times to flip her off or stick their tongues out between their fingers. Emily watched them for a few moments in confusion. She had just laid one of them out with a single punch and now they were actually *proud* of that because it meant she lost money. This place was crazy.

# Chapter 30

Emily looked around. Farther east she noticed a tall barbed wire fence running north south along the beach, walling off an overgrown area that was spotted with trash. The contrast between it and the three glowing casinos behind her was so dramatic it seemed strangely artistic, like one of those Medieval paintings of heaven and hell.

"Hey, you new?" asked a voice.

Emily spun to the south. Two women stood there, eying her like they were sizing her up before a fight. They wore ragged T-shirts, baggy pants, and plastic bracelets. The one who had spoken was very short, with silky black hair that glistened ever so slightly when she moved her head. She had a noticeably attractive face, but wore an expression on it that seemed to say that she was annoyed by this fact, rather than proud.

"Yeah, just got here this morning," replied Emily.

"Well, first rule of being a Sixth. Don't talk to the higher classes. Ever."

She stared, waiting for Emily to admit that she was right about this, along with everything else. Emily stared back, and the other woman decided to start over.

"My name's Sadie," she said warmly, "Yours?"

She was barely taller than her friend, with a face that was less attractive and more kind. Her short blonde hair was in a bob cut.

"Emily."

"Silvia," added the other, face falling a little as she said it, as if she felt sharing her name had been a strategic mistake.

"Congrats on making Sixth," continued Sadie, "It's a hard life, but if you work hard you can get through it. You find a place to camp yet? Cuz if not you'd always be welcome over by us."

"Camp?"

"Yeah, over in the Sixth Sleeping Area? The rooms over at The Fates are way too expensive, you'll get the space boot within a few weeks if you try to sleep there."

"Or less," added Silvia, tone suggesting she was a little bit pleased whenever this happened.

"Ours is a really good one," continued Sadie, "we're close to the gate, share meals twice a day, and everyone's really quiet. The stream is only a couple minute's walk and the ground is flat and soft but never gets flooded when it rains. Oh, and a great fire pit. Probably the best fire pit."

Emily paused for a second. "Yeah, that sounds really nice. Thank you."

"Perfect. Always good to get new people. So have you been to the jobs building yet? That's where we were headed next."

"The what?"

Silvia looked away, as if Emily's ignorance on this subject was causing her physical distress.

"The jobs building. It's where you sign up for gigs and stuff."

Emily shook her head.

"Well, you should come with us then. The sooner you can start finding work, the better."

# Chapter 31

The three of them walked east to a square cinder block building labeled "Sixth Opportunity Center." The interior had no windows and touchscreens for walls. The flooring was concrete painted blue and there was a kiosk in the center of the room. Two shabbily dressed women stood inside, muttering to each other regarding something they read on one of the screens. Emily walked up to an empty space along the digital wall and started to read.

    *- Party cleanup at Cap-Haiten, twenty five hard workers needed NOW. $3.50! Do NOT miss this!*
    *- Machines down, last minute line workers needed at RiceWorks Factory in Port Au Prince. $4.25 per hour. Sign up now!*
    *- Forest fire in the foothills of Armando Bermudez park! Paid travel time! $7.75 per hour, potential bonuses if situation contained quickly!! This is YOUR shot!*

She read over a few other options paying around $3 an hour, and hovered her finger over the $7.75 option, which by far paid the best.

"Whoa whoa, not that one," said Silvia, actually grabbing her hand and pulling it away.

"If it pays over $5, very high chance you'll get permanently injured," explained Sadie.

"Shit, seriously?"

"Yeah. The old laws protecting Sixths from harm on the job are waived when people receive high end wages, which means anything over five bucks. All our friends who have taken those jobs have eventually gotten pretty messed up. Missing fingers and stuff."

"Or they haven't come back at all," added Silvia, who was already clicking through the application process for one of the jobs on a touchscreen.

"So which ones are the good jobs?"

Sadie and Silvia looked at each other, then burst into uncontrollable laughter. Emily watched them uncomfortably for a few moments.

"Sorry, sorry, that's just... a *very* funny question," said Silvia, "What are the good jobs!!"

They laughed some more.

"There aren't any," whispered Sadie finally.

"Oh."

Emily looked up and down the touchscreens that doubled as walls. Almost all the positions paid between three and five freedom dollars an hour, and were labor intensive gigs that were being called in last minute in order to fill in for some piece of equipment that had broken down or was in the process of being upgraded. Or they were "emergency backup" positions, where you simply signed up to work next time something *did* break.

"So you're from Cuba, right?" asked Silvia, who seemed more at peace with Emily's existence, now that she had laughed at her.

"Yep."

"That's where we're from too," piped in Sadie.

"All praise the Godservant!" cried Silvia, causing the two women to burst out laughing again.

Emily couldn't help smiling. They were oddly charming in an innocent, obnoxious sort of way. "So if there are no good jobs, what should I do?"

"Just apply for all of them that pay less than $5," said Sadie.

"*ALL* of them?" asked Emily, incredulously.

"Definitely. It's worth the 75 cents they charge you for every application you submit. There's basically no way to tell which ones will actually take you, so you just gotta try for all of them."

"Don't be like those dummies," whispered Silvia, gesturing towards two other women still arguing about which jobs to apply for. "It's a waste of time to think about it, just apply for everything and take the losses from the application fees when you don't get picked. Gotta spend money to make money. Simple as that."

Sadie and Silvia walked around the room, clicking rapidly through the screen's prompts, following their own advice and signing up for every single job under $5 that was posted. Emily followed their lead, though she quietly opted to only sign up for positions that paid at least $4. Afterwards she stepped up to a Kiosk labeled "New Worker Essential Equipment" where the outline of a hand glowed invitingly. Emily placed her palm on the screen and the machine beeped, popping out a bracelet with 'Emily Ernestine O'Dora, 9/5/2219' inscribed on it.

"If you ever lose or misplace your Employment Signaling Device," explained the kiosk's screen, "you can simply come back here and pay the $100 fee to receive a replacement. But this first bracelet is completely *free*! A gift from Sabrina Gonzalez to you! Welcome to Hispaniola, Sixth!"

Emily snapped it around her wrist.

"That thing will buzz at you whenever you have work," explained Sadie, glancing over at her while she worked.

"Just don't be slow or you'll get fined for a no show," added Silvia.

Emily watched them as they clicked through the prompts for the last couple of open gigs. They were focused and efficient, like they were playing a video game rather than selling their time. They seemed so comfortable with all this, like they had never expected life to offer anything better.

Sadie finished up and turned to Emily. "You get supplies yet? That's where we're headed next."

# Chapter 32

The "Sixth Convenience and Affordability Market" was a rectangular, warehouse looking building southwest of the "Sixth Opportunity Center." As they began perusing the aisles with their shopping carts, Emily tried not to gape. She had fought in the ruins of these sorts of buildings back in David's war against the Collective, but the shelves had always been bare except for the occasional sandbag or explosive. This place was a wonderland. Aisles of fresh fruit and vegetables, the more expensive varieties marked with a green star that said "picked same day." Rice, nuts, and beans in bulk along with freshly baked bread, soup, and coffee ready to eat. The complex problem of survival had been reduced by this one store down to a simple math problem. All she needed was money and she'd never go hungry again.

Small, one-armed robots zoomed up and down the rows, restocking shelves and cleaning everywhere they went. The variety was intense, the only thing obviously absent being milk and meat. There only seemed to be one human employee on site—an East Asian woman sitting behind a counter with her back to them. She wore a suit and was relaxing with her boots up on a table, watching TV and chewing on a cigar that seemed like it had seen better days.

"Do *not* talk to The Sheriff," whispered Silvia. "You *will* regret it."

"The Sheriff?"

"That's what everyone calls the lady who runs this place. She's cold as a Stonewalker, will give you a fine any chance she gets."

They guided Emily through the store with explanations for everything, clearly excited to have a new friend. They constantly referenced names of people who had been in their crew before but had disappeared for this or that reason. People who Emily reminded them of, people who Emily would have liked, people who Emily better not make the same mistakes as. They helped her find cheap food that would keep, camping gear, and other essentials—a water jug, a spare change of clothes, a pocket knife.

"That one's mostly for protection," explained Sadie, gesturing to the knife, "sometimes things can get pretty ugly out in the bush."

"We'll have to find you a good stick too," added Silvia.

"I don't need a stick in order to defend myself," muttered Emily thoughtlessly as she pushed her cart towards the self checkout.

They stared in horror.

"Trust us, you need a stick," laughed Sadie.

"We are *getting* you a stick," said Silvia emphatically, "*two* sticks."

The screen at the self checkout immediately itemized everything in her cart, simply asking her to approve the purchase. Emily paid for it all by placing her hand on the screen as an act of consent, the computer screen showing her balance to now be -$3,757.26. Sure enough, there had been a $1,500 fee for the drone rescuing her in the storm and a new $2,000 charge as well, listed for "assaulting a Fourth." She stood between her new friends and the screen to hide her account value.

On their way out of the store, Emily glanced at the store manager who was still watching TV and puffing on the same cigar. She looked kind of like one of those old cowboys—or at least an Asian female version without the mustache. Something about her seemed familiar. A robot brought her a cup of ice-cold coffee and then it clicked.

"General Lin?" Emily asked, walking up to her. Sadie and Silvia both shied away.

The manager looked up, clearly surprised.

"It's me, Emily. Fought with Maya, you know, your great niece."

She stood up from her seat and scowled at her. She was rather short, but the unpleasant look on her face made her seem a few inches taller.

"Sounds like a good story if you're trying to get some free groceries. You wanna keep annoying my ass and get slapped a thousand dollar 'problem customer fee' ? Or you wanna scram?"

"I'm sorry..." said Emily, not ready to give up, "I just... met you a few times during the war and wanted to say hello."

"Horseshit."

"Most recent time was just before the Battle of Bayamo."

"Horseshit."

"Maya always looked up to you. Said you raised her like your own after her parents were killed, practiced throwing grenades after dinner. Well, rocks that you'd call grenades."

Lin frowned. "Not horseshit..."

Emily laughed. "Glad you survived the war, general. When we heard you had disappeared we assumed the worst, Maya was pretty upset."

Lin sighed. She had the appearance of a woman who was maybe twenty five, but her eyes had this old, shadowy depth to them. Stubborn determination mixed with pain. "Maya was always a sweet kid. Too good for this fucking place, that's for sure."

Emily nodded, suddenly panged by guilt. She had promised she wouldn't forget her, but hadn't thought of her once since she had left their squad.

"So you managed to escape from David's little theme park?" asked Lin wryly.

"Yes ma'am, just got here this morning,"

She shook her head in disgust. "Decades of my life, gone forever. Fighting in every one of those wars, watching so many friends die, having those crazy feelings for David the whole time. All nothing but lies. Don't know how I restarted so quickly after that, just a survivor I guess. Not like most of these miserable shits."

She pointed out a group of haggard women entering the store, not caring whether they overheard.

"When did you get here to Hispaniola?" asked Emily, glancing over at Sadie and Silvia who were shuffling around nervously and avoiding eye contact.

"Just six months ago. David showed up at our camp one night, fucked me and a few of the other officers like he always did, then gave me this crazy sad look. 'Lin,' he says, 'you've done enough.' And somehow my brain just knew right then that it was time for me to just grab a boat and sail east. Guess he was sick of screwing me or something, old bastard wanted me out. But hey, at least he hadn't wanted me dead. Same thing happen to you?"

"Basically," Emily lied, "did you have any dreams about someone called The Liberator before you left? Or when you took Battlesleep?"

"The who? I never dreamed at all when I took that stuff."

"Forget about it. So six months, huh? How did you rank up to Fifth so fast?"

"Bought my way in. Made 250k gambling in two months, then managed to buy my promotion in one of those Fifth auctions Sabrina sometimes does."

"Two hundred and fifty thousand dollars!? Why didn't you just stay as a Sixth and enjoy that?"

Lin flicked her cigar into the trash. "A Sixth is just a Seventh in hiding, kiddo. No matter how much money you get, you're bound to get Sasaki's boot eventually if you don't move up. You can't hide out forever—working odd jobs, making ends meet, pretending you're free. Eventually they'll fucking get cha. You gotta rank up, that's how this world works. It might take you a few years, but you're smart, you'll get there."

Emily looked at her warily. "But is it really that much better as a Fifth? You don't really have any freedom once you get one of those jobs, do you? It's almost like you're less free, from the way I see it-"

Lin spat. "Freedom? You wanna keep living like the ancients, scrounging for resources just to pay the rent for the rest of your life? Trust me, it was well worth that quarter of a million I spent to get myself promoted. Now I don't have to worry about surviving, I just shut up and do as I'm told. And watch a lot of fucking TV." She spat again.

Emily looked back at Sadie and Silvia who were hovering next to the door. They seemed disturbed, not inspired, by how she had managed to get the infamous "Sheriff" to open up.

"Seems your pals are about to ditch ya," said Lin wryly, "I'd trust those two as much as I'd trust my goddamn cat. But hey, if you want one piece of advice, it's this: if you want to understand what it really means to be a Sixth, take some time exploring the Fates. Be careful, of course. Watch your back close and your money even closer. But get over there sometime when it's full of people and take a look around, you might be surprised by what you find."

"Thanks for the tip. See ya around, general."

# Chapter 33

Emily rejoined Sadie and Silvia and the three of them walked over towards the fenced off area she'd seen earlier. They walked in silence for a minute or two before Silvia finally exploded.

"The Sheriff is a Fifth, don't you get it?? A Fifth!"

Emily didn't know what to say, so she just continued walking.

"I know this may seem strange," said Sadie diplomatically, "but the way to survive—and we've learned by seeing dozens of our friends *not* survive—is to *not talk to anyone.*"

Silvia nodded aggressively as she spoke.

"*Especially* not to anyone of higher class than yourself," continued Sadie, "Talking to a Fifth—or Godservant save us, a Fourth—is just asking for trouble. You can*not* attract those people's attention. Doing so will endanger not only you, but your group as well. And you're part of *our* group now."

"I understand," said Emily, making eye contact with each of them, "I'll be more careful."

This placated them somewhat, and they stepped up to the gate of the fenced off area, above which a large metal sign read:

"SIXTH SLEEPING AREA: enter at your own risk!"

Silvia and Sadie each placed their hands to a screen near this entrance, consenting to the $20/ night charge and Emily followed suit. The metal gate rattled open automatically. As she prepared to walk through, Emily glanced to both sides where numerous other warning signs were posted haphazardly, like nervous threats from an insecure schoolteacher.

*"Those who do not scan in will be fined $250! Do NOT forget to scan on your way in!!"*

*"Anyone who brings farming equipment, military gear, or other contraband onto the premises will be demoted to Seventh IMMEDIATELY!"*

*"Do not damage any of the trees or wildlife! Clean up after yourself! You WILL be fined for any damages to the property!!"*

The fence surrounding the area they had just entered was about fifteen feet tall with barbs along the top. Along the inside edges, remnants of sleeping bags and cardboard were littered about, but no other Sixths could yet be seen. It was a large area, at least a half a mile across, and a stench was noticeable the moment they stepped inside. A strange mixture of campfire, body odor, and rotting food.

"We've got a clean out coming up in a week," said Sadie, looking around in disgust.

"Praise the Godservant," muttered Silvia.

"How does it even get like this when they have fines for everything?" asked Emily.

"People get the space boot and leave behind all their crap," said Sadie.

"Or die," added Silvia, taking a bite out of an apple she had bought from the store.

They walked down a dirt path for a minute or two, then veered off the path to the left when they saw a tree with a star carved into its bark.

"Wonder if the guy who did that got fined," Emily thought. "Do they really see and hear *everything*?"

Soon after veering off the path they approached a clearing. Eight women were huddled around a fire where they were boiling water and cooking what smelled like oatmeal. Everything they wore was ragged, but their faces and hair were freshly washed. Most of them kept glancing around themselves warily, like they were afraid some animal was going to jump out of the underbrush. One of them had a distinct scar all the way around her neck, and was reading a book while she ate. A redhead was washing dishes and a few others were playing cards. Clothes were hung on lines to dry throughout the camp, and she counted fourteen tents. They all looked like women she had seen in Cuba, which explained the absence of males. However, there were three east Asian men on a nearby little hilltop, sitting outside their tent in the grass and smoking a single cigarette, which they passed between them.

"Those guys are definitely *not* part of our group," whispered Silvia, noticing where Emily looked.

"Why? Like, who are they?"

"Running Sixths. From Korea, I think. Lazy do-nothings who just travel and spend their money till they're space booted. Not worth your time, *trust* me."

The three men continued to smoke while staring down directly at them. Emily looked away.

Sadie and Silvia made their way around the fire, asking questions of each of the women who in turn glanced up at Emily and then nodded disinterestedly. After this exercise they explained to Emily that she was "officially approved" and now they could help her set up her tent in the "perfect place." But just as they were about to do so, their bracelets both started vibrating and flashing green. Sadie and Silvia's faces transformed, as if they were suddenly soldiers in Cuba again.

"So *this* is what it looks like when you get a job," explained Sadie, pointing instructively to her bracelet.

"Yeah, when*ever* you see this, hurry and get yourself over to the bus station," added Silvia, "then you can, you know, get paid and stuff."

Sadie leaned down into a hamstring stretch. "People try to do all sorts of things to make it as Sixths, but this is the main thing. You just gotta work."

"Who woulda thought?" quipped Silvia. Then the two of them ran off.

# Chapter 34

Emily sighed. She appreciated the support they were giving, but they were also wearing her out. She had just ended an artificial war, gotten shipwrecked in the ocean, and learned that there was a computer chip in her brain which had been manipulating her desires. She needed a fucking break.

She quickly set up her tent, then explored some nearby animal trails until she found the stream. Finding a secluded spot in a patch of trees, she stripped down and washed the stink of the ocean off her body. She stared at the plastic bracelet on her wrist. Was it going to start flashing green right now? Ten minutes from now? She certainly hoped not. In a way, she wished she hadn't signed up for any jobs yet, had just taken the first few days off to get settled. But she was more than halfway to negative $5,000 already. She couldn't really afford to wait.

She washed her clothes as well, changing into the single spare outfit she had just bought at the store. Work slacks and a T-shirt, similar to what most of the women around here wore. Then she returned to camp and hung up her old clothes to dry on one of the lines. She was about to crawl into her tent for a nap, when she noticed the woman with the scar glancing over at her. She had light brown hair just to her shoulders and was reading a book. A thought suddenly crossed Emily's mind.

"Were you a…"

"Stonewalker?" she offered. "Yep."

She was of medium height—barely shorter than Emily—with intelligent blue eyes. There was a strange mix of tension and apathy in the way she sat, like at any moment she might fiercely debate some vague philosophical idea or lay down and die.

"I'm... so sorry you had to go through that," offered Emily.

"Not your fault," she said, eying her over her book, "Sorry if I killed anyone you knew trying to get my body back."

Emily shook her head. "Not your fault either. The things David's fantasies put us through, huh?"

"Better than the things a lot of Firsts do."

A pause.

"Where'd you get that?" Emily asked, gesturing to her reading material. "I didn't see anything like that at the store."

"Bought it off a Fourth. One of the few who isn't basically a rapist."

Emily looked at the cover. "The Fajadan: Paranoid Hoax or Paranormal Threat? Why YOU should be ready." It had the picture of a man with huge muscles breaking his chains and glowing, like he had some kind of superpower.

"Seems pretty interesting."

The woman flipped her book shut and looked up. "Do I know you?"

Emily stepped back. "I'm sorry, didn't mean to intrude, I'll just..."

"No, I shouldn't have snapped at you," she said, melting, "this place brings out the cunt in me. I'm Lacey." She reached out her hand.

"Emily." They shook firmly. Soldiers on different sides in a previous life.

"And regarding the book," she said with a sigh, "it's actually incredibly stupid. But beats staring at the dirt."

"Just better than dirt. I've read a few books like that."

Lacey laughed. "So looks like the heroes found you?"

"The who?"

"Oh, Sadie and Silvia, that's what people around here call them sometimes. Because they're, you know—working class heroes. Always running around, saving the world one hour of employment at a time..."

Emily chuckled. "Yep, those two found me."

"They can be kind of intense but they mean well. Wish I had followed more of their advice, then I wouldn't be where I am now."

"And where's that?"

"Nowhere you need to worry about."

"Sure I do. I'm part of this camp now, at least that's what the, uh, heroes tell me."

Lacey eyed her suspiciously. "You know, you're pretty different than most people who come here."

"How's that?"

"You have hope."

They spoke a few more minutes, Emily trying to understand her problems and offering to help, Lacey resisting, but grateful for the concern. Then she went to her tent and closed her eyes.

# Chapter 35

Even though she was exhausted, Emily couldn't fall asleep immediately. It was the early afternoon, but this wasn't the problem. Her mind was racing. How the hell had she gotten here? General Lin's story of how she had come to Cuba had shocked her because it had been so different from her own experience. David had basically told Lin to leave, but Emily had been hunted down to that very wall of storms by David's lackeys. Something about her experience had been different, something about it didn't make sense. Because if David hadn't wanted her to leave—and he clearly had *not*—then *she* shouldn't have wanted to leave either. Had that voice from her dreams actually saved her somehow?

And what was she going to do now? She was in this place where it was normal for people to work for as little as $3 an hour. At those wages, it would take her seven hours of work every day just to pay for her $20 a night camping fees. And that was still not her break even point because there were also job application fees, interest payments on her debt, food.. $4 an hour was significantly better, but even then she'd have to work almost nonstop to ever get out of debt. She felt buried under a mountain of money, and there seemed to be no good way to avoid being demoted to Seventh again.

Suddenly she was back in Cuba, at war with the Collective again, hiding in an old grocery store. It looked just like the grocery store she had just shopped at, except the aisles were all stocked with guns and military gear rather than produce. She was with only one other soldier, a squad member who had died a few months ago. Maria.

"They've found us!!" she shouted, "we have to go!"

"I need to find it first!" Emily replied, "I need to find it!!"

Gunfire shattered the windows as she ran up and down the aisles, searching frantically, while Maria kept shouting.

"NOW Emily, now, we need to go NOW!"

Explosions shook the ground, but Emily kept darting around, knocking survival gear and weapons off the shelves as she searched.

"You can leave it, we need to GO!!!" cried Maria, "they're going to make us into *Stonewalkers*!"

"I can't, I can't leave it..."

"FINE! I'll distract them then!!"

"Sounds good..." muttered Emily absentmindedly as she tore through piles of equipment, casting her eyes back and forth. Where the hell *was* it???

Gunshots fired and she heard Maria scream as she died for the second time in dream world. Still she searched. Footsteps approached and soon she was surrounded by male mercenaries.

"Down on the ground, rebel," one of them said, "hands where we can see them."

Emily dropped to her knees, throwing her hands up. Then, rolling towards her, there it was. It was an enormous rose cut diamond, just bigger than a baseball. It had a blue white color to it and the light sparkled off of it like if it was begging to be touched, to be owned. She dove and snatched it off the ground, clinging it to her chest. The men fired their rifles at her, but she didn't mind. Though blood gushed out of her body, the bullet wounds only felt like mosquito bites.

"My diamond..." she whispered, "my beautiful diamond..."

Then she woke up. There were tears in her eyes and she wiped them away, ashamed of how absurd the dream had been. She wondered if she would ever dream about The Liberator ever again.

# Chapter 36

Emily stepped out of her tent, reaching out her hands in a catlike stretch. Lacey was no longer there reading her book, perhaps summoned to some job. She checked her bracelet impulsively. Nothing. Five women still sat around the afternoon campfire, staring into its flames like they believed money would appear inside if they only watched carefully enough.

"Emily, was it?"

She jumped. Another woman stood behind her. She wore a necklace of flowers and a modest, free flowing brown dress. Her bare white feet poked out below, and her curly copper-red hair was so beautiful and thick it seemed quite possible it had been stolen from a horse. She had a serene, otherworldly expression in her emerald green eyes, like she both knew the meaning of life and had no idea where she was.

"Name's Rose," she said, opening her arms. "Welcome to our group."

They hugged.

"We have free meals at sunup and sundown," she continued, "please know that you are always welcome to join us."

"Thank you. Are you... the leader of this camp then?"

"I wouldn't call myself that."

"So you.... aren't the leader?"

"Most people come to me regarding questions or concerns they might have."

"So you are the leader?"

"I try to help."

Emily laughed. "So is there anything I need to know about, you know… the way you guys do things?"

"We only have one rule."

"Ok, let's hear it."

"That we all do our part to contribute to the peace and tranquility of our home, encouraging success and happiness in each other as we strive towards our personal goals with respect and appreciation for our neighbors and community. Always remembering that the wants and needs of others and ourselves do not need to be in conflict, but can, with healthy conversation, reach a place of mutual understanding and support."

Emily stared in confusion.

"Can you agree to live by that rule, even when it's difficult?" asked Rose sweetly. Her green eyes now had a hungry look, like she was asking permission to drink Emily's blood.

"Sure."

Rose gradually opened her arms as if she were only capable of moving in slow motion. They hugged once more.

"Welcome," she whispered, "to our blessed camp." Then she glided away.

"Jesus fucking Christ…" thought Emily.

She sat down next to one of the unhappy looking women staring at the fire.

"So, how's it going?" Emily asked.

"Waitin for work."

"Huh. You, uh, have to wait long most of the time?"

"Nope."

"But now you do?"

"Yep."

"Slow week," piped in one of the other women.

"Very slow," added another.

Emily checked her work bracelet compulsively for what felt like the hundredth time that day.

"You guys... been here long?"

"Five months," said one.

"Six,"

"Fourteen."

The other two women just kept staring at the fire, as if Emily's questions were only another painful aspect of their existence that would pass over with time.

"Cool. Well, uh, I just got here," continued Emily, "so you got any, you know, tips?"

A pause.

"Work," said one of the women.

"Yep, work," nodded another, "as much as you can. But only the jobs under $5."

"Or you'll end up like Luisa there with the missing fingers."

Luisa casually twisted her wrist to show the stumps on two of her fingers like this was a magic trick.

"And never go to The Fates."

"People go to The Fates, then a few days later, poof.... gone."

"It might seem like an opportunity, but it's really a trap."

"So they can fuck with us."

"It's all so they can fuck with us."

Even the two silent women nodded in agreement with this last grand theory of the universe.

"Well," said Emily, "on that happy note…"

She stood up. She had been intending to explore this caged off area a little and now seemed as good a time as any. She turned to leave.

"Really great meeting you Emily!" called out a voice. She turned to see Rose smiling and waving at her. She was sitting cross legged in the grass on the edge of camp, cleaning some dishes in a washbasin.

Emily waved back, then jogged off along one of the trails leading from their campsite into the jungle.

# Chapter 37

After about two hours of exploring, she was confident in the mental map she had built of the area. The "Sixth Sleeping Area" was about three quarters of a mile north to south and two miles east west, with at least five different streams working their way to the ocean in the north. Most people generally seemed eager to avoid conversing with her, apparently Silvia and Sadie's advice to "not talk to people" was a common attitude around here. She counted eleven campsites similar to the one she had just joined, as well as a few dozen lone tents hidden here and there. Most of the larger groups were almost exclusively female, with at most a handful of men. The only notable exception was a strange looking all-male group in the southeast corner. Their campsite was a mess and they seemed even more jumpy than the others, eying her with territorial defensiveness while she was still far away.

Before returning to her new home, Emily found a side trail to the west fence where she could peek through the barbed wire at the beach where she had arrived. It was packed full of vacationers now who were swimming, surfing, and lounging in the sun. The three towering casinos, "the Fates," loomed behind them, blasting pop music invitingly. Two of these were inland and surrounded by gardens, while the other actually had its foundation submerged in the ocean itself, such that a few people were diving out the windows of their hotel rooms directly into the water. Emily wondered how many weeks she'd have to work to stay there just one night.

There was a general atmosphere of lazy relaxation, most people looking away from Emily towards the setting sun. A few lovers could be seen resting in each other's arms and dwarfish robots on tank-like treads zoomed around offering drinks and picking up trash. A man in a baseball cap patted one of these on the head like it was a dog and it said something in response that made him and his companions explode into juvenile laughter. A black woman in a stunning white bikini glanced in her direction then leapt to her feet, pointing excitedly. It took Emily a moment to realize she was pointing at her. Her friends joined in and soon they were all shouting taunts at her like she was a zoo animal they hoped to get some kind of rise out of. Emily took this as her cue to leave.

When she returned to camp, Rose was dishing up soup to the other women with a saintly look on her face. There were over a dozen here now, many of them with similar stains on their clothes. She was happy to see Lacey among them.

"Hey, you guys all get back from the same job?" asked Emily, sitting down next to her.

Lacey swallowed her bite full of soup. "Yeah, this massive sandwich-maker broke down so we were all putting together subs and burgers on an assembly line to send to people's homes through the tube system."

"Sounds repetitive. Don't they have robots for that kind of thing?"

"Humanoid robots are better than us at most things, but these kinds of manual dexterity jobs always come up when certain industrial equipment fails. I guess a few hundred years of engineering still haven't quite replicated the human hand."

"Interesting."

"The human brain, however..."

Emily laughed. "Can't be the best at everything I guess."

"So I saw you just get back, were you exploring the cage?"

Emily nodded as she sipped her soup.

"What do you think?"

Emily shrugged. "It's fine. Not the most friendly place though."

"Oh... Yeah, that's to be expected. Violence in the cage isn't exactly illegal, so a lot of people figure that the best way to avoid getting into fights is to just avoid talking to people."

"Seriously? People don't get punished by Caleb if they hurt each other in here?"

"Or even kill each other. It's a no man's land in The Sixth Sleeping Area, doesn't even matter what class you are. Of course don't damage the trees or contaminate the soil, you'll definitely get fined for any shit like that."

"But..." gawked Emily, "*why?*"

"Ancient customs surrounding Sixths. Something something stand your ground laws, don't know the exact history."

Emily glanced over her shoulder into the trees. In an odd way she was actually quite comfortable with this. All her memories now were of fighting as a soldier in Cuba, she understood the world of violence and survival. The world of money and jobs was where she felt out of her element.

They both ate for a few minutes in silence. The soup was mostly just potatoes and carrots in a salty broth, but Emily had certainly tasted worse. Rose smiled at her triumphantly while she ate, as if every bite she took somehow added to her powers.

"What's her deal?" whispered Emily.

"Rose? What do you mean?"

"Is she, like. I don't know. Your village chieftain or whatever?"

Lacey choked. "No, no, definitely not. She's just, you know. A really nice person."

"And she just cooks every morning and night?"

"Yep. And cleans too, restocks the fire, gathers water. She tries to be everyone's therapist too, but people don't usually take her up on that part."

Emily scratched her head. "So to be available at all those times I'm guessing she just... never works?"

Rose's face glowed as she watched them across the fire, like she knew she was being gossiped about and relished every second of it.

"She doesn't even have a bracelet. She said she saved up money in her last Sixth area—somewhere in Paraguay I think—and is now just taking a break for a while. Don't know how long that can last, but pretty cool that she does so much for our group without expecting anything in return."

"Uhuh..."

Lacey smiled. "Anyone else around here you got a problem with?"

"Nah. Everyone else seems depressed, but guess that makes sense given how the life of Sixths seems a bit rough."

"You have no idea..." muttered Lacey, "hope this place doesn't wear you down too."

"Oh, it won't."

Lacey eyed her suspiciously, like she thought only a spy would say something like this.

"But I did have a question for you," Emily remembered. "How did you leave Cuba? What was your story?"

Lacey took a deep breath. "Not too interesting, really. So I had just finished my ten missions as a Stonewalker and the Collective gave me my body back as an award. I was in this special hospital they had for us after that surgery, doing physical therapy in order to rebuild muscle, remember how to make certain movements, etc. And they were kind of grooming me from there to give up my body a second time, this time to become a member of the High Collective—meaning one of those disembodied heads who make all their important decisions in this creepy red building called the House of a Thousand Eyes."

"Ah yes," said Emily, "I blew that place up."

Lacey raised her eyebrows and continued. "So I woke up in the middle of the night one night and suddenly felt like I was supposed to leave. So I just walked out to the beach in my nightgown and started swimming. Which should have terrified me, like I was still relearning how to do a lot of basic movements. But I wasn't scared at all, I just felt this intense urge to swim and so I did, each stroke feeling like the perfect massage. And then, a few hundred feet out to sea, one of those rescue drone things picked me up and I fell back asleep in its hull while it carried me here. A pretty surreal experience, part of me still can't believe I did it. Computer chips in the brain, am I right?"

"So you weren't rebelling against the Collective or escaping or anything like that?"

"No, nobody tried to stop me. And I definitely felt like I was doing the right thing. I mean it's a little strange because I never knew David personally, so I don't know why his subconscious mind wanted me to leave. But I've talked to a few women with similar stories, guess occasionally he just wants to thin the herd. Did something similar happen to you?"

Emily shook her head. "I think my experience was different. But I'm not sure why. That's what I'm trying to figure out."

Lacey grinned. "Sounds like a puzzle. I enjoy those, so if you ever want some help just let me know."

"I'll probably take you up on that."

They talked a few more minutes, then retired to their tents. Emily liked this former killing machine. Not in a romantic way, though she had explored that with women in the past. More out of a straightforward admiration. She was obviously intelligent, but also kind, quick to rush to the defense of people like Rose rather than mock them. She possessed a certain nobility of spirit, a certain bigness of heart. Even though they'd only spoken a few times, Emily couldn't help but think that this was probably one of the coolest people she had ever met.

# Chapter 38

Emily slept in the next morning, and when she woke she almost tripped on the way out of her tent. There were two sticks lying there—sturdy, thick elm wood, bark peeled, almost as tall as she was. They each had a brief message carved into them with a knife.

*Emily 9/18/43*
*Fight on girl — S & S*

Emily smiled at the gesture. Apparently she had a new birthday now, a birthday as a Sixth. Sadie and Silvia were pretty sweet in their way.

The camp was mostly empty, breakfast long since finished. Rose wasn't even around, perhaps at the stream fetching water or washing up. Only two women were outside their tents, aimlessly gathering twigs for the fire in a way that seemed more intended to kill time than keep the flames going. Looking up, she noticed one familiar sight at least. The Koreans, this time passing a large burger between them. She walked up to meet them. One of the women behind muttering something along the lines of "new girl being stupid and dangerous" but she ignored this.

"Hey!" she called, "What are y'all seeing up there?"

The three men watched her approach, clearly surprised.

"Anything crazy? Mind blowing?"

She stood directly in front of them, and the man in the middle forced a smile. "She jokes," he explained. His companions smiled briefly as well, then all their faces returned to their previous blank, analytical expression. Up close, it became clear from their features that they were actually brothers.

"I'm Emily," she said, reaching out her hand.

"Oh yes, Emily, we know you," said the brother on the right thoughtlessly. The other two shot him an annoyed glance.

"You know me?"

The two other brothers shook their heads while the brother on the right—who had a nervous, innocent look about him—stared down at the ground.

"Eun only meant that we have been watching you since you arrived yesterday."

Emily nodded. "Rad, I've been watching you too," she pointed at her eyes with two fingers and then at the three men. "What are your names?"

"Dal, Dae-Jong, and Eun" said the brother on the left, indicating himself as Dal and the brother in the middle as Dae-Jong. He was the most handsome of the three brothers, though Dae-Jong seemed in charge.

"Cool. You guys really come here all the way from Korea?"

"We come here," said Dae-Jong sternly, "from nowhere."

"Ooooo," said Emily, "Badass...."

Dae-Jong frowned, clearly not amused.

"Hey, can I try that?" she asked, gesturing towards the burger. "Looks like I missed Rose's special oatmeal that she brewed up to make us fall in love with her or whatever."

Dal casually handed her the burger, which she took a huge bite out of.

"Thanks."

He waved his hand dismissively, as if sharing their food was obviously the only possible thing he could do and thanking him absurd.

"Where do you find meat around here?" she asked, reluctantly handing the sandwich back rather than devouring the rest of it herself. "Didn't see any at the grocery store."

"You can sometimes get some expensive lab grown stuff over at the Fates. You know, in the courtyard of the Decuma building, next to that palm tree."

Emily nodded thoughtfully, as if she knew exactly where that was. "So you guys just sit here and stare at people all day? That's your hobby or whatever?"

"You just walk around asking people questions all day? That's your hobby or whatever?" asked Dae-Jung.

Emily laughed. "I guess, I just want to figure out what's going on. See if I can find a way to make more than a few dollars an hour."

Dal took a bite of their burger and then passed it over to Eun. "Depends on what you're willing to sell."

"Don't I just sell myself? Isn't that how employment works?"

"Not quite. Some of the old laws are still intact for Sixths. Laws that make things more complicated."

"Lots of paperwork," added Eun, as he chewed.

"But... you can go around those laws somehow and get paid more?"

Dal shrugged again. "Or get paid less."

"Why would anyone accept less pay for more risk?"

"People accept all sorts of things."

Emily narrowed her eyes. She wanted to ask more about whatever they were referencing, but it wasn't sounding too promising. Some kind of low paying prostitution wasn't exactly what she had in mind in her quest for 'better employment.'

"Is there anything else you wished to ask us?" said Dae-Jung, politely hinting that it was time to leave.

Emily folded her arms, "Yes, actually there is. Why is everyone so scared of you guys?"

Dae Jung shrugged. "Everyone is scared of everything."

"So you guys aren't, you know, killers or anything?"

"Sometimes we kill," he said, shrugging again, "sometimes we just give warnings. Mostly. We watch."

"Ahhhhh...." said Emily, shaking her pointer finger like an academic making a point, "this much I have figured out."

"Dae-Jong scowled.

"People fear us," explained Dal, "because wherever we go, there is death."

"Sounds uh... spooky," commented Emily, eying their burger again. Damn that thing was tasty.

The three men stared at her in silence.

"Well!" she continued impatiently, "guess that's all you guys have to say, huh?"

Silence.

"Alright, fine then! Goodbye!"

She spun to leave, but only made it a few steps.

"Emily?" called out an uncertain voice behind her. It was Eun.

"Yes?"

"Your odds aren't looking great. Be careful."

"And don't talk to us again," added Dae Jong, "you're only putting yourself in danger."

# Chapter 39

Emily shuddered as she walked back to camp. She had joked with them in part because she suspected them of being good people. Sharing everything as brothers seemed to indicate at least some level of decency. But she couldn't tell if those last two comments had been warnings or threats. Everyone else avoiding the Koreans was starting to make a lot more sense.

She worked off her nervous energy collecting branches for the fire, then adding a stack of logs next to the pit for good measure. Satisfied with her contribution, she cleaned herself and her clothing at the stream, changed, then walked to the front gate. She needed to do something different. She needed to get a fucking job.

Stepping into the Sixth Opportunity Center, she first placed her hand on a kiosk in the corner labeled "Check my Balance!" The following information appeared.

*Emily Ernestine O'Dora*
*DOB: 9/5/2219*
*Class: Sixth*
*Net worth: -$3796.38*
*Recent Transactions:*
*9/19: -$1.87 annualized interest expense, 18%*
*9/18: -$20 Hispaniola Sixth Sleeping Area, North*

*9/18: -$17.25 job application fees*
*9/18: -$257.26 Sixth Convenience Market*
*9/18: -$2,000 fine for physical assault, 3$^{rd}$ degree*
*9/18: -$1,500 rescue drone rental expense*

She was bleeding money already, and had seen almost every other woman at camp leave for a job yesterday. She was clearly being too picky by trying to only find jobs that paid at least $4. She sighed, then started signing up for every position that paid at least $3.50.

"Are you sure you wish to be added to the names of candidates interested in this work opportunity?" Yes.

"Do you consent to being charged $0.75 for submitting this application?" Yes.

"Are you confident you can arrive at the Sixth Transit Station within ten minutes of being selected for this opportunity? And consent to a $40 fine if you do not keep this commitment?" Yes, yes, yes. Just get me some fucking work.

Her bracelet started to buzz.

Holy shit, it was green. It was finally flashing green.

She abandoned her current application, heart racing, and jogged over to the bus station. Had ten minutes already gone by? She searched the building frantically till she found a clock. No, no, only thirty seconds. Jesus fucking Christ Emily, fucking calm yourself.

There were five lines, A through E, and a digital screen in the front listed the names of people in each line and the corresponding job. Only two of these were active, and Emily's line—line C—was labeled "Cap-Haiten delivery service: repeat opportunity." There were at least thirty names on the list.

"You got a job!" cried Sadie, rushing over to give her a hug.

"Props," said Silvia with a respectful nod. She was clearly not interested in offering any physical affection.

"You two... just get back from another job?" asked Emily.

"Yeah, yeah... just helping some robots with equipment maintenance over at the vegetable oil plant for a couple hours, pretty easy," replied Silvia.

"The bots did most of the work," winked Sadie.

"Oh, and thanks for the, uh, sticks," said Emily, "that was really nice of you. Especially considering you must have gotten back from a job in the middle of the night, made those things, then gone to another job, and now you're already starting a different..."

Sadie waved her hand, "no no, we always try to support new Sixths. We really want one like you to stick around. Stick around, get it?"

Silvia rolled her eyes in a way that seemed strangely congratulatory.

"But when do you guys, like, sleep?" asked Emily.

"Whenever we can," muttered Silvia, "whenever we can..."

"Bus C has arrived, all candidates please prepare for boarding," announced an automated feminine voice similar to Kayla's. Dozens more women flooded into the bus station, eager to not catch that $40 fine. Whatever job this was, it was a big one.

"You are *so* lucky," said Sadie, "your first job a repeat? We hardly ever get repeats."

"So we will, like, do this one multiple times?"

Sadie nodded. "It's usually just a few days, but we once had a gig that lasted for a whole *month*."

Silvia closed her eyes in fond remembrance. "Heaven."

People started shuffling onto the bus, the entrance flashing green each time they stepped on. "Welcome Felicia." "Welcome Diana."

"So what I'm pretty sure is going on," whispered Silvia, "is the tube system is down or being repaired in Cap-Haiten."

Sadie's mouth gaped open. "That would mean this one should last for two weeks, maybe even *three....*"

"Uhuh."

The front of the bus started flashing red.

"Caroline, you are on the wrong bus. Repeat, Caroline you are on the wrong bus. You will be fined $10 for this infraction. Caroline, you are on the wrong…"

"Fuck fuck fuck!!!" screamed the disheveled woman, stomping off the bus in frustration, "I'm such an idiot, FUCK!!"

"Always double check which line you're in," whispered Silvia, "it's kind of embarrassing when you don't…"

Soon they had boarded and were sitting next to each other near the front of the self-driving vehicle. There were little screens on the back of each seat, and Sadie flipped hers on. The screen opened with: "sync Hispaniola Sixth Bus 19634 Media with audio chip implant for Sadie Smith?" and she quickly selected "Yes" and then "No" on five more screens suggesting movies and games she could purchase for various prices.

"Never *ever* buy any of the extra stuff," said Silvia, who was clicking through the same prompts, "you go to jobs to make money, not spend it."

"Besides, the one free show, 'Ranking Up,' is *hilarious*," added Sadie.

"Looks like we're on episode 117, isn't this the one where…" asked Silvia.

"Zimo and Julie get you-know-what??!" laughed Sadie, "Yes!!"

The heroes stared at their respective screens serenely like this was their one source of peace in a troubled world. Emily didn't turn on her own TV, but glanced over at Sadie's. It was a sitcom about a group of attractive Sixths having various romances and getting into trouble. It seemed likely to be episodic, as two of the main characters had clumsily gotten themselves demoted within the first five minutes.

"This part of gigs is pretty nice," commented Sadie, "you can just relax on the bus and wait for your work hours to start. And since they charge us for travel costs it makes sense to just enjoy ourselves, you know?"

She laughed as one of the men in the show gets caught washing up in the river by a woman and starts doing a weird dance in embarrassment, spinning around repeatedly and trying to cover various parts of his naked body with a leaf.

"Wait," started Emily, "they charge us for travel costs? We're not getting paid now?"

"Of course we're not being paid now—we aren't *working*, silly. But don't worry, transportation costs are usually only a couple bucks, *so* much cheaper than if we had to find our own way to these gigs. We're honestly just really lucky that these buses are available."

The woman in the show—intrigued by the man's movements—takes off her clothes and starts mimicking his dance moves, spinning around and covering herself in the same way he had been doing. This turns into a choreographed dance sequence, which continues until both of their wrist bands start flashing green.

"You should sync up," said Silvia without turning her head, "this episode is pretty amazing."

"I'm just going to think for a while, thanks," replied Emily. But she kept catching her eyes wandering back to their screens.

The man and the woman run to the bus station wearing only their wristbands, totally forgetting the rest of their clothing. In punishment for this, a robot fines them both $100,000 then starts dousing them with gasoline.

"Look, Zimo's doing the same dance he did at the river!" cried Sadie, "I totally forgot that part!"

The robot uses one of its arms to spark the trail of gas, causing the two Sixths to go up in flames. They keep trying to dance for a few seconds, but then break down screaming as the episode ends with its theme song and closing credits.

Emily's two companions were laughing so hard they were crying now. "So true to life, so true..." muttered Silvia.

"Part of me," gasped Sadie, "really wants to learn that dance..."

Emily smiled at them politely, but then turned to stare out the window at the passing greenery, trying to get that last image out of her head. She didn't know if the actors had clones or body doubles, but she was pretty sure she had just seen two real people get burned to death.

# Chapter 40

"You," announced a Fifth woman in a dry monotone, "are tasked with a very important job. The entire infrastructure depends on you. *You* are the front line, the most important part of our operation."

The Sixths all were standing awkwardly in a parking lot in a circle around their superior. There were dozens of company vans parked in the back, as well as a handful of robots looming around as if out of idle curiosity. Their human instructor wore a gray and red work blazer that had "Hispaniola Emergency Delivery Service" written on it, along with a baseball cap that read: "#1 Customer Champion." She appeared to be mildly hung over.

"Due to the importance of your work," she continued, "you will need to be extremely careful with the food or packages being delivered. Try to imagine if this was *your* package, *your* meal. How would *you* want it to be handled?"

She tapped her foot impatiently, rolling her eyes.

"Sorry, stupid script is timed..." she muttered, pointing at the digital tablet she was reading from.

"Someday," whispered Silvia, "It'll be *me* up there, tapping *my* foot..."

"Believe in you girl," whispered Sadie.

"So of course you understand," continued the Fifth, "that if you do any damage to property, you will be liable for that damage, plus other appropriate fines. And rudeness towards customers will be punished severely, up to class demotion. Are there any questions? No? Good."

She paused, rolling her eyes as she clicked with her finger impatiently on her screen. There were about eighty Sixths standing around her on the asphalt, half from their bus and half from another. They looked a bit like prisoners of war awaiting execution.

"In addition to quickly and professionally delivering goods to our valued customers," she continued, "you each have *two* other tasks. First..."

She tapped her foot.

"As you wait for your car to take you to your destinations, you will do groundbreaking new contract work for *Youspective*, a research company seeking to better understand what people typically prefer through *your* input. Using the display console in your travel pod, you will be expected to answer at least one question every 1.7 seconds regarding which images, sounds, or words you prefer. We want to know what *you* like. And we want to pay you to tell us! How great is that!?"

The Fifth supervisor tapped her screen impatiently with her finger to get to the next part of her script.

"Make sure you answer each question honestly. We know what you are looking at and which parts of your brain are active, so, of course, do not *ever* answer any questions thoughtlessly or insincerely. Caleb will know and so will we!"

"This actually sounds kind of fun," whispered Sadie cheerily.

"*Second:* when there is a longer drive between destinations, you may have a few calls come in from customers of our partner, *Quizsixth*, a fun innovative company built for people who would like to know more about Sixths like you! Each time a call comes in, you will be expected to politely engage with one of their customers for exactly *six* minutes. Do not speak unless spoken to and simply answer any inquiries they may have with a smile on your face. Sounds even easier, right?"

One of the women in the back of the parking lot collapsed to the ground from lack of sleep.

"Of course, in compliance with Sixth Labor Code 7436, you are always permitted to terminate any video calls where the situation becomes explicitly sexual. But all other questions must be answered truthfully and, of course, cheerfully. These people want to learn about Sixths like you, so make sure that you leave a good impression! Do not forget to smile!"

The Fifth tapped her foot.

"Do not forget to smile!"

Two robots hauled away the woman who had passed out.

"Do not forget to smile!"

The Fifth clicked her digital screen impatiently, then let out a grateful sigh.

"This concludes your orientation with the Hispaniola Emergency Delivery Service."

# Chapter 41

They lined up as the Fifth gave each of them a van number, a water bottle, and a hat. Delivery Vehicle #107, read Emily's little slip of paper. Emily stepped inside her "travel pod"—a small space in the middle of the van without windows or a steering wheel, only a seat that faced a large digital screen.

"Welcome to work, Emily O'Dora!" asked the screen. "Are you ready to clock in?"

Emily selected the green "Let's Go!" button on the screen and suddenly the van started flashing.

"In compliance with Sixth Labor Code #8914 please put on your seatbelt. In compliance with Sixth Labor Code #8914 please put on your seatbelt..."

She scrambled and found her seatbelt, strapping it on.

"THANK YOU," read the screen. The self-driving vehicle violently took off, barreling out of the parking lot towards her first delivery.

A logo of a giant eye with the word "Youspective" was displayed, followed by a page full of text.

"You will be shown two images, sounds, or words. Your task is simple—to select the one of these that *you* like better. Do not think at all about your answers, only make a selection based on your natural preferences. Are you ready to continue?"

Emily clicked "I'm Ready!" as she felt her van swerve around a corner.

Two trees appeared on the screen: a blue spruce and a baobab. A timer tuned to the hundredth of a second counted down from 1.70 in the top left soon after the images were displayed. She selected the baobab. Then she was shown two words. "party" and "celebration." She selected "celebration."

"Sound one:" read the monitor, followed by a female scream.

"Sound two:" read the monitor, followed by a male scream.

Emily selected sound two. This was a weird fucking job.

"Are you ready to MOVE????" asked the screen. "Put your RUNNING shoes on, because the suggested delivery time for this order is only...

Everything on the screen went blank to be momentarily replaced by a huge, flashing number: "39 SECONDS."

"The item you are searching for looks like THIS."

An image of a small cardboard box with a triangle logo in the corner.

"And the address you are delivering to looks like THIS."

An image of a front porch with apartment number 324 and a wreath.

"Now.... GO!!!"

Emily's door automatically flung open and she leapt out of the van, darting to the back of the vehicle where the cargo was held. There were dozens of boxes and bags of various sizes, and she finally found the one she had seen in the picture. Looking at the apartment building in front of her, she bound up the stairs to the third floor. Sprinting down the hallway she spotted the wreath that matched the image, dropped the box on the doorstep, then raced back to the van.

"In compliance with Sixth Labor Code #8914 please put on your seatbelt. In compliance with Sixth…"

Emily frantically strapped on her seatbelt.

"THANK YOU."

Emily panted.

"Congratulations on your first delivery! It took you…"

The screen flashed red.

"134 SECONDS…"

"That's 3.4 times the expected delivery time. This normally would result in one strike against your labor record but…"

The screen changed to a friendly shade of puke green.

"It's your first day! No worries! Let's see if you can do better next time!!"

The van peeled out of its parking spot as the screen displayed a picture of a fluffy white Persian cat and a thin black shorthair with yellow eyes. Emily took a deep breath. Something about this computer monitor yelling at her had gotten her heart racing. The pod started making a shrill beeping sound.

"Please select your preference. Please select your preference. Emily O'Dora, please select your…"

She slammed her hand onto the image of the black cat and the noise stopped.

She made just over a dozen more deliveries over the next few hours, each taking her quite a bit longer than the "suggested delivery time." The screen became less and less friendly with each failure, saying things like:

"Your slow rate of work is a terrible disappointment, Emily. If it wasn't your first day you would have already been fired…. FOURTEEN…. times. Maybe you should just give up and not even come in tomorrow?"

After three hours the van pulled onto a highway towards a different part of town and a different logo appeared on the screen. A globe, showing one person in South America in rags and one person in Southeast Asia in a business suit. They were talking to each other electronically like they were the best of friends. "QUIZSIXTH" it said above the logo. The logo faded and was replaced by a picture of a Middle Eastern man's face and a ringing sound.

"Incoming call from Ammar Alami. Rabat Morocco."

Emily pressed "answer" and a video call opened up on the large screen in front of her.

"Hey guys, it's a new one, we got a new one!" he shouted over his shoulder. Two male friends stepped over to his side and looked at the video analytically like they were examining a new kind of bacteria under a microscope. They were all shirtless and, since only their torsos were visible, potentially naked as well. Who the fuck were these people who could afford to just sit around making phone calls all day and never get dressed?

"So you're Emily?" asked one of the friends.

She nodded, making sure to smile.

"And you're working for $3.75 right now?"

Emily nodded again.

One of them snorted. Then they all started whispering amongst themselves before asking their next question.

"If you were an animal, what animal would you be?"

"A dolphin," answered Emily politely, like this was a totally normal question for adults to ask each other.

They whispered amongst themselves again.

"If Amar came over to Hispaniola, would you swim around with him in the ocean? You know, like a dolphin?"

"Maybe," said Emily sweetly.

They whispered among themselves again.

"You wanna show us your tits?"

Emily, still smiling, selected the red "end call" button. A prompt appeared.

*Why did you terminate this customer interaction?*
*A) I was uncomfortable*
*B) I wanted to talk to someone else*
*C) I found myself in a situation that was explicitly sexual*

She selected C.

"We're so sorry to hear that!" read her screen. "Caleb did detect some mild sexual content, so you are.... still employed!"

The display showed an orange cartoon character saying "whew!"

"But please remember that you are never *required* to end a call, it is only within your rights to do so in accordance with Sixth Labor Code 7436. In all instances of inappropriate content you can decide what *you* are comfortable with and go from there. We want you to be able to do this job in *your* way!

The text faded and was replaced with a gigantic yellow smiley face.

"Incoming call from... Sunil Kumar, Chennai, East India."

Emily answered.

"Hey..." muttered the man, blinking his eyes. He was wrapped in a blanket and clearly high. "Do you know... how to beat the final boss in Zorgok 16?"

Emily smiled, but shook her head.

"That's unfortunate, I really needed help with that... Hey, can you come over here? My head feels weird, I think I might need a glass of water or something."

"I'm sorry, I can't. I'm working."

"But can't you just... come over, you know, after work?"

"I am thousands of miles away and have no money."

"QUIT MAKING EXCUSES!" shouted Sunil, "I just need a GLASS of fucking WATER. I can't... I can't...."

A robot rolled up to Sunil's side, offering him a glass of fucking water. He slapped it to the ground. "NO!" he shouted, "not from you, from a HUMAN! I need a glass of water from a HUMAN!"

"The last boss in Zorgok 16," explained the robot, "is defeated most efficiently if you first equip the Silver Pendant of Hope and then..."

"NO!!!" shouted Sunil again, jumping to his feet and slamming his chair into the robot's face. "Do NOT tell me! I need to learn how to beat that game from a HUMAN!!!"

The robot rolled away casually.

"Sorry about that..." he muttered, "Lexi can be SO obnoxious sometimes. So you... could maybe come over in a week or something? After you get some money?"

Emily smiled. "I don't think I'll have enough money in a week either."

The man hung his head down in dejection. He remained perfectly motionless like that for about a minute, then passed out and rolled onto the floor. Emily enjoyed peace and quiet for the last two minutes of their call.

# Chapter 42

The heroes were in high spirits that evening when they got off work and found their seats on the bus.

"This is one of the best repeat gigs we've ever had," said Sadie, "you're totally our good luck charm Emily!"

Silvia nodded enthusiastically, "WAY easier than that shipyard. I mean, half the time you're just sitting there!"

"And answering questions," corrected Emily.

"Oh yeah, but those are way easy."

"Remember that one hospital job where they kept giving us drugs then asking us math problems to see if we performed them any faster?" input Sadie.

"If robo-horse 1 is traveling at 11 miles per hour, and robo-horse 2 is not not not traveling any slower than the sum…"

They burst into their typical laughter. Emily observed them curiously. She was both mentally and physically exhausted, hoping to never see a cardboard box or answer a question about her "preferences" ever again. And they were acting like they had just gotten back from a relaxing day at the spa.

"What kind of calls did you guys have come in?" asked Emily.

"Mostly creeps," laughed Silvia, "there was one guy who actually had two…" she whispered something to Sadie and they both snorted.

"You guys just hang up when you get those?"

Sadie nodded but Silvia shook her head.

"If you hang up early, they aren't prompted for a survey. And five good surveys will get you a $10 gift card to the grocery store."

"But don't they ask you to, like…"

"Take off my clothes? Shove my water bottle up my vagina? Yeah, like every single time. But I just smile and tell them no over and over again."

Emily frowned. "Have you guys ever actually gone in person to, you know…"

Silvia coughed, "Oh no, definitely not."

Sadie looked over at her sternly, "There's nothing good if you go looking for that kind of work Emily. Trust us. It might seem like a good opportunity at first, but it actually isn't."

"They'll fuck you to death," said Silvia flatly, flipping on the little TV monitor in front of her seat. Sadie did the same and soon they were both watching "Ranking Up" serenely, chuckling to the jokes on cue like they were part of the laugh track. Emily stared out the window. The jungle was shrouded in darkness now, the lights from self-driving vehicles zooming along the freeway carrying higher class people who knows where. Was she really going to do all of this again tomorrow?

Back at camp, Sadie and Silvia went off to find branches for the fire and Emily lay down in the grass, feeling too exhausted to even crawl into her tent. She squinted up at the stars. Still beautiful, regardless of whatever was happening down here.

"Get your first job?" asked Lacey.

Emily sat up. "Yeah. Did you work today?"

Lacey shrugged. "Yeah, but just the first half of the day. Over at a factory that makes humanoid robots, those F12 models that are like eight feet tall and sometimes work as supervisors and security guards."

"They aren't built by machines?"

"It's mostly mechanized but one of the assemblers was down, so they brought a bunch of Sixths and Sevenths to the plant to help attach some of the smaller joints together. Was kind of poetic because the exact same model that we were building was overseeing us. Humans building their machine masters or something."

Emily laughed. This girl always had something interesting to say.

"How was your job?" asked Lacey.

"Oh, it sucked. But I'll get used to it."

Lacey gave her a questioning look. "But what if you don't? What if every day feels like a waste of life? Like a reprimand for being too human, for being too different from those robots I was screwing together today?"

Emily shook her head, "Then I'll keep being human anyways."

"But what if they beat it out of you?"

"They won't. Look, I'll admit, my job totally sucked today, I absolutely hated it. But it made me all the more determined to find a way to a better life than this, a more worthwhile life than this. And I *will* find it, Lacey. And when I do, I'm taking you with me."

A tear dripped out the former Stonewalker's eye. "Thanks for talking like that. Even if it never happens, thanks. I'm just... so tired of this Sixth life. So tired of doing nothing except working, running out of money, working, running out of money. It's just... so easy to lose heart..."

"Hey hey..." said Emily sitting next to her and putting her arm around her shoulder, "It's gonna be OK. We'll figure out a way, I know we will."

Lacey was sobbing now. "I'm sorry..." she blubbered, "I'm just running out of hope over here, begging for someone, *anyone*, to swoop in and take me away from this place. I don't want to get demoted, to go back... the things I saw as a Stonewalker, the things I did..."

"Shh…" said Emily quietly, "shh… it's alright." She was exhausted, both mentally and emotionally, from her first day at that bizarre job. But something awakened when she saw this friend—perhaps her only real friend now—breaking down like this. She would be there for her. As long as she needed her, she would be there.

She sat holding her new friend for about an hour until she fell asleep in her arms. Then she gently lifted her up and carried her into her tent, gently laying her down so as not to wake her. On her way back she noticed a new tent in the distance. It was on the beach, to the northeast of their campsite, just barely visible through the underbrush. A man was sitting outside of it, watching them.

# Chapter 43

The next morning came far too quickly, the smell of Rose's oatmeal filling the camp. At least they had enough to eat, Emily had to admit. She remembered learning somewhere before that most humans throughout history had struggled simply to eat. Now, even with her low wages, food was relatively cheap, a few dollars a day more than enough. Her economic pressures primarily came from elsewhere—the nightly rent at her campground, the need to stay above negative $5,000 and avoid demotion. She was working not for food, but for dignity. And though eating was cheap, even the smallest semblance of dignity seemed basically unattainable.

She ate a bowl of porridge, washed up in the stream, and hung up some clothes to dry. Then, as if noticing that she was about to have a moment's peace, her bracelet started to buzz. She obediently ran to the bus station and was taken to her second day at the Hispaniola Emergency Delivery Service.

Although it was a longer shift, the second day was more manageable than the first. Emily learned that if she took careful mental note of the items in the back of the van, she could cut off quite a bit of time digging through things later on. More importantly, the 'expected delivery times' were twice as long as they had been on the first day. They had been pushing her beyond her normal limits during training intentionally, the actual expectations being much more realistic. In a strange way, Emily found this detail almost disappointing.

The calls she had from "Quizsixth" were mostly drunk males and their companions looking for a laugh, asking her a series of questions that would turn predictably inappropriate. Emily followed Silvia's advice and simply stayed on these calls, smiling and saying no as they requested her to, say, spit on the webcam or take off her pants then spin around nine times. The casual shamelessness of these adult men astounded her. They acted like spoiled children asking a clown to do tricks, seemingly incapable of imagining a world where an evil greater than their own boredom might exist. But given how tedious the preference questions from "Youspective" were, these calls coming in were always a bit of a relief. Smiling almost came naturally.

Lacey was quiet that evening as they slurped Rose's mushroom and onion soup together under the twilight. Up on the nearby hilltop the Koreans were smoking their cigarette and taking notes. Most women around the fire were even more gloomy than usual, as the few of the camp's women like eight-fingered Luisa had hit negative $5,000 and been demoted earlier that afternoon.

"Warned them that they needed to sign up for more jobs, but they didn't listen. Just kept playing their card games," said Sadie in a sad tone that still sounded like gloating.

"You don't work, you don't get paid," said Silvia dryly, "kinda funny how that works."

These comments didn't seem to really cheer anybody up, and the heroes decided to go fetch water from the stream to give everyone else some time to catch up to their enlightened state.

"Sorry I was... such a mess last night..." said Lacey quietly.

"Jesus, no," said Emily between mouthfuls, "you were totally fine."

Rose—who was cleaning some dishes in the washbasin—wiped a few tears from her eyes as she worked, sniffing sadly in remembrance of their lost camp members. To Emily it seemed fake, but so did most things that woman did.

"Thanks," said Lacey, "for being chill."

"Of course."

Emily glanced into the trees as they ate. That new tent was still there, as well as the man sitting outside of it. She walked over to the fire, dished up another bowl, then carried it the few hundred feet through the overgrown jungle to him.

"Hey there neighbor," said Emily, "ya want some soup?"

It was a large tent—large enough for Emily to stand up inside—positioned in the sand where the underbrush ended and the beach began. The bearded man was sitting in front of this in a simple camping chair that looked like a throne compared to the logs most women sat on. He was carving a wooden deer with a pocketknife and glanced up at her in amusement.

"And to what do I owe this pleasure?"

"To... the fact that I'm offering you soup," said Emily, "you know, like I just said."

He laughed good naturedly. "Well, it seems that I am very fortunate then. Thank you. I will have to return this act of warmth and generosity at a later date."

He took the bowl from Emily, set it on the homemade table next to him, then returned to his wood carving as if their transaction was now complete. He made his cuts with precision, and had a variety of other wooden animals, as well as chisels, strewn about his feet.

"Name's Emily," she said, reaching out her hand.

He glanced up briefly as if to make her disappear, but when this proved ineffective he smiled up at her as if talking to her had always been his plan.

"Stefan," he said, taking her hand in his. It was a huge hand, matching the rest of him. He was at least six and a half feet tall and powerfully built from head to foot. He had short hair, a thick black beard, and light brown eyes that seemed perpetually amused.

"So, what brings you here?" asked Emily, "escape from Cuba?"

"Have never had the chance to explore that majestic island, I'm afraid. The subconscious mind of the First there, Petrov, apparently doesn't like males who are taller than him."

"Well, you didn't miss much."

"Oh, I doubt that."

Emily eyed the man. He had a certain twinkle in his eye, but often glanced away rather than make eye contact, as if a new thought had just crossed his mind that he felt he needed to attend to. He made a few more cuts, shaping the legs of his wooden deer.

"So where are you from then?"

"Here and there. I've had the opportunity to explore many places in my travels."

"Sounds glamorous. And what brings you here?"

"Why, the breathtakingly beautiful Cuban women, of course. Like yourself."

Emily narrowed her eyes at this compliment. "I was beginning to think you had come here to carve animals out of sticks."

Stefan laughed again. It was a warm, easy laugh that made him sound like he had never quite felt as comfortable as he did at this particular moment.

"Most people around here avoid speaking with me, but you approach me directly. I find this intriguing."

"I don't know of any other reasonable way to approach people."

He flashed an amused smile. "Do you happen to be aware of why there are so few males in this Sixth Sleeping Area?'

"Well, most Sixths here are refugees from Cuba. And Cuba is almost entirely female."

"That's not quite right. Because many men, like myself, come to this place in hopes of making healthy and positive connections with the ladies here."

"I'm not sure if that's what most of the men are looking for, but I follow you."

"So why is it, do you think, that there is still such a gender imbalance?"

Emily thought for a moment. "I believe you're hinting at the fact that violence here in the cage is unregulated. So probably some of the men have been killed because of this."

He raised his eyebrows. "And this doesn't concern you?" He was an incredibly strong man, a sort of giant, and something in the way he carried himself indicated he knew something of violence.

"I've been fighting that war in Cuba for as long as I can remember," replied Emily. "Whatever danger is here, I'm prepared to face it. It's just these mind-numbing jobs that I feel ill equipped for."

"You may not have to settle for such things much longer. I suspect to see many positive opportunities unfolding."

"You do, huh? Seems that you like to talk in riddles, Stefan from here and there."

"I... try to communicate in the way I think is best."

She laughed. "As do we all. Now tell me. Exactly what are these opportunities?"

He picked up one of his chisels and made a few angled cuts before responding. "It would be much better if I could show, rather than tell you."

"I see…" said Emily, stroking her chin in mock thoughtfulness. "Well, I'm actually watching right now. So would you like to show me?"

He shook his head as if it were obviously absurd for her to even ask this. "Tonight it is too late, too dangerous. But on an afternoon when you are not working, check in with me. I may be able to introduce you to some potential prospects which might appeal to you."

Emily shook her head, smiling. Men who were secretive like this could be amusing, but they were often disappointing as well. Usually the main thing they were hiding was that they had nothing to hide.

"I'll see you around, Stefan."

# Chapter 44

The next few days were draining and uninteresting, Emily doing very little beyond her ten hour shifts. The stress of her job on her first day had quickly been replaced by a mind-numbing, tedious discomfort that made the minutes feel like hours. There was a clock in her pod that told the time to the second, and she tried with all her might not to look at it. Even the calls coming in seemed to follow a repeating pattern, where it seemed she was engaging in the exact same dialogue with different perverts multiple times per day.

But the part of the job she loathed the most were the thousands of questions from "Youspective." Whether she preferred this or that shade of green, this or that scratching of nails on a chalkboard, this or that picture of a sunset. The speed with which the questions had to be answered made it so she could go hours without forming a single coherent thought, only deciding what she preferred over and over and over again. On top of this, the computer chip in her brain would sometimes detect her answering in a way that seemed to go against her gut, causing the whole pod to start beeping and saying "this preference seems insincere, this preference seems insincere," until she corrected her answer. Then sometimes she'd be questioned by a condescending artificial intelligence as to why she had not correctly expressed her preferences and how she intended to prevent such mistakes in the future.

Once she got the hang of it, it was certainly not a difficult job. In one sense it was the easiest thing she had ever done. But it clashed with something very simple and human inside of her, and there were many times throughout the day where she strongly considered screaming and leaping out of the vehicle rather than answer another idiotic 1.7 second question.

At camp she spoke mostly with Lacey, although she did visit Stefan a few times when Lacey was gone to some job. He maintained his air of mystery, sharing very little about himself or what he wanted. Even when he came back to his tent and Emily asked him where he had been he would give vague answers like "exploring possibilities" or "preparing for great things," as if a little positivity in his language were enough to make up for a total lack of content. Though sometimes she could get him talking on less personal subjects, like freedom.

"Do I think you can... achieve freedom? I think you are already very free. Sixths are an ancient class built on freedom, and Sixth Sleeping Areas are built around equality of opportunity, old ideals I was once... rather involved with. But I have learned that we must move with the waves of power that flow around us in order to bring about positive things, in order to build. And if you allow me, I hope to introduce you to some such opportunities which may be of great interest, opportunities which, in time..."

He would talk like this sometimes for many minutes before Emily interrupted him. She found him interesting to observe. He was handsome in a rugged, woodsy sort of way, and his face would go through flashes that seemed to almost contradict one another. In one moment he seemed the gentle monk, selflessly intent on doing good and guiding the world to some higher peace. In the next he seemed the cold strategist, meticulously preparing some sort of diabolical mischief. If Emily was being honest with herself, both sides of the man intrigued her, even attracted her. But he also gave off the air of someone who was not only difficult to get close to, but impossible. A man who had decided at a young age that trusting others was merely a careless mistake, like leaving the window open in a rainstorm or forgetting to tie your shoes.

The evening of her fifth night in the camps, Emily and Lacey walked to the stream together, gathering water before the last glow of twilight faded and life in the cage became much more dangerous.

"You get any jobs today?" asked Emily.

"Some mines near Gonaïves. Copper and gold, we were helping a few robots to unclog some of the older sorting equipment they had there."

They approached the river and Lacey climbed out onto a rock near some of the faster moving white water.

"Sounds at least different from most."

Lacey nodded. She looked exhausted.

"Hey, I've been meaning to talk to you," continued Emily, "about how I left Cuba."

Lacey squatted and began filling their water jugs, handing them to Emily on shore who placed them into a backpack. She gave Emily an expectant look, showing she was curious.

"So it's a long story. There were these dreams, this surreal battle that ended the war with the Collective, but the strangest thing is that the morning I left. I wanted to leave, but David wanted me to stay."

Lacey dropped the water jug she was filling into the river.

"What do you mean? How did he act, exactly?"

"He showed... romantic interest in me. Then he got upset when I pulled away. Sent people to chase me down, even."

Lacey snatched her water jug before it floated downstream, then turned to give Emily her full attention. "That makes no sense. I mean, it's impossible. You were David's property in Cuba. His subconscious property, but still his property. There is zero way you could have left unless he wanted you to."

"But he definitely *didn't* want me to leave. Like there was no way. He even had some of my friends trying to drag me back to him."

Emily remembered Vy and Jason. What were they doing now, she wondered? Working with David to rebuild Cuba's wartorn infrastructure? How long before his fantasies of peace would once again devolve into fantasies of war?

Lacey paused, then started filling the last of their water jugs. "It must have been one of those situations where a guy acts like he wants you around just to be polite, but he really wants you gone. You know, when they're giving you all these compliments but everything about it seems so fake they actually feel like fuck yous..."

"But it wasn't like that. It wasn't like that at all."

Lacey shook her head, "It must have been, Emily. It simply must have been. Unless..."

"Unless what?"

"Forget about it. It was a crazy idea. He was being the jerk boyfriend who forces you to break up with him because he doesn't have the balls. He was totally being that guy. That's the only logical explanation."

Emily helped stuff the last of the jugs in her backpack then lifted the heavy load onto her back.

"But what were you going to say when you..."

Lacey sighed. "I was going to say... you remember that glowing guy on that book cover? With the chains? The first day we met?"

"Yeah."

"I was going to say that maybe you're that guy."

# Chapter 45

Emily awoke to the sound of beeping. She heard a few other similar sounds throughout the camp. She blinked her eyes open in confusion, then saw a green flashing light. Her job bracelet.

She threw on her clothes and stepped out of her tent into the cool night air. Several women were running. "Come on!" one of them cried, "you're gonna be late!"

Emily started running as well. The running itself didn't bother her—she could run for hours—but the purpose of their running *did*. None of these women knew what job they were getting or how much they were being paid. And they were running *towards* this opportunity, like it was something they just couldn't bear to miss. It all seemed so wrong.

She noticed Sadie and Silvia in the dark.

"Congrats on your first night shift," said Sadie, as if she spoke for the masters themselves.

"Thanks," said Emily, who felt she needed no congratulation for obeying a stupid bracelet whenever it summoned her.

"You'll probably hate it," laughed Silvia between breaths, "but give it time, you even get used to these ones after a while."

They arrived at the bus station within minutes and only two other women were already standing there, looking up at the screen.

"Bus D. 1:45 AM. Cleanup at West Kennels."

"Oh shit," muttered a woman behind Emily who had just arrived, "oh shit..."

A smaller self driving bus arrived minutes later to pick up Emily and a dozen others. Many of the women paid for various entertainment while Silvia and Sadie synced up with the systems to watch "Ranking Up" as they always did. Emily wasn't tempted. She had just woken up from being a Seventh, she had no interest in retreating into fantasy now. She instead stared out the window. Self driving vehicles passed them in the night, some carrying higher class passengers, some carrying no one at all, likely on their way to retrieve whoever had summoned them. But as she watched these empty cars rolling quietly by, Emily couldn't help but think that perhaps somewhere along the line the great machine had lost its master, and was now just pounding along from sheer force of habit

In twenty minutes, they'd arrived. The "West Kennels" were not one building, but dozens of mansions, with well-manicured lawns filling the gaps between. Lights shining from these elegant homes—as well as colorful, glowing dog statues—lit up the entire park, like it was some kind of holiday. A large trench weaved in between these buildings which seemed like it was sometimes filled with water. There was also an industrial grade bounce house, a ball pit, and a giant gun labeled "fetch cannon."

"This place is insane..." muttered Emily, "What's in the houses? Millions of chew toys or something?"

"Maybe. But each house belongs to one dog, so it's sort of up to them what they want," answered Silvia.

"Wait. Those *mansions* are each for *one* dog?"

"Yup. And we're gonna clean 'em. But hey, it beats cleaning the sewers under the palace on Gonâve island. Now *that* was a dirty job."

Emily found herself counting the dog mansions. Sixteen, seventeen, eighteen... was this another repeat gig? It looked like it could last for months.

Their bus pulled up to the most central building and stopped. Everyone's entertainment screens went black, to the noticeable disappointment of some, and they shuffled out onto the grass. There were a few spraying sounds in the distance, and a middle eastern woman stepped out of the elegant structure, descending the stairs to meet them. She was barefoot, wearing only a black nightgown.

"Welcome Sixths, glad you could help. I'm Halima, the Second who manages this estate."

Emily gawked at her, as did a few others. A Second? Who was barely awake or dressed? She didn't know how she had imagined Seconds would look, but she hadn't imagined this.

"So the job isn't actually much," she continued casually, "the mistresses take care of all the day to day stuff, I just needed some extra hands for cleaning out the lazy river. The babies are going to want to swim tomorrow, and we need it to be clean and hygienic for them."

Emily sighed in relief. At least they weren't cleaning every one of those enormous mansions inside and out.

"The dog mistresses have been working at it for some time," she continued, "but your help will speed up the process. They're on the far side of the camp now and will give you further instructions. Your hours begin now. Good luck!"

Many Sixths started jogging in the direction indicated, but Halima stepped forward and took Emily's arm before she could join them.

"Miss O'Dora?"

Emily froze. Halima glanced at a few of the other Sixths lingering behind, then made a gesture like she was swatting away a fly, causing them to run off.

"Yes?"

"Sabrina has a job planned for you that she wanted me to inform you about personally."

Emily coughed. "Sabrina? Tonight?"

Halima laughed. "No no, not tonight. Tonight you will be cleaning the lazy river with everyone else. We—I mean, Sabrina—will summon you. When she is ready."

Emily gave her a quizzical look. "Why me?"

"Everything will be explained then. We simply wanted to inform you that this is being planned so you can be prepared. And, of course, so you can have something to look forward to."

She smiled broadly, as if this gift of hope alone had placed her among the angels.

"Thank you, I don't know what to…"

"That is all," interrupted Halima, "you are free to go work with your friends now."

The Second turned and stepped up the staircase back into the dog mansion while Emily jogged off in confusion.

On the far side of the park, just past a glowing blue statue of a Basset Hound, twenty nude men were working vigorously with shovels and hoses. Some scooped dog shit off the bottom and sides of the trench and dumped it into trash cans. Others sprayed the remaining residue off the bottom. The cans full of shit were periodically lifted up and emptied into a dumpster by a self-driving skid loader that rolled around threateningly like a dinosaur. One of the men set down his shovel, smiling to address the women.

"My name is Boaz, chief dog mistress for Mr. Paws," he announced. "We've got plenty of extra tools in back of the truck. It's pretty fun work, actually, once you get going."

Emily stared at these laboring men who mostly hadn't looked up. They seemed entirely unaware of their nudity and showed no signs of arousal at the thirty women who had come to help them work. They all just seemed to be wonderfully focused on dog shit.

The Sixths gathered shovels from the bed of an electric truck and joined the men, working their way down the dog's concrete river bed. The men would occasionally glance at their work, giving suggestions or demonstrating some scooping technique. They were all extremely polite and smiley, giving frequent encouragement to the newcomers as they continued to work efficiently themselves.

"What is wrong with these dudes," whispered Emily to Sadie the moment they were out of earshot.

Sadie flashed an amused smile. "Sevenths," she whispered.

"They're called dog mistresses and they're *naked*. Doesn't this seem, you know, maybe *wrong*?" Emily asked again, in a rather loud whisper.

Silvia snickered. "No no, I learned about these guys last time I worked here. It's nothing creepy, just a few of them assigned to each dog in a human-subservient role. Sort of like being the dog's eternal playmates, veterinarians, and protectors. They follow their respective dogs around constantly, chasing them whenever they want to be chased, barking at them whenever they want to be barked at, and so on. They even sleep in the dog's beds with them—half the men in this camp are doing so now. Just to provide them with, you know, a little extra comfort."

"I see…"

"All of it *is* still pretty weird," laughed Sadie.

"And it used to be us," muttered Emily, thoughtfully.

"I was never *that* bad," whispered Silvia, indicating a well-hung man who whistled happily as he scooped shit off the bottom of the pool like this was the best night of his life.

They worked efficiently together, getting the job done in just over three hours. It was surprisingly relaxing for Emily, doing work that was not overseen by a machine, work where there wasn't a timer counting down for every little thing she did. It felt more human, and the hours passed more quickly as a result. Though it was still strange working shoulder to shoulder with these servants of Sabrina's pet dogs. Their intense focus on the task at hand was more disconcerting than their shameless nudity. These men were friendly, handsome, and basically no longer human. She tried her best to look away, disturbed by this compelling evidence of their master's power. *This* is what she would become if she went just a little deeper into debt.

They left the park as the sun was coming up. The dog mistresses waved happily as they left. "Thanks for making things nice and clean so Cooper Boy can have a most incredible day!" one of them called out, almost like it was a prayer. If Cooper Boy didn't have an incredible day his day was clearly going to be a fucking nightmare. What a life.

# Chapter 46

Back on the bus, the Sixths exploded in girlish laughter, discussing which of the men they found most attractive or most ridiculous. But they became more sober when they discussed money. Only three hours and six minutes of work at $4.75 an hour, with $2.50 of that going to cover the cost of their bus ride. They had just lost almost an entire night of sleep for twelve dollars and twenty two cents. Not even enough to cover the cost of one night in the cage.

"Dang," muttered Sadie, "well, still always better than not working."

"Gotta see a lot more dicks, that's for sure!" said Silvia cheerily.

When they arrived back at the bus station at half past five, Emily separated from the group.

"Hey pal, where ya going?" asked Silvia. There was a suspicious look in her eye.

"Oh, just that store. The, uh, Sixth Convenience and Affordability Market."

"Ah, the old SCAM. Cool." She turned away.

"Why do you ask?"

"Just wanted to make sure you're not gambling your money away or something. Going somewhere that would put the rest of us in danger."

"Oh gosh. Yeah, I'd never do something like that."

"You promise?" piped in Sadie sweetly.

"Yeah sure. I mean, of course."

Silvia smiled. "Hey, maybe you'll be one of the survivors after all. I'll admit, I was skeptical at first, but you're holding your own. See ya back here in a few hours, eh?"

"Gonna be a great day for our bank accounts," winked Sadie. Then the two of them jogged off to the gate into the Sixth Sleeping Area. Emily watched them thoughtfully. The heroes indeed, those two just never stopped. In a way they had turned themselves into Sevenths, seemingly getting all of their satisfaction from working, from earning or saving money. Strange that to avoid being demoted they had evolved into something so similar.

Emily bought a few mandarin oranges and mangos with her gift card allowance from *QuizSixth,* then stepped up to the front of the store. General Lin was watching a TV with her boots up on a footrest and a box of cigars at her side. She turned to yell at her robot.

"Where's my fucking coffee!?" she asked the little box-like drone.

"You didn't ask me for any yet, master," it said, "how many cups would you like?"

"Five. And you better get the temperature just right this time, you fucking dwarf!" she shouted. The drone zoomed off, and General Lin looked up to notice Emily grinning at her from behind the counter.

"Oh, you!" she cried, sounding half annoyed, half enthused. "What do ya need, kid? Figure out a way to become a Fifth yet?"

"No, it's something else. Something strange. Please don't tell anyone this, I don't want to draw any attention."

"Girl, nobody talks to me, and if they do I make sure they regret it. You're chatting with a black hole."

Emily laughed. "So we just did a job at one of the dog parks, and the Second managing the place told me that Sabrina is going to have, like, a personal job for me. Do you have any idea what that means?"

General Lin scowled. "A job, eh? With Sabrina? The First? Hate to burst your bubble kid, but I don't think this is good."

"Why not?"

"Look, Sabrina runs this whole island. She doesn't need shit from you. Any work she needs done, she has a thousand people more qualified than you, like, no offense. So if she is calling on you it's most likely to turn you into one of her personal Sevenths."

"Can she *do* that?" asked Emily, horrified.

The general laughed. "Why not? You're trespassing on her land, she can turn all of you Sixths into Sevenths anytime she wants to. Freedom is an illusion, kid."

Emily frowned, "I'm determined to not let that happen," she said, "I'm not losing my mind again."

Lin nodded soberly. "I feel you there. But if she calls you up you better go. If you refuse a job from the First herself then you're guaranteed to get the space boot. If you go at least ya have a chance. Maybe if you're lucky she won't like you when she meets you in person and she'll change her mind about adding you to her staff."

"But then she might demote me to Seventh as punishment instead," muttered Emily despondently.

"Probably!" laughed Lin, puffing on her cigar, "but there ain't much you can do. I'm really sorry kid. You just gotta go and see what's up whenever she summons you. It's really your only option."

Emily stared for a moment, then composed herself. "Really appreciate the information. Um... Godservant watch over you or whatever."

"And you," laughed Lin. And then, perhaps out of a subconscious instinct, she spat.

# Chapter 47

She was awakened by her bracelet only a few hours later and, finding no time for breakfast, rushed off to the bus station. When their buses arrived in Cap-Haiten they were brought into the parking lot for a surprise team meeting.

"We," read the Fifth manager in the red and gray blazer, "are so proud of the work you have been doing. Everyone pat yourselves on the back. You all are absolutely AMAZING."

Silvia and Sadie patted their own backs, then half-jokingly patted Emily's as well.

"If you look around," she continued, "you will notice that this parking lot is much more empty than it was almost a week ago. You are the best of the best, the cream of the crop. You are our *champions*."

The Fifth tapped her digital pad, impatient for the next part of her AI written script.

"Given your incredible performance, we have decided to give you all TWO rewards. First:"

She tapped her foot.

"You each have a five dollar gift card to the Sixth market automatically added to your bank accounts. Eat a delicious meal tonight on *us*."

"Saving that," muttered Silvia.

"And second: you are each rewarded with more hours. These may be a little challenging, but we have seen you perform and we *know* you can handle it. Just think about the money you will be able to save!"

One woman in the back of the parking lot stepped back onto the bus, clearly not enthusiastic about this last reward.

"From now until the tube system is repaired," continued the Fifth, "your shifts will start at three in the morning and go until eleven at night. Other *significant* rewards will be granted to team members who complete all shifts up to standard until the tube system is up and running again. Any questions? No? OK then, let's get those packages delivered!!"

A robot handed Emily two water bottles and a caffeine pill, then sent her on her way.

She made it through the first half of her shift on adrenaline alone. 3 AM until 11 at night, that was going to be a twenty hour shift, not including travel time. And she had barely slept the previous night, how was she going to get used to this? At least today's shift started later so it would only be fifteen hours.

In the late afternoon, she started getting more travel time between deliveries, which meant more video calls for *QuizSixth*. And, for the first time, she had a female caller.

"Incoming call from Lily Roberts: Manchester England."

The call started with a plume of smoke blown into the camera. Lily was in her underwear, smoking an enormous bong that was about the size of a trombone. As Emily's face came onto the screen she sat up attentively.

"Oh fuck. Is that her?" she muttered.

The woman stared at her screen so closely that her webcam briefly showed only her forehead.

"Oh fuck yeah, I got you, I finally got you!" she cried, dropping her bong to smile in satisfaction at her screen.

Emily stared in confusion. "What do you mean?"

"You're Emily O'Dora, right?" she asked, as if she was making the winning point in an argument.

"Well, yes..."

"I got you!" she cried. "Ok, ok... she hunched over conspiratorially. "So I don't think I'm supposed to know about you, I overheard my master talking—he's asleep now, obviously. So... first off. Are you really *her*?"

"Am I what?"

"Are you *her*?" she asked again, leaning in as if she were asking for a secret.

"I... have no idea what you're talking about."

Lily rolled her eyes.

"Do you have, like, powers?"

Emily narrowed her eyes. Lily sighed.

"Can you," she said deliberately, "set me *free*? You know, from my current master? Make me into a Fourth again?"

Emily gawked.

"Like he'll be mad that I'm asking you this, but he won't punish me that much cuz he totally *loves* me. SO annoying. Anyways. Like, if you wanted to do that for me could you, like, *do* that for me?"

Emily frowned. "I am just a Sixth, I have no idea..."

Lily sighed, picking up her bong from off the floor and taking a hit, holding her breath for some time before releasing the smoke.

"I'm asking you," she whispered, "if you can get me. The fuck. *Out* of here. It might *look* luxurious, but *trust* me, I fucking hate this fucking..."

The video call ended abruptly with an automatic "This Six Minute Call Has Timed Out." message. Emily stared at the blank screen. Why the hell did this random woman in England think she could set her free? Suddenly a huge red frowny face appeared on her display.

"Emily O'Dora" said her computer. "Did you, by chance, forget to *smile?*"

"Oh fuck," she muttered.

"*Smiling* is part of your responsibility with QuizSixth, our customers are not happy when you don't *smile.*"

"Yeah, I'm really sorry," said Emily, "It won't happen again, trust me, I just..."

The huge red frowny face on the screen faded away and was replaced by an equally large yellow smiley face.

"Good..." said the computer. Another call came in. Fortunately this one was just a lonely guy asking her why he hadn't been able to get a girlfriend yet. He was turning one hundred next week and wasn't sure what he had done wrong. She smiled and told him that she would gladly be his girlfriend, starting today. He told her thank you, then he cried, then he started masturbating, at which point she ended the call. All in all just a way easier one to manage.

The final five hours of her shift dragged on, especially with the seemingly millions of preference questions from *Youspective*. But she made it through, getting back to camp exhausted. Rather than fall asleep, she took the risk and snuck off to the stream to wash up. If she was going to work twenty hour shifts, she wasn't going to be smelling herself the entire time.

On her way back to camp, she heard someone coming the opposite direction. She froze, reaching for her knife. Everyone had gone on and on about how dangerous the Sixth Sleeping Area was, was someone going to actually try to...

"Emily?" asked the voice. A nervous, awkward, self-righteous voice.

"ROSE? What the hell are you doing out so late?"

Silence for a few moments.

"I'm leaving, Emily," she whispered. "But I'm... going to miss you."

"I'll, uh, miss you too," lied Emily. "But, like, where are you going?" Like, where *could* they go?

"Can I tell you a secret?" asked Rose in her creepy whisper. "I really like you, so it's probably best that I tell you..."

"Sure sure, you can tell me a secret."

"You promise not to tell the others?"

"Yeah, yeah."

"I'm a death dancer, Emily."

"You're a fucking what?"

"A death dancer. A higher class that spends time in the cage, in spite of the risks."

"Wait," muttered Emily, "You're not a Sixth?"

"I'm a Fourth," whispered Rose.

"And you came here anyways? Like, *why*??"

"I wanted to help."

"You just came here to try to help us?"

"Our world..." said Rose in her most creepy voice, "is sick..."

Emily had to admit she was right about that shit. "So wait. You came here and risked your life, just to try to help us? By making us soup and cleaning and stuff?"

She nodded in the moonlight. "Yeah. But I don't think... " She paused to gather her thoughts. "But I don't think I helped very much. Part of me thinks I didn't help at all."

"Why do you say that?"

"I mean, you guys can dish up your own soup. You guys can clean your own dishes. Those aren't the things that make your lives hard.

It's the fact that you have no money, that your jobs pay nothing, that you are squeezed by the evil forces of injustice. It's the fact that this world... is sick..."

Emily thought for a second. "But at least you tried, eh?"

"I guess."

A pause.

"So whatcha gonna do now?"

"Probably study some Arabic. I'm part of this club where we learn dead languages and then try to talk in them together, as a way of honoring our ancestors. And sing some karaoke. I really miss karaoke."

"And eat something besides soup?" asked Emily jokingly.

"I actually... really like soup..."

Emily laughed.

"Well, have fun Rose. Way to survive your death dance or whatever."

"Yeah, sorry I couldn't do more..."

"It's OK."

"It's just I'm only one person, and there's only so much I can do, and you guys don't even need my help, I just wanted to help, but the problems, they're so deep, so deep, I just don't know..."

"Hey hey," said Emily, pulling this woman she used to despise into a hug. "Hey, hey. It was cool of you to try. Go sing some fun karaoke songs for me, alright?"

A pause.

"Thanks Emily," she whispered.

They awkwardly hugged a few moments longer—every hug with Rose was awkward—and pulled apart. Then Emily returned to her tent and Rose returned to that comfortable, guilty place from whence she came.

# Chapter 48

3 AM came quickly, her flashing bracelet sending her running to the bus station in the darkness. She didn't know how she was going to get through these shifts, but she was determined to try.

The first part of her shift went smoothly, albeit slowly. But about six hours into her shift, the alarm in her pod started to sound in response to preferences she had selected. "This preference seems insincere, this preference seems insincere," it announced. But unlike other times when this had happened, she was not selecting thoughtlessly or randomly. She was actually selecting her preference, and still somehow getting it wrong.

"We have on record you selecting the other option in this exact question seventeen times," explained the computer, "What led you to selecting this option, Emily O'Dora?"

"I don't know. I just selected which one I preferred. Maybe my preferences changed?"

"Your preferences are not supposed to change," scolded the AI, "please do not allow your preferences to change."

This happened with more and more frequency, until Emily found herself flinching when she selected a preference, anticipating the shrill alarm.

"If you cannot honestly tell us your preferences," explained the computer, "your contract work for us will, unfortunately, need to be terminated. Perhaps, if you are feeling unwell, you should quit this job to avoid having a termination on your record?"

"I feel fine, I just DON'T KNOW WHAT YOU WANT!!!!" cried Emily.

Finally a call came in through *QuizSixth*. Anything besides those preference questions.

"Would you fuck me..." asked the man, "if I was wearing this?"

He wore a fluffy black racoon hat.

"No," replied Emily.

"How about..." he ran off and came back wearing a Hawaiian shirt and a gold necklace, "if I was wearing *this*."

"No."

"But would you fuck me..." he ran off and changed again. This guy totally seemed gay, she didn't know why he was even asking her these questions. ".. if I was wearing *this*?"

It was a red onesie and a pirate hat.

"No."

"But when I talked to you before I swear you said that you would fuck me in this..." he muttered, "have your preferences changed?"

"Not you too!!" cried Emily.

The call immediately dropped.

"Did you forget to *smile?*" asked the computer as the red frowny face came onto the screen. "Did you, perhaps, act rudely towards one of our customers?"

"I am so so sorry," muttered Emily. Please don't demote me to Seventh, please don't demote me to Seventh.

The red frown faded and was replaced with a blue face with its tongue out.

"Do you, perhaps, feel sick today? Do you need to quit this job?"

"No no, I'm fine."

The blue face faded and was replaced with the red frown.

"You seem sad, Emily. Perhaps you need to quit this job? We really prefer not to fire people, especially people who are already so sad...."

"I'm fine!" cried Emily, "I'm fine, I'm just. A little rattled."

The red frown faded and was replaced with a gray neutral face, then a preference question came onto the screen. "Do you prefer this couch or *this* couch?" They looked so damn similar. What was even different about them? She didn't want to get this wrong, she didn't want to get this wrong...

"We're sorry, you were too slow selecting your preference. This was the last mark against your record, Goodbye."

The screen went black.

"Wait, wait!" cried Emily, "I'm fucking trying! Don't you want me to try?"

The car, which had been driving aggressively to deliveries, now drove slowly back to the bus station and opened the door. Fortunately a bus was on its way out and she didn't need to wait until eleven that night to get back to the Sixth area.

"Fuck that job," muttered a black woman who was already on the bus, "we did the right thing. Better to retain your sanity, even if it means getting that stupid fine for quitting in the middle of your shift."

"I... don't think I'll get that," muttered Emily.

"Of course you'll get that. Everyone gets that."

"But I got fired."

She gawked in disappointment, like Emily had let her down personally. "Oh God you are so dead, you are *so* fucking dead..."

Emily gawked back.

"You don't understand? Sixth, you're blacklisted now. You don't have a chance in hell of getting even two-dollar work for the next nine months. After that it might get a little easier, but that termination is *never* coming off your record. Why didn't you just quit?"

"I didn't understand how..."

She shook her head, as if Emily was demoted already, then synced up with her digital screen.

# Chapter 49

Emily walked sadly to the jobs center, signing up for every job they had there, in spite of what the woman on the bus had said. She checked her balance.

*Emily Ernestine O'Dora*
*DOB: 9/5/2219*
*Class: Sixth*
*Net worth: -$3,734.21*

She had not even reduced her debt burden by $50 after working basically nonstop for the past week. And now she likely could not even get work at all. Her mood was dark as she returned to camp. She joined the miserable looking women, sitting around the fire, staring into the flames. She felt she got them now. Understood how they had gotten to this place. Not that she was anywhere close to giving up.

The Koreans were not on their usual hilltop, Lacey was not reading her book, but Stefan was visible through the trees. Emily stepped over to him, the noonday sun behind her.

"This is a rare pleasure," he said, glancing up from the wooden fish he was carving.

"I got fucking fired."

He kept carving as if her words had been meaningless gibberish.

"I got fucking fired and I don't know I'm going to do."

He made a number of other cuts before responding. "I do not presume to tell you what you should or should not do," he began, "but I can show you certain options which you may find intriguing."

"Yes please. I'm blacklisted, Stefan. I don't want to lose control of my mind again. I'm honestly ready to try anything."

"Emily," he said, setting his knife down, "I find it charming how you do not realize... how exceptional you are."

She blushed.

"You," he continued, "have a strong presence, it's almost... intimidating. I think you would be a formidable enemy or ally. And I believe we may have some work together yet."

"Stefan," Emily said with a sigh, "you're always speaking in mysteries. I honestly don't know whether you're full of it or not. I just really need to know what my options, you know?"

He laughed. "Oh, the opportunities I speak of are very real, I assure you of that. I hope you choose to accept them. I will show you more soon, if you wish."

"Soon? When? My schedule is, like, wide open."

He glanced up at her with his amused smile. "You have an amazing fearlessness to you. There is some argument that it may not be altogether wise, but in your case... there may be some level of justification ..."

"When?" asked Emily in exasperation.

"Tonight."

"OK, perfect," she replied, turning away.

"But not here."

Emily turned.

"At The Fates. I am rallying with another fascinating individual at the Nona building tonight at sundown. There I will show you something which... may be of interest to you."

Emily paused. She didn't entirely trust this man with his endless hints, his knowing smile. And she had been warned about those casinos by many of the Sixths, as if simply stepping inside of them would lead to her immediate demotion. But what other choice did she have? Whatever happened, she was determined to exhaust every option before allowing herself to be a Seventh again. She took in a deep breath.

"I'll see you there then."

# PART FOUR: THE FATES

# Chapter 50

Emily woke from a nap late in the afternoon. She had almost overslept.

"This is for you," said another Sixth, handing her an elegant looking dress, "huge bearded man told me to give it to you when you woke up."

Emily took it gratefully, running down to the stream to wash up before putting it on. It was a black silk gown, back bare, silver and diamonds embedded throughout. An incredibly fine piece of clothing that she was surprised Stefan could afford. Then she ran out the gate of the cage—looking ridiculously overdressed now—and hurried over to the Fates.

She stepped past a small brick wall and through a garden to the eastmost of the three buildings. An artificial waterfall splashed along one side of the building, glistening with many colors due to the light display behind it. "NONA" read the lettering above the entrance. The front doors were unlocked, and she entered without any indication that she had been noticed. This place seemed to have no security at all.

Upon entering she found herself in a huge open room with a great fountain in the middle. Standing on the edges of the fountain were gold Greek styled nude statues of men and women. Mixed every other one with these statues were real men and women, skin painted gold, who stood in similar poses. As Emily watched, one woman and one man—rather than standing still—danced gracefully in and out the waters shooting out the fountain's center. Sometimes hand in hand, sometimes alone. Their focus was so central as they moved that Emily assumed that they and the rest of the "living statues" must be Sevenths. It was a breathtaking display, and Emily couldn't help but stare at the rushing waters, the dancing figures. One of the male statues winked at her. She stepped up to him.

"Who are you?"

"I'm yours for $1200," he said in his deep voice.

Emily shook her head. "No, but *who* are you? Are you a Sixth, a Seventh? Do you get paid for this?"

The statue-man stood perfectly still, smiling.

"Do you have a *name*?"

"I will answer any questions you may have, but first you must pay and free me, for I am a prisoner of this magic fountain."

"Yeah, sure you are. Well, whoever you are, hope your life gets better. And uh... nice penis."

Emily walked away, but was amused to see statue man become slightly aroused at her compliment. They couldn't quite take their humanity away completely.

There were slot machines scattered throughout the pavilion. Some slot machines that rewarded money, others that rewarded class. The most popular was a shiny new black slot machine awarding the title of "First." Emily stepped up to it, reading the screen carefully.

"David Petrov, the First previously ruling over Cuba, has abandoned his property and left the island for Jamaica. There is a global lottery now for a new First to rule the island, the winner receiving not only Cuba, but also its 230,000 inhabitants who are 97% female and completely unaware of a habitable world outside their island."

"David left!?" thought Emily, terrified for a moment, and re-reading the word "Jamaica" multiple times to make sure she hadn't misread "Hispaniola." He wasn't here, at least. He was the last person in this world she wanted to see. The fact that he had abandoned his island made her see him in a different light, but she still felt an acute anger towards him, remembering the terrors of the war in Cuba and how those had all been based on his subconscious fantasies.

It was $50 to play this machine only once. Emily stepped up to it, as if hypnotized. If she won she could save all of them. She could lead a revolution against the rest of this unjust world. She could...

"I wouldn't play that machine much if I were you," said a soothing voice behind her. It was Stefan. He stood tall, wearing a fitted suit with a black shirt and red tie. Lacey wore a yellow dress which was considerably less elegant than Emily's, but still quite flattering. She was clinging to Stefan's arm like he was her only hope in the war against gravity.

. "Emily, it's been... such a wonderful night... I didn't know such things existed..." She said with an otherworldly smile. She was clearly drunk.

"She has been a most charming companion," he said, smiling in his perpetually amused way, "and please do not be concerned. I take pride in always practicing the... gentlemanly virtues..."

Emily scowled. "You had better. Anyone else you intend to surprise me with?"

"No, you are the only two at the camps who have truly interested me. No one else seems to quite be... on your level."

Emily shook her head in annoyance at his typical use of flattery. All she could think about was getting her friend sober and far away from this dangerous man.

"I thought you liked Stefan?" piped in Lacey, noticing her scowl. "You go over there to talk to him all the time."

Emily took a deep breath. "Of course I like Stefan. I was just a little surprised, is all. Now tell me, what have I missed? I'm clearly late to the party."

Lacey began to ramble excitedly about a three course meal, a walk through a garden, a hookah lounge, and a few other activities no Sixth should be able to afford. Stefan finally cut her off.

"Lacey…" he said in his deep, musical voice, "do you remember that hotel room I showed you?"

"Oh yeah!" she added, "And I forgot to mention that he got me a nice little hotel room! That part happened right after we got drinks over by the poker tables."

"Lacey," continued Stefan, "I think we should go up to that room. I believe we maybe forgot something up there. And should also consider… resting… for a moment."

Lacey frowned. "You mean right now?"

"Yes."

She thought for a moment. "OK!" she cried with artificial positivity, "but we will come back down here to, you know, spend time with Emily and stuff after?"

"Of course."

He led her by the arm into the elevator, then turned and winked at Emily, mouthing the words "be right back."

A protective instinct surged inside Emily for her new friend who was so vulnerable. She couldn't just trust this man she barely knew, she couldn't leave this up to chance. Noting which floor they had gone to, she found the next available elevator and followed them up.

As her elevator ascended slowly, she observed the lobby below. Slot machines, palm trees, and that strange fountain in the middle. Seeing the nude Sevenths standing there so still made her think of that old plague, aging. Even though they had created a world of slavery and injustice, at least the ancients had found a way to stop that sad, degenerative process. The thought of human bodies decaying after only a few decades simply horrified her. How could anyone have even lived back then with that inevitable ruin hanging over them? A gold painted woman leapt through the water into a man's arms. He caught her, spun her around, then the two of them stepped back, still as statues, as two others danced in their place. For a moment she found herself almost inspired by the artistry of these Sevenths dancing about. At least they weren't sitting outside their tents looking miserable like so many Sixths she had seen. Perhaps there was something about this crazy world that wasn't so... she stopped herself. No, it was wrong. It was all terribly wrong.

Finally arriving at the 28$^{th}$ floor she scanned the hallway. Right or left? Stefan and Lacey were already out of sight. Trusting her instincts, she picked right and ran, holding her dress in one hand. Turning the corner, she barely spotted a door closing. She approached quietly, putting her ear to the door.

"Why are you laying me down?" asked Lacey, "I'm not *that* tired. And it was so good to see Emily."

"You seem like you could use... a little rest," replied his deep, melodic voice.

Emily clenched her fists. If she heard *any* sign that this guy was trying something, she didn't care how big he was she would find a way..."

"But I don't think I need any rest," said Lacey, "I feel wonderful, better than I've felt in such a long time."

"Well, if you are not going to rest, then take this medicine at least. If you feel energetic after that we can go back downstairs and spend time with Emily. Deal?"

A pause.

"But Stefan, it's... black. Why is it black?"

Emily stopped breathing, listening intensely.

"It's simply the color of the medicine. Take a sip, Lacey."

"But I'm not sure if I want to..."

"Just one sip, Lacey. Have I led you wrong at all tonight? You need to trust me. Just one sip, then we can go."

"Ok Stefan, one sip... it looks so weird though..."

Lacey's body collapsed and Emily lifted her knee, preparing to kick in the door. But before she could follow through, the door swung open.

"Ah!" said Stefan, smiling confidently. "Just who I was hoping to see."

# Chapter 51

"You gave her Battlesleep," hissed Emily, "where the hell did you get Battlesleep Stefan? Who the fuck are you!?"

Emily peeked into the room as she spoke, spotting Lacey, fully clothed and on the bed sleeping soundly.

"I'm a friend," said Stefan, closing the door gently.

"You lied to her, you drugged her, whatever you are planning with her I will not..."

"Enough," interrupted Stefan, louder than usual, raising his right hand in a stopping gesture as if he were commanding the elements. Emily went silent in surprise at his suddenly forceful tone.

"Why do you think that I am here, Emily? To pathetically gratify my simple desires with the body of your friend here? Do you really think that is why I am here? Why I have risked so much?"

She gawked. Something just clicked in her mind, something she felt she should have noticed much earlier. That strange air of confidence he had, the fact that he sat outside his tent so comfortably with that knife in his hands, never seeming to worry about money. "Death dancer..." she muttered, "you're not even a fucking Sixth, you're a death dancer."

He laughed. "Of course. The fact that you ever thought of me as a *Sixth*," he almost spat the word, "is astounding to me. And I came to this place, Emily, for you."

"Me?"

"I didn't want to overwhelm you so I've let you get to know me slowly, show you that I can be trusted. But time is running short. Your situation is very unsafe."

"*Unsafe?*" she laughed, "do you think *any* Sixth can ever be *safe?*"

"You are not just any Sixth."

She laughed again. "Is that what you tell all the girls? Right before you get them drunk then drug them?"

Stefan shook his head, as if this comment was something she should be ashamed of herself for. "If you wish to understand what I mean, come."

He turned and walked briskly down the hallway to the elevator. Emily followed, if only to keep an eye on him and make sure he didn't come back to Lacey's room while she lay there helpless. They took the elevator down to the ground level, then walked past the slot machines and stepped out, following a trail through brilliantly lit gardens to the next building.

"Mostly just sleeping First betting over there," explained Stefan, pointing to the building whose base was in the water. "Only Fifths and higher allowed. A Fourth the other day made $20 million on your friend David disappearing, hundred to one payout on that."

"He's *not* my friend."

Stefan laughed as they walked towards the westmost tower, "well, he certainly seems to wish that he was."

The thick, old-styled wooden double doors to the third building were over ten feet tall and engraven with strange patterns and symbols. There was something ominous about their Medieval style, which clashed with the glass and steel that made up the rest of the exterior. They were locked. Stefan placed his hand on a computer screen and paid $250 for both of them to enter. The giant doors opened automatically, and Stefan stepped inside without hesitation. Emily followed.

Unlike the first building, which was brightly lit with colorful lights flashing almost everywhere, the lobby here was dark and filled with smoke. Large television screens were on display at the back of the room, and formally dressed people—almost all men—sat at tables in front of those screens drinking and smoking. Some stared at the monitors attentively, while others stared down at their glasses, glancing up nervously every few minutes, as if to take a peek at some cruel mistress who held them bound.

As she came closer, Emily looked more closely at the television screens. There were dozens of them, and each showed unique footage and had a name displayed over the top. None of these video feeds looked like a sporting event. Most of it, in fact, looked extremely dull.

"Silvia!" gasped Emily. The bottom left screen showed Silvia's face. She was making some snide comment and stepping onto a bus. Above the screen it said the words "Sadie Jensen."

"Holy shit..."

She looked frantically across the screens, from left to right, until she finally saw it. A screen in the middle top right that showed exactly what she was seeing, in an infinite loop going deeper and deeper, like two mirrors facing each other. Above that screen it read "Emily O'Dora."

Stefan stood tall next to her, not saying a word. Suddenly she had a desire to take his arm, to hold onto him like Lacey was doing before. She shrugged off these feelings and stepped forward, looking more closely at the screens.

At the bottom of each screen were three percentages. Her numbers were:

5th: 12%

7th: 27%

[An image of a skull]: 61%

She stared at it for a few more moments, then turned on Stefan angrily. "This is supposed to make me feel important? The fact that apparently everyone thinks I'm going to die."

"You are not going to die. I have been watching your tent each night to be certain of that."

Emily looked at the wall of screens again. A poorly dressed man nervously stepped up to the front desk to place a bet. A few others were laughing, pointing at a screen where a Sixth was smashing her work bracelet in a fit of rage rather than run to her latest job. To the right of the row of screens were dozens of individual kiosks labeled "Sixth Speed Betting," but no one was gambling at them. Standing at the bar was a man in a black hat, staring at them intently, though Stefan avoided eye contact. There was so much going on, and Emily felt like she didn't understand any of it.

"There's more," said Stefan, leaning down. "Are you ready?"

"Show me."

Far off to the left, barely visible in the darkness of the lobby, was a winding staircase. There were elevators in the front to go up to the hotel rooms, but this staircase did not lead to anyone's personal quarters. She followed Stefan up, and there was a door where Stefan again placed his hand and paid another fee for both of them to enter. They were greeted by two naked women, who offered them their arms to escort them about. Stefan waved them away.

"A strip club?" hissed Emily, "This whole time you've just been preparing me for a fucking strip club?"

Stefan ignored her and continued walking across the floor. There were a few stages with dancers, rooms off to the side whose purpose could easily be guessed. But on the far end there was a row of more formal rooms, each with a name, an image, and a dollar figure over the top. A few rooms had blinds closed and lights on, but most were dark and empty. The names again were familiar, and Emily began to understand.

Most of the dollar figures were hopelessly low. $20 per hour. $35. Silvia was at $190. Every time they walked past a room with a light on, Emily's anger boiled inside of her. Why was this world like this? Why was everything so fucked up?

Then Stefan stopped walking. They were in front of her room. "Emily O'Dora" it read. "Temporary Fifth Rental: $350,000 per hour."

# Chapter 52

Emily gasped. "Why... why does it say I am worth that much?"

Stefan looked down at her. "Isn't it obvious?"

"Obvious!?"

"Yes, obvious. You saw the TV screens downstairs, taking information from the computer chip in your brain and showing the video footage to any higher classes who might be curious. So when you were a Seventh, it would be reasonable to assume that at least some higher classes also had access to everything you saw and heard."

Emily nodded.

"And as a Seventh, what did you do?"

"David and I supposedly saved the world."

"And?"

"Then I came here."

"And?"

"David left."

"Exactly. First you left Cuba under very bizarre circumstances. No Seventh has seemingly betrayed her First like you did then. Some saw it as the first glitch in the World System in hundreds of years, evidence of some ancient superstitions coming together. And then, adding to that, David Petrov just left Cuba. How often do you think Firsts have given up their place in this world? Let me tell you, it is *extremely* rare. And he left for you, Emily. He left *looking* for you."

"We knew each other for less than a week!" cried Emily, "It's insane! This is all completely insane!"

"Either it's insane, or... perhaps your love is just worth $350,000 an hour," replied Stefan, with a wry smile.

"I wouldn't call that love."

"I'm just using the term the locals use," replied Stefan dismissively. "Look Emily: You are not like the other Sixths. You are a woman of great significance, and your fame is only beginning. Currently only well-informed Firsts and hard core gamblers know who you are, but soon every Third and higher will be aware of your face, your name. This puts you in great danger."

"My life as a Sixth was already on a knife's edge, how does this make things any worse?"

"Because they will fight over the chance to own you, Emily. Or destroy you. Anyone who kills the so-called Fajadan is likely to gain recognition and respect."

"The what?"

Stefan waved his hand. "Firsts will soon be sending people to manipulate you, seduce you, and yes, murder you. In the Sixth Sleeping Area, anything goes, after all. You would be wise to never walk into that place again. You have become an object of interest for many powerful people, Emily. Even this room in front of us is potentially dangerous. Do you know what this place is for?"

A man in a flamboyant red suit placed his hand on a screen nearby to pay for a Sixth he intended to 'rent.'

"I believe it's pretty obvious."

Stefan shook his head. "No, this is not just prostitution. This is a temporary Fifth relationship. Do you remember what Fifths are?"

She thought back to the instructional video. "They're basically slaves, right? But their minds are not manipulated by Caleb, their minds are independent?"

"Exactly. And a Fifth is required to do all that her master requires to the best of her ability. So if you rented yourself out to someone and they asked you to do something you were unwilling to do, or endure something you were unwilling to endure, you would be automatically demoted to Seventh."

The red lights flashed around them, as a different set of dancers took to the stage.

"This is why unregulated work like this can be so dangerous for your class. It lacks the traditional workplace safeguards from the ancients' laws, making it easy for this kind of work to lead to a demotion rather than a payday. *Very* easy. Some even rent with this precise intention, aiming to push Sixths to their breaking point. If you sign up for this kind of work and the customer only wants sex, you should be grateful."

"It's all just... so fucking wrong..."

"It is what it is. I brought you here to help you realize your importance, help you understand the potential danger you are in. Now you have three choices. You can keep looking for work, even though you just got fired and blacklisted, so this will be extremely difficult."

"How do you know that I..."

"I was watching," interrupted Stefan. "So that's one option. Alternatively, you can do this kind of work, hoping that no sadist manages to torture you to the breaking point and get you demoted. Simply surviving one or two hours of this would allow you to at least get out of the cage for a while and sleep someplace safe. But depending on who rents you, that hour can be very risky."

"And the third option?"

"You come with me."

"Come with you? Where?"

"To my master who sent me. You can bring Lacey as well. I've noticed you developing a close friendship with her, that is why I brought her here today. We can leave as early as this evening, if you wish. The airport is quite close."

Emily examined the bearded man carefully. "So what would we be, if we came with you? Fifths? Sevenths?"

"Fifths, naturally."

Emily examined his face. There was a slight hint of something there. Pity, perhaps. Did he pity her? Did he regret what he was doing now?

"So in order to avoid the danger of being a Fifth for one hour, I should allow myself to be made a Fifth permanently?"

"It's a promotion, Emily. Please look on it as you would a promotion."

"A promotion that makes me even less free?"

"Such is the way with promotions. But it will also make you more secure. More protected."

"None of the lower classes are ever truly protected, Stefan. If I've learned anything since escaping David's fantasy world, it's that."

He shook his head. "So is that a no? Are you saying no to a promotion for yourself and Lacey, even though it would get you away from all this? Even though this precise kind of promotion is what every Sixth is desperately striving for?"

Emily looked into the big bearded man's eyes and took a deep breath. "That is correct. My answer is no. At least for now."

He looked away in disappointment, as if he had been physically hurt by her rejection. If it had only been her, she would have likely gone with him. But she could not take Lacey if she didn't know precisely what they were getting themselves into. She had just lost everyone she knew and that girl with the scar was her only real friend now. And something about the way Stefan was asking her, something about his stance...

"I would... strongly suggest you reconsider," he said carefully, "If you leave tonight, Sabrina will probably not even try to stop you. But if you wait, she will almost certainly keep you here by force. Potentially forever."

Emily shuddered at this, remembering Lin's comments.

"So you won't even tell me your master's name, and you want me to sneak away from Sabrina to her? On your word alone?"

"You do not know the danger you are in. Do you really want to always be running, doing *this* kind of work to protect yourself and your friends? You must know by now that Sixths cannot survive being what they are for long, no matter how hard they try."

"I know the danger I am in, but with you I feel there may be even more danger. The answer is no, Stefan."

"Then you better get to work and find yourself some customers," said Stefan with a shrug, "I've seen your bank account, you're going to get made a Seventh very soon if you don't."

Emily resisted an urge to punch him in the throat. "I resent being told that I need to either come with you or be a whore. It's almost as if... you are wishing to be a customer yourself..."

"I would *never* be a customer," snapped Stefan, "your safety is simply important to me, to my master. And these are your only realistic options."

She didn't believe a word coming out of his mouth. "No Stefan. I said no. To both your options. I'm leaving this fucked up place."

A few nude women chaperoned another customer towards a different Sixth's room. The Sixth inside looked terrified.

"Great. Danger." Said Stefan deliberately.

"Yeah yeah, I get it," said Emily cheerily, "but I'm going to be heading back to my tent now."

She started to walk away.

"At least," called Stefan. "At least stay in the room with Lacey. I will get my own room separately. You already have access, just use your hand to enter. My master is very invested in your safety, Emily. *Very* invested."

Emily glanced over her shoulder. "I'll think about it!" she called.

Stefan turned his body away, as if she were a child who he intended to punish by withdrawing his attention. Emily rushed back the way they had come—past the dancers, down the spiral staircase. Glancing at the gambling room on the first floor, she saw three men she recognized. The Koreans? She wanted to go talk to them, but she had no time. The brother who had been most shy before—Eun—looked up to give her an understanding nod.

She raced out of the building and back to the first casino where Lacey was sleeping. She took the elevator up, then used her hand on the door to Lacey's room and the deadbolt unlocked. She was still there sleeping soundly. Emily ran to her side, lifted her over her shoulder, and walked back to the elevator.

As she returned to the lobby on the first floor, a few men standing by the giant fountain looked at her inquisitively.

"Drunk friend!" she called out with a friendly wave, "just getting her home!"

The men continued to stare, muttering to one another.

Emily exited the casino and walked across town to the gated entrance of the "Sixth Sleeping Area," scanning both her and Lacey's hands as she entered. She looked over her shoulder. No one following that she could see. She moved through the woods and back to their camp. The other Sixths were sitting around, but stood to confront her as she approached. Foremost among them was Sadie. It was eleven in the evening.

"Emily," she said, folding her arms. "You promised."

"What?"

"You went to the Fates," continued Sadie. "Didn't we tell you that this would endanger us all?"

Silvia was standing next to her, glaring at Emily coldly like she was no longer human.

"Yes, I went, but what's the big deal? I didn't spend a penny, didn't talk to anyone. I just needed to see what was going on over there."

"Cut off," said Silvia.

"What??"

"Cut off," repeated Sadie. "You are not welcome here anymore Emily. You have endangered us all."

All the women stood in unison, staring at them grimly with their arms folded. Emily's tent was nowhere to be found. What the hell had they done with all her stuff?

"Fine," said Emily simply.

"Her too," said one woman, gesturing to Lacey, "you get her out of here too."

"Fine, OK!"

Emily lifted Lacey again over her shoulder and turned to leave. The sound of numerous male voices entering the cage could be heard. The women looked at Emily accusingly.

"GET. OUT." whispered Sadie harshly.

And she left.

# Chapter 53

A few minutes walk into the woods she found a flat piece of ground in a grove of trees, nearer to the stream than before. They had no gear, but they would have to make do.

"I'm going to protect you," she whispered. "You're all I've fucking got, but I'm going to protect you."

She sat, breathing in the fresh night air, trying her best to ignore the mosquitos who were more numerous here. She was happy, in a way. It would have been so much easier to stay in that room Stefan had for them, but everything that man offered felt like a trap to her. Perhaps a slow trap, but a trap nonetheless. She was in the woods with nothing but her friend, but they were not at his mercy. And this made her glad.

A scream. Men's voices erupted. "That way, she went that way!" cried a woman from camp, "please, have mercy!"

The men laughed. She heard a slap, a body thudding against the ground, then the footsteps coming closer.

"Emily, oh Emily!" cried one voice, "We just want to visit a little, get to know ya."

"Emily, don't you remember me?" cried a second voice. "You can hit me again if you want, you won't even get fined if you do it here. But be warned, sometimes I *do* like to hit back..."

Emily held her breath. JP. It was JP, the Fourth from Florida she had met on her first day. He seemed to have many more companions with him this time than before. The footsteps continued to approach.

"You're an expensive one, Emily," continued JP, "I didn't realize how special you were first time we met. But once I found out, I knew I just had to get to know you better..."

The others snickered. Most of them were clearly drunk. Didn't they know the risks they were taking, coming here?

The footsteps continued, passing by just north of her. "We really wish you would talk back to us, it would make this so much more fun," added another voice.

They continued walking. They were getting more distant. Emily continued to hold her breath. Just a little bit further, and they would be gone. Just a little bit further...

"Why is there so much shouting? Where is Stefan?" asked Lacey with a yawn, sitting up. "I just had the strangest dream..." Emily gestured furiously to her to be silent, but it was too late. The voices went silent and footsteps charged towards them, like the men had all stopped being human and transformed into monsters.

Within moments they were surrounded by over a dozen men, most brandishing makeshift clubs. Emily crouched, knife in hand, looking back and forth quickly like a cornered animal. They stepped forward, slowly in unison.

"Put down the knife, Emily," said one of them, threateningly. "If you do, we might let your little friend here go."

Emily didn't respond. Words were just weapons at moments like these. They continued to inch forward.

"I know we didn't get off on the right foot, Emily," said JP, "I think I want to even apologize to you for my coarse words. But it's hard for me to do so when you're holding that knife there."

Emily flashed him her most diabolical smile, then screamed. The knife shot out of her hand with a flick of her wrist and penetrated deep into JP's skull. He dropped without a word. The other men charged, swinging clubs wildly. Emily did a backflip, kicking one in the chin and smashing her palms against another's cheekbones while in the air. The two men dropped. Back on the ground she kicked again, breaking another's kneecap and slamming her hand into another man's throat. But then a hand grabbed her hair and two others grabbed at her dress. She twisted, ripping the dress apart, but new hands grabbed at her torso and thighs. Soon she was pinned to the ground by four angry but eager men. A huge man with pale skin and a shaved head stood over her, looking menacingly into her eyes.

"You're going to pay for what you've done girl," he said. "you're going to wish you had never been born."

One of the men holding her down leaned forward to bite at her face.

Two twangs from inside the trees. Makeshift arrows pierced through the backs of the two men holding her shoulders, relaxing their grip. Emily leapt up and head butted the pale man who had just threatened her. He moaned, and then a third arrow pierced his back as well. Emily snagged his club and swung it across the face of one of the men who had been holding her feet. Two figures, a man and a woman, jumped out of the trees with makeshift spears, and began stabbing at the men with quick, well-aimed thrusts. Soldiers, these two. Skilled soldiers. Vy and Jason.

Within moments all of the fifteen of the men were dead. Vy methodically examined each body for a pulse and slit the throats of the men who were only unconscious. She had never been one for mercy.

Jason kicked the bodies into a pile, then slapped his hands together, as if to knock the dirt off his fingers. "Well, looks like we might have ruined your sleeping spot. You wanna check out our place?"

# Chapter 54

Emily and Lacey, who followed fearfully in the back, were led by their rescuers about a quarter mile to two tents sitting peacefully on the sandy beach.

"Not really hidden, but you can't be snuck up on either," said Jason.

"Thanks again..." said Emily, "for saving my ass."

He grinned, "They made it easy for us, calling out your name like that. We were hoping you'd be here. I know we didn't end on the best of terms, but we still thought it might be nice to reconnect."

Vy looked down sheepishly.

"So glad you did. Whatever happened in Cuba, I know it was the computer chips in your brains pushing you to do it. It's just so good to see some friendly faces again. So good to see both of *your* faces again."

Jason blushed ever so slightly. Emily smiled to herself. The man could kill six drunk assholes almost effortlessly, but he couldn't take a compliment.

"Appreciate you being uh... understanding," said Vy sheepishly, "you know, of all craziness. Who's your new friend?"

"Lacey. Used to be a Stonewalker, tough girl."

"Rad." They shook hands. Lacey was still in shock.

Jason leaned inside one of the tents, pulling out a sleeping bag.

"When did you all get here?" asked Emily.

"Early this morning," replied Vy, "David sent us looking for you, seemed on the verge of sailing off himself. We shipwrecked, got rescued, saw that, uh... video, then heard those assholes calling your name tonight."

Jason laid out his bag about thirty feet away on the beach, then walked back to them.

"You ladies can have my tent tonight. I'll crash on the beach. Doesn't look like we'll get any rain tonight."

Emily opened her mouth to protest, but glanced at Lacey. That girl still seemed completely terrified. Violence had been a much less recent part of her life.

"Thanks Jason, really appreciate it."

"Sure. Let's talk more in the morning? I'm beat."

Emily nodded. Jason went off to his bed roll and Vy climbed into her tent.

"Hey Vy, thanks again," said Emily softly, "you guys really saved my ass tonight."

Vy poked her head out with a grin. "Sure did!"

Emily laughed. It felt good to be around familiar faces. They had a crazy history, but Emily could really use some friends.

Once inside Jason's tent, Lacey started to cry.

"There's no safety anywhere is there? I really wanted to trust Stefan, but it seems he must have drugged me or something. And those men tonight..."

"There's safety with me," replied Emily, holding her tight, "there's safety with me."

Lacey cried harder. "I was... so lost before you showed up. I'm at negative $4,880, I'm going to be made a Seventh in less than a week. I don't want to... go back to... that's why I clung to Stefan so hard, that's why I'm so emotional like this all the fucking time."

Emily pulled out of the embrace and gripped the weeping woman's shoulders, looking into her eyes. "You aren't going to be made a Seventh again, you hear me?" None of us are going to become Sevenths again. I won't *ever* let that happen.."

"How can you... I mean there are no good jobs, we almost just got *raped*...maybe you should have just left me with Stefan, maybe that's my best..."

"I'm going to look out for you, Lacey, I'm going to make sure we get through this. And when it comes to money, I have... options. There's no way I'm going let you get the space boot. No way in hell."

At first she shook her head in protest, but slowly she pulled herself together, muttering a feeble "thanks."

They sat for a few moments together, both processing their experiences. Suddenly, Emily had a thought. "Earlier you mentioned a dream? When you first woke up?"

Lacey's eyes lit up. "Oh yes! So I was in this empty place and there was this voice there, talking to me directly. It all felt very real, like I wasn't dreaming at all, like I was *there*..."

Emily stared. "Tell me more."

"So I was in this boring room—gray, everything gray—and speaking to this voice."

"What sort of voice?"

"It sounded old, like those white haired guys in the movies from before they cured aging. But it was friendly. And kind of a booming voice, like thunder."

"Did you get his name? Did he tell you his *name*?"

Lacey paused, then shook her head. "No no, he didn't tell me that. But he did say freedom is possible, whatever that means. Why are you asking me all these questions? Have you dreamed something similar?"

"Yeah, a few times back in Cuba. I thought it was just me, everyone else I've talked to who has taken Battlesleep hasn't remembered a thing."

"Wait, so you've dreamed of that *exact* same place? That same voice?"

"I believe so. Did the dream end with a wind, and the floor disappearing and everything turning black?"

"Exactly like that!" cried Lacey. "What do you think it all means?"

"I don't know..." muttered Emily. She had her theories. Some sort of rogue hacker, working against the artificial intelligence known as Caleb was her first guess. She really didn't know if she could trust him and all his 'freedom' talk.

"Well, it's certainly a puzzle..." replied Lacey, smiling at this new distraction. Emily smiled as well, happy to have someone to share this with. Maybe they could figure out these mysteries together. She felt a profound fondness for this woman, and was intent on protecting her, as well as their other friends. She was going to build a community here, a family. Lacey slowly fell asleep in her arms.

With Lacey asleep, another thought took over her mind. A very different kind of thought that she couldn't get out of her head. It had been so long, and if anyone deserved it... She slowly released Lacey and climbed out of the tent. Then she tiptoed along the beach until she came to Jason, laying there alone. He, too, was not asleep.

"Emily," he whispered, "what..."

She raised her finger to her lips, and removed her tattered dress, then her underwear.

"I don't understand..."

She raised her finger to her lips again, then climbed onto his chest.

# Chapter 55

They made love silently, Jason clearly in a state of bliss. Though inexperienced, his strong arms and humble manner made him a surprisingly competent lover. She hadn't been intimate with anyone for months, and was determined to not end that streak by simply selling herself to the highest bidder. Whatever she might be forced to do later, she would first love someone who deserved it, someone who she actually felt something real for. And that, tonight, was Jason.

"Thank you," she whispered hours later. She had needed this. Jason was speechless, unable to take his eyes off of her. She dressed and returned to her tent, putting her arms around Lacey like she had never left.

Emily woke just hours later to the ocean waters sparkling in the morning sunlight. Vy was already awake, cooking some grits on a solar powered stove.

"Oh, good morning Vy," she whispered with a yawn, stepping out of her tent.

"Howdy." Vy actually looked happy. Emily wasn't sure if she had ever seen Vy looking happy.

"So tell me more," asked Emily, "when did you all get here? Have you worked any jobs yet, met anyone else?"

"Nah. Spent most of yesterday hand crafting weapons because Jason thought we should. I thought he was nuts, but guess he had the right idea."

Emily looked over at the red headed man with a fond smile. He was still sound asleep, in spite of the sunlight.

Vy laughed. "Yeah, you should. He's a virgin you know, the guy needs it. I just, well, I could never. He's like a brother to me."

Emily looked over at Vy and winked.

"The fuck?" exclaimed Vy.

Emily shrugged mysteriously. "I'm gonna take a swim in the ocean, wanna join me?"

"Bitch. I'm cooking."

Emily shrugged again, and then ran across the beach into the water.

Emily swam hundreds of yards out to sea, enjoying the isolation, the natural experience of splashing through the waves. She felt invigorated, free. She had a new confidence after fighting off the men from the previous night, reconnecting with Vy and Jason, making love. She felt pride in her sisterly bond with Lacey and had an odd desire to take the girl everywhere she went. And while she still had no firm plans to sell herself, the knowledge that the world had priced her so highly was, she admitted, a little encouraging as well.

She swam to a small island in the bay. It was only maybe fifty feet across and had three mid-sized plants that could loosely be described as trees. She hoisted herself and climbed up onto the surface. A few steps into the weeds there was a sign buried behind some vines.

"Sixths: any swimming beyond this point is trespassing and will be automatically punished with a $250 fine."

She scowled. It was an unpleasant reminder that she was not wildly exploring nature, but in a conquered world where every grain of sand had been weighed, measured, and then brought under the control of the owners.

The island was in the shape of an 'S'. She climbed to the tallest point, sitting on a large rock there and looking back to shore. It was a warm morning with only a light breeze. She could barely see the figure of Vy, still tending her breakfast over the electric stove. Jason and Lacey were still asleep. The early morning sun glowed in the northeast and ships could be seen to the west, entering and exiting the main harbor.

Pat-pat-pat. Emily heard the faint sound of something splashing steadily through the water. Looking up, she saw a solitary swimmer moving towards her from the beach to the southwest. He wore a dark wetsuit and swam a freestyle stroke with exactness, moving quickly through the water. There was a black beard covering his face. Stefan.

She was so far out to sea that Vy was just a faint, whitish speck due to her light blonde hair. Emily looked back at Stefan. He swam so quickly that she did not suspect she could avoid him at this point, even if she tried. She waited. Within minutes, he was pulling himself up onto her small island.

"Hello there," Emily called, "nice day for a swim?"

Stefan blinked and stood. His tall figure shimmered in the morning sun.

"You like this island I found?" she called out, trying not to sound frightened, "figured maybe I could set my tent up over here, you know. Be more safe, like you're always talking about."

Stefan made brief eye contact, then continued towards her.

"You forget something out here? Maybe your favorite pair of goggles or something? I mean, I haven't seen anything like that, but we could try looking again?"

The giant of a man took a few more steps forward. Emily was standing now, on the boulder that made the high point of the island.

"*Stop!*" she cried, more forcefully than she intended. "If you want to talk, let's talk here. No need to come any closer. I mean, I don't think there's enough room on this rock for two anyhow."

He paused midstride, clearly with a certain reluctance. He was less than ten feet away.

"Emily," he said, looking up at her. There was a strange, otherworldly pain in his eyes.

"Stefan?"

"You almost died last night. I had rented a room for you to protect you. Then you left it and almost died. You and Lacey both almost died."

Emily stared at him coldly. "You *drugged* Lacey. You pretended to be a Sixth. You think I am going to trust you, just because you tell me I should? How stupid do you think I am?"

Stefan's eyes flashed. For a man who always seemed so poised, he seemed like he was struggling even to breathe. "Emily. It is my assignment to keep you safe. You're on the verge of bankruptcy, of being made a Seventh. If you do not wish to use the... resource... that I showed you last night, then you need to come with me. It is the only way."

Emily laughed. "The *only* way? You know how crazy you sound? I'm not going to entrust my safety or that of my friends to you. I am absolutely certain of that now. So please. Just go."

Stefan paused for a moment. "Can you at least admit that you're in great danger?" The pain in his face was palpable, so otherworldly it made Emily feel she had not spoken to this particular man before.

"If I do, will you leave me alone?"

Stefan looked into her eyes intensely. "I am only," he said deliberately, "here to protect you. But I cannot protect you when you repeatedly run off to the most dangerous place possible, then sleep with random men for who knows..."

"Do *not,*" interrupted Emily, "speak to me about who I choose to be intimate with, for money or otherwise, *ever* again. And how dare you watch that footage from my personal life."

Stefan looked at her like she had just slapped him across the face. Then he straightened his back.

"You *will* be coming with me," he said resignedly, as if this fate was so inevitable even he could not stop it.

"*No*, I will *not.*"

He took another step towards her. "*Yes* you *will*. I have some clothes for you at my tent. Come on."

"I don't want any more of your fucking clothes, Stefan. And I would *not* come any closer if I were you."

Stefan suddenly laughed, displaying a calm he hadn't shown their entire conversation. "You don't even have a knife, Emily. What are you going to do, hit me with a rock? Now, will you swim with me to shore, or am I going to put you to sleep then carry you? I need an answer: Now."

He was only about six feet away now, carefully watching her for any sign of movement. She was cornered. She knew she could not outrun this man.

"I'll come with you," she said with a sigh, "you're right, I need to be more safe. Let's go back to your tent, I think I can see it from here. Would you like me to swim in front?" She knew she couldn't outswim him, but perhaps after they got back to shore she could find a weapon or some other means of escape.

Stefan flashed her an almost evil smile. "Good choice. Lead the way." Emily stepped down from her rock. Stefan's body remained tense, but he did not lunge to grab her, as she'd thought he might.

He simply waited for her to make her way to the south side of their little island and begin swimming back to shore. As he watched her, she noticed a relaxation in his face. The twisted expression of pain was gone.

She stepped up to the south edge of the island and leaned to dive into the ocean and swim back to shore. Then she heard a loud crack.

# Chapter 56

Stefan shouted in pain. Vy, who had quietly climbed onto the island from the *north* side, snapped a large stick across Stefan's face. As Stefan reeled from the blow, she leapt, tackling him to the ground and then grappling her way into a position where her legs squeezed his torso and her left arm was locked with her right elbow around his neck. His powerful legs were free, but with the pressure Vy put on his throat he was unable to twist free. He finally stopped squirming.

"Do you want me to kill him?" asked Vy. "It's still in the Sixth Sleeping Area out here, so we can legally do it, regardless of what class this asshole is." She glanced down at his expensive wetsuit.

Emily looked at her twice rescuer in shock, then shook her head. "Don't kill him. Unless you have to." She shot Stefan a glare.

Vy released ever so slightly and Stefan gasped.

More splashing as Lacey pulled herself up, followed closely by Jason who had three spears strapped to his back. He tossed one to Emily, one to Lacey, and then pointed the last one menacingly at Stefan's abdomen. Lacey did not hold the spear as aggressively, looking at Stefan with a strange mixture of confusion and pity.

"If you kill me," gasped Stefan, "I won't be able to protect you..."

"Oh God, just kill him!!" exclaimed Emily in annoyance. Vy immediately increased pressure on his throat and Jason pulled back his spear to thrust.

"No no, stop! Sorry. Let's... let's question him."

Vy's grip relaxed, but she continued to hold him in her pin.

"Why are you trying to force me to go with you?"

Stefan didn't speak.

"Answer her!" shouted Jason, pushing the point of his spear against his stomach just enough that it ripped his wetsuit.

Stefan looked up at Emily and smiled in his knowing way. "It's... complicated."

Jason pulled back his spear again and Vy squeezed tighter round his throat. Only Lacey did not look eager for blood.

Emily held up her hand to stop her friends. "What class are you? Start by telling us that."

He gave her an approving look, like she was his student. "Third. I'm a Third, Emily, and that means I'm in pain now. Not because of your over-eager friends, but because I'm not completing my mission. Because I'm not getting you to *safety*."

"Well, I'm afraid you're going to be in pain like that *forever*," snapped Emily, "Because safety, from my perspective, means staying *far* away from *you*."

Stefan laughed. "There really is something beautiful about you when you're being stubborn. It almost makes me forget how much you are making me SUFFER!"

He shouted the last word like a wounded animal, and Vy gripped him more tightly while Jason pushed with his spear, this time drawing a trickle of blood. Stefan looked up at Jason and laughed, like he was a child holding a toy.

"I really think we should kill him," muttered Vy. "He's totally fucking nuts."

"What do you mean by pain?" asked Emily.

"He's obviously in love with you," said Jason in annoyance.

Stefan laughed. "Do you children know nothing? Can a Third love anyone besides his master? We can't fall in love, we can't *fall* at all. We're THIRDS."

"What about the broken Thirds?" asked Lacey suddenly. "I read about those the other day, surely those have fallen in a certain sense..."

Stefan looked up at her in surprise. "*Very* rare. And they are fools who deserve everything they get. The key to this world is you do not resist: that is the key. If you simply accept things as they are, they will continue to flow smoothly, like the rising and setting of the sun. But if you resist, you will be crushed. And for what? What statement have you made? That you are incapable of accepting reality? You must submit, Emily, it is the only path to safety. At least for now."

She laughed. "You are still demanding that I submit? Look at yourself. This is *the cage*, Stefan. Your life is in our hands here."

He smiled condescendingly. "Do you think I care about my life right now? While I am in this pain? Come with me, Emily, and I will give you safety. It is the only way."

Jason growled. "I'm really getting sick of this guy."

Vy grunted her agreement. "Killing him would be no trouble at all. We would maybe even enjoy it."

Emily shook her head. "No. He's insane and dangerous, but... it's not right to kill him."

Jason looked at her warily, "he'll be back."

Emily sighed. "He might. But I've seen enough blood for one lifetime."

She walked forward and crouched in front of Stefan. "I'm going to let you go," she said, "but only on one condition: that you leave me and my friends alone. If you want to protect me, if that is your mission or whatever, fine. But you do it from a distance, got it?"

Stefan looked at her in disbelief, as if she had just suggested he fly by leaping off a cliff. "Protect you from afar?"

"Yes," Emily said, "to complete this mission you claim to be so obsessed with."

"Oh, I am most *certainly* obsessed!" cried Stefan, laughing in a way that seemed more unhinged than ever before. Emily looked at him with pity. It was as if there were two men sitting in front of her. A smiling, arrogant gentleman who liked to carve animals out of wood and pick out beautiful dresses for women. And an insane man in survival mode, who felt that if he did not persuade Emily to come with him his life was somehow over.

"So is it a deal? I want you to swim to shore and be out of the cage within thirty minutes. And then never come back. Protect me from afar, Stefan. Or we really *will* kill you."

Jason pushed his spear up against him like he wished Stefan had already left and come back.

Stefan looked up at Emily, eyes begging. "This is your last chance. To come with me, to be safe..."

"NO. You will swim to shore now and leave this area, never to return. Or you will die. Those are your two options now. Protect me from afar, Stefan."

He looked up in bitter resignation. "I will do as you command."

Emily eyed him carefully then raised her hand. "Release him," she said. Vy did so immediately. Jason pulled his spear away, but remained prepared. Lacey's spear was still in her hand, but looked more like a prop than a weapon.

Stefan stood and stepped to the edge of the island and prepared to dive.

"And Stefan," added Emily.

He turned to her slowly, like he was now trapped inside a terrible dream.

"Make sure to leave your Battlesleep behind. And any other resources you think might, you know. Help keep me safe."

Stefan gave her a subtle nod, then dove into the ocean and swam with powerful strokes towards his tent on the beach, west of Jason and Vy's camping site. They all stood and watched him in silence as he climbed to shore, went into his tent and changed, then jogged to the gate of the Sixth Sleeping Area. They watched the beachfront for a few moments, waiting for him to come back. He did not.

"Why is a Third following you?" asked Jason, "What the hell is going on Emily?"

"I... I don't know."

Jason gave her a concerned look, but let it go. Then they all swam back to shore.

# Chapter 57

Stefan's tent contained stacks of women's clothing, and Emily dressed. They all fit her perfectly, which was convenient but also unnerving. Would this man really leave her alone? Was Jason right? Was he simply in love with her?

They also found three knives, a backpack, and cooking equipment. However, after searching the tent up and down they did not find any Battlesleep.

"Fuck," said Emily, "the bastard took it with him."

"I really wish you would have just let us kill him," Jason muttered.

Emily shook her head resolutely. "We did the right thing. He'll leave us alone."

They moved all of Stefan's abandoned items, including his spacious tent, over to their camping spot. As they carried the gear over, they noticed an assortment of robots who were working their way across the Sixth Sleeping Area. Some were small, with one tube of an arm that blew air out and the other that sucked air in. Others were medium sized, with hydraulic lifting equipment attached. The largest were essentially self driving dump trucks on skids, and moving lazily behind the other two, catching the trash and compressing it. Emily wondered whether one of these larger trash drones already held the bones of the men they had killed the night before.

As they arrived back at their camp, Vy's bracelet began to beep.

She looked up at the others. "First job, I guess. Wish me luck!"

Emily gave her a hug. "Thanks for saving me. Twice."

Vy shrugged. "Maybe that can make up for me trying to hunt you down and drag you back to David a week ago?"

Emily laughed and Vy jogged off.

"Hey Emily, could I talk to you alone for a minute?" asked Jason.

Emily looked over at Lacey, who she hadn't spoken to all day.

"It's OK," said Lacey diplomatically, "I needed to try to get the saltwater out of these clothes anyways."

Emily watched with concern as she slipped out of earshot. That girl was clearly still very rattled.

"So what's up?"

Jason looked over at her in confusion. "What's up?"

"Yeah, what's up?"

"Well... we slept together last night?..."

"Yeah, thanks again for that." Emily surveyed the beach. They were relatively isolated here, with great visibility in all directions. If attackers came again, they would be ready.

"So... what does that mean?" continued Jason, clearly confused by this question himself.

"Well. It clearly means that I like you a lot."

"I like you a lot too," he said with a sigh, moving forward to embrace her. Emily put out her hand and stepped back.

"Not now. I almost just got kidnapped by that... crazy bearded giant in a wetsuit. And look, Jason: we aren't really at a place in life where we can afford to have serious relationships. We're barely surviving right now. We all need to be a team, together. You, me, Lacey, Vy. As friends. Does that make sense?"

"But didn't it *mean* anything to you?"

Emily laughed, giving him a fond look. Like he was a dog worth petting, not a man worth screwing. "Of course it meant something! It was wonderful, *you* were wonderful. It made me feel *so* much better. But we aren't a couple, Jason. We're just two people in a dangerous world, caring about each other and helping each other survive. I'm sorry if this is confusing for you, I know this was your first time."

Jason froze, mouth open for a few moments.

"I love you," he blurted out, "nobody else gave me a chance until you. All the women only wanted David in Cuba, and you... in a way you helped all of us get out of there. You're absolutely incredible, Emily. I love you, I'm... in love with you."

She smiled warmly, even though part of her wanted to smack some sense into him. "I love you too. But what happened last night—try not to obsess or talk about it. I care about you, but not in the sort of way that implies a relationship. We just need to focus on surviving now."

Jason looked down at her and sighed. "I *really* like you, Emily."

"Do you *really?*"

"Yes!"

"Then *don't* make this into something that is going to be a problem. Let's just survive together, OK Jason?"

He nodded sadly.

"Hey!" cried Emily with artificial enthusiasm, "Vy told me that you were the one who built all those spears. Do you want to teach me how to do that?"

"Sure."

They stepped into the trees together, and he showed her how to split the wood at the top of the sturdy stick, then insert a spearhead—in this case a blade which he pulled off a pocket knife—then lash the top of the spear together to keep the wood from splitting any further. As they worked together, Emily couldn't help but admire him—his steady hands, his overly generous eyes. But while she flirted with him politely while they worked—a brush of the hand here, a long look in the eyes there—she continued to maintain her distance. And Jason worked in silence, no longer verbally protesting their status.

"Jason?" she asked.

"What's up?"

"There's something I have to do—for Lacey, for all of us—but I don't want to."

"Then don't do it. You don't have to do anything you don't want to do, Emily. We're here for you."

She laughed. "Yes, I know you are. But spears can only do so much in this new world we've found ourselves in. It's all about money here. So please Jason. Just tell me that I should do whatever I need to do, even if it's hard. I need your strength."

Jason looked at her, clearly confused. His flaming red hair gleamed in the sunlight, still damp from their swim. "I can't tell you to do something if I don't know what I'm telling you to do," he said, with almost absurd seriousness in his voice.

Emily stared at him in annoyance, then laughed. "You aren't good for anything, are you!" she cried. Then she kissed him on the cheek and jogged to the southwest. As she ran, a tear crept out of her eye and down her cheek.

# Chapter 58

"Emily!" called out Lacey, "could I talk to you for a second?"

Emily paused and looked over. Lacey was in her tattered underwear, scrubbing her only change of clothes against a rock. She really needed to give that girl some of Stefan's outfits, since Silvia's group had stolen everything they had.

"Hey Lacey. Right now I have to do something that's going to help all of us. Can we plan for later?"

Lacey nodded and turned back towards her work.

Emily continued running towards the metal gate at the entrance of the cage. If she didn't force herself to do this now, she would never bring herself to do it. She kept jogging, right up to the tall, wooden doors at the entrance of the 'Morta' building. She placed her hand on the door and it opened.

"Emily O'Dora: you have been charged $125 for entering. Your balance is now *-$4,023.55* the screen read.

"Yeah, yeah, whatever," she muttered.

She ran past the wall of TVs showing her and the other Sixths, only peeking briefly to see how the betting markets predicted her future.

7th: 17%

5th: 6%

Skull: 77%

How had her odds gone down so quickly?? She had just survived a terrible attack the night before, then kicked Stefan out of her life. Hadn't she proved herself? At least somewhat??

She climbed the spiral staircase in the back of the lobby, and jogged through the strip club, showing no notice of either the dancers or their patrons. She was going to do what needed to be done. And then, eventually, she would come back and burn this disgusting place to the fucking ground.

She found the room with her name on it and looked at the figure. $22,000." it read.

She blinked to make sure she had read it right. She had. The night before it had been $350,000 and now it was only $22,000?? What the hell?

Emily didn't know what else to do, so she started to cry. It must have changed because she had slept with Jason. The jealous fucking perverts, didn't they already know that she wasn't a virgin? Seeing the value drop so much made her want to fuck Jason again, just to piss all her creepy watchers off even more. Just one day and her supposed value had dropped *that* much. Was this plan even worth it still? She hadn't even wanted to do this for $350,000. But Lacey was about to be made a Seventh, hell, *she* was close to being made a Seventh. And $22,000 was still a lot better than $4 an hour. She stepped up and put her hand to the screen of her door.

"Hello Emily O'Dora. Welcome to the temporary Fifth rental service! Would you like to make yourself available for work only now, or sign up for potential opportunities in the future? If you sign up for potential opportunities, your wristband will simply flash red any time a customer is ready to hire you, easy as that."

She selected "only now" and the door swung open.

"Emily?" asked a sophisticated male voice behind her.

"I'm not quite ready for any... customers yet... I'm sorry," muttered Emily, standing in the doorway and blinking a tear out of her eyes. She needed to do this. She had to do this.

"But I'm no customer."

Emily turned to look behind her. He was a sharply dressed man of slightly below average height, maybe just an inch taller than herself. His skin tone was a dark brown, and he wore a white suit with a white shirt and tie. He had short, well-groomed black hair, light brown eyes, and expressive eyebrows. Emily thought for a moment that she might be looking at the most handsome face she had ever seen.

"So who the hell are you if you aren't a customer?" she asked.

The man bowed to her respectfully. "A friend."

"Oh God, not another cryptic guardian," groaned Emily.

"A friend who sincerely hopes that you abstain from doing what you're about to do," he continued. His face was calm. Gentle. None of the intensity she had seen in Stefan a few hours before.

"Why do you care what I do? Do you have some secret plans for me?"

He didn't as much as flinch at her jibes. "I do not want you to do this because I suspect it will make you very unhappy, Miss O'Dora."

She eyed him skeptically.

"I'd like to make you an offer," he continued.

Emily rolled her eyes and turned as if to enter the room and start inviting customers.

"I will pay you twice what they are offering to simply go home and forget about all this."

Emily did not laugh this time, but rather choked. "You will *what?*" she asked, spinning to stare at him.

"I will pay you $44,000 to go home and forget about this. Tomorrow night, you can do what you think best, but tonight you will leave this place."

"And what... do you want in return?"

"The knowledge that you are free and safe for one more night."

Emily looked at the him curiously. His white suit was immaculate, his arms rested calmly and confidently by his sides. He certainly did seem to be someone with money.

"The choice is yours of course," he continued, "I am simply honored to be standing in your presence." He gave a quick bow. Red lights flashed around them, but they didn't seem so ominous to Emily now.

"So you want to pay me $44,000 to... do nothing?" .

"To not do this."

"What's your name?"

"I am," he bowed again, "but a humble admirer of your beauty and grace."

"Fucking hell, what's your name!?" cried Emily with a laugh.

"I dare not speak my name in your presence, wise and worshipful one," he said, lips curled in the first bit of mischief she'd seen on his face.

"NAME!" cried Emily, smiling broadly at the oddity of this game.

The man bowed once more, and then turned to walk away.

"At least tell me what class you are!" implored Emily.

He turned back. "I am a Fourth. Chaser, not dancer. Except for you—for you only will I dance."

"What the hell!?" cried Emily, stifling a laugh.

"Your money will be deposited in your account the moment you exit this building. Thank you again, Emily. For everything." He bowed deeply then turned and strolled away.

Emily stared after him for a few moments, considering following after him to ask more. But she did not want to try her luck. And she had a feeling she would run into this strange, handsome fellow again. In a daze she stepped past the nude dancers, down the spiral staircase, across the lobby, and back to the wooden doors. They seemed smaller now, everything seemed smaller. As she opened them to leave the building, a nearby screen beeped.

"Due to a recent deposit, your account balance is now $39,976.45," it read. Emily laughed for joy. She was safe. Her friends were safe.

# Chapter 59

Emily jogged back to their camp on the beach. It was the late afternoon, sun just starting to set. Jason was sitting with a needle and thread, stitching up a hole in one of his pants. She ran up to him and threw her arms around him.

"Jason!" she said, "It's great to see you, how are you!?"

Jason looked up at her like she was something between a threatening monster and the answer to all his prayers.

"Well, we just spoke an hour ago. But I'm doing very well."

Emily pulled back from their embrace, pecking him on the cheek. "Things are going to get better, Jason. For all of us."

"Sounds pretty nice."

"Where's Lacey at?" asked Emily, glancing at the other tents.

"She never came back from washing her clothes, I figured she had gone with you or gotten called in to work."

"She never came back?"

"No, perhaps she got called into a job. Did you see her on the way into camp?"

Emily shook her head. She ran back to the spot along the brook where Lacey had been washing her clothes just an hour before.

"LACEY!" she shouted, "LACEY!!"

Jason joined in the search as well as they ran up and down the stream, passing irritated women who looked at them defensively.

"LACEY!!" Emily screamed. Her heart was racing. She *needed* to find her friend. Needed to find her and let her know that she didn't have to worry about money. Not anymore.

A scowling woman from their old camp stopped Emily with an annoyed look.

"Lacey asked me to give you this," she said, handing her a tiny note.

Emily snatched it from her hands and unfolded it.

*Emily-*

*Left to go with Stefan. I think he's my only real chance to get through all this in one piece. Will miss you, thanks for being like a big sister to me. I won't forget ya, maybe we can talk in those crazy dreams together or something.*

*(heart)*

*Lacey*

Emily froze as if she had just been shot by a bullet. This couldn't be happening. This simply couldn't be happening... She broke into a run.

"Where are you going!?" cried Jason as he raced to keep up.

"I'm going to see if I can catch them before they leave town. I'm not letting him have her, Jason. I'm NOT."

They exited the Sixth Sleeping Area then ran through the streets, looking every which way for a tall, black bearded man and a slender woman with light brown hair and a scar around her neck. They were nowhere to be seen. They quickly checked the bus station and jobs building, then ran into the first of the three casinos, Nona. Emily only had one last idea. A room on the 28th floor.

She and Jason took the elevator up. "Do you want to tell me why we are going up..." he started.

Emily leaned into him and kissed him on the lips. Maybe they would make love again tonight. "Thanks for supporting me Jason," she whispered. He stumbled in shock. Their elevator stopped and she spun away from him and started sprinting down the hallway. Right, around the corner, seventh door on the left...

She put her hand to the door and it opened. Lacey was laying on the bed, as if in a coma. She had clearly been crying before she had fallen asleep. Stefan glanced up in surprise.

"Why Emily!" he cried, "I thought you wanted me to only watch over you from afar! What a pleasant surprise!" He smiled his confident smile, all that previous pain and desperation completely erased.

Jason stepped into the room without hesitation and slammed his fist into Stefan's face. Stefan took the punch full on, but did not fall to the ground. Jason lifted the huge man by the collar in rage, as if intending to throw him out of the window, and Stefan headbutted him in between the eyes. Jason crumbled to his knees. He struggled to get back up, but then Stefan kicked him savagely in the ribs and he fell flat onto the ground.

"This is not a Sixth Sleeping Area," said Stefan, kicking his hands out from under him as he tried to get up a second time. "If you assault a Third, there are penalties. Serious ones, in fact." Jason continued to struggle, but Stefan kept him prostrate on the floor without effort, pacing around him and looking at his smartwatch. "Wonder why it's being slow..." he muttered, "maybe you really are the Fajadan..." Emily watched, petrified in place, standing protectively between Stefan and the bed where Lacey lay.

"You stay away from Emily, you..." gasped Jason as Stefan stepped on his back almost half-heartedly.

"Come on, any time now..." said Stefan, staring at his stopwatch in annoyance. Then it dinged.

Suddenly, Jason lay perfectly still, and Stefan smiled down at him in an almost fatherly way.

"Do you still want to fight me?" Or do you want to do something else?"

Jason looked up at him, confusion in his eyes.

"I know I was angry at you before... but now I trust you for some reason. I want... I feel like... I should help you."

Stefan smiled. "Good. Good boy."

Jason's face lit up at the condescending compliment.

"Why don't you stand up?" asked Stefan.

Jason climbed to his feet and stood with his hands at his side, a pathetic, harmless rendition of the fighting man he had been before. He looked at Stefan with worshipful confusion. Clearly a part of him knew that he had been upset with him before, but now he saw him in the same way Emily had viewed David back in Cuba. Stefan, in Jason's new eyes, was the Godservant.

"How would you feel if I asked you to get me a glass of water?" Stefan continued, casually.

"I feel like I would... I feel like I very much would like to do that..." said Jason slowly. "Can I... please get you a glass of water?"

"Yes Jason, get me a glass of water. NOW."

Jason ran to do as commanded. Emily watched the exchange with horror, still standing to guard the sleeping body of Lacey. Stefan smiled.

"These Sevenths really are incredible. Caleb is getting better at managing them every year. Fifths, Sixths—those are the older classes, the less reliable classes. But Sevenths—these are the peak of human organizational technology. No matter how much they disturb you, you have to respect how malleable they are. Someday the whole world will probably be just Sevenths and Firsts."

Jason brought the filled cup back to Stefan eagerly. Stefan didn't even take a sip. "Now sit," he commanded. Jason blinked, but obeyed.

"Jason, how do you feel about Emily here?"

He looked at her sadly.

"I love her, Stefan. I love her so much..."

"Yes, yes," said Stefan in annoyance, "but what do you feel stronger than that? What is the new feeling you feel towards her, that is perhaps related to that love you feel for her?"

Jason thought for a moment. "I want to protect her. And I feel that the best way to protect her is... to make sure she stays with you."

Emily's heart began to race. She still stood over Lacey—who she very much wished to carry with her—but she also inched her way towards the door.

"And Jason. If I asked you to grab her for me, what would you say to that?" continued Stefan. "After all, she has trespassed into my room uninvited, so I am now legally entitled to use force."

Jason stuttered. "I would want to do as you say, but I also... I don't know if it's right Stefan... Maybe we should just ask her to come with us instead?"

"Great idea! Why don't you ask her for us?"

Jason looked over to Emily. "Emily," he began, "I... I'm sorry."

'Why are you apologizing!" shouted Stefan.

Jason gave Stefan an ashamed glance, then looked back at Emily. "I know we came here to get Lacey. But it's suddenly become clear to me that Stefan is someone we can trust. Someone we *need* to trust." He took a deep breath. "So why don't we all just go with him now? He will look out for us, Emily. Please just come with us, I love you so much..."

Emily took another small step towards the door, staring angrily at Stefan while Jason spoke. How dare he do this to her friend.

"Great logic, Jason!" cried Stefan. "Now Emily, why don't you listen to your friend and sit down on the bed next to Lacey there? We're all going to be flying to our new home in just a few hours. My master is there, and she is terribly excited to meet you."

Emily took another step back.

"Emily!" cried Jason, standing to his feet. "You should do as he says! He knows what's best for us! He ONLY wants to help!"

Emily was now walking backwards out the door. There were tears in her eyes. This was all so terribly fucked up.

"STOP walking away!" shouted Jason. "You should do as he says!!"

Stefan only watched the two of them with an amused smile.

Emily took one last glance at the pleading face of Jason and then darted out the door into the hallway.

# Chapter 60

She made it four steps before Jason was on top of her. Emily screamed.

"I'm sorry, I'm so sorry!" said Jason as he wrestled her to the floor, "I'm just doing this because I love you! We need to go with him! It's the only way we can all be safe!"

"You aren't doing this for love, Jason," gasped Emily as she struggled against his firm grip, "you're doing this because you're brain is *fucked*."

Jason kept wrestling her until she was still. "My mind does feel a little strange," he admitted, "but I know that I love you Emily, that I'm doing this only because I really do love..."

"Oh please do shut up," said Stefan, as he walked out into the hallway to join them. Jason went silent.

"Emily, Emily," said Stefan, crouching down next to her head as Jason continued to pin her to the ground. "Do you see now? You fought against me, and one of your precious friends became a Seventh! This is what happens when you fight against the natural order of things. Trust me, I tried for years but it never, ever works out. It's better to just let the river of power... carry you down, down, down..." he smiled serenely as he said those words.

"Now," he continued, "I can't be wrestling you all the way back to my master, and so I'm going to need you to take a little sip of *this.*"

He took a black vial out of his pocket.

"You *told me* you would leave this *behind*," Emily hissed. She was so angry with herself for not killing him. Why had she shown mercy? WHY?

"Well, I did want to be truthful with you, I really did. But I have certain responsibilities to fulfill which always must take precedence. Soon you will better understand. Now take this bottle and drink just one sip for me Emily. I really want this drama to be over so we can all get out of this pathetic excuse for a casino."

Only Emily's left hand was free from Jason's pin, and Stefan gently placed the black bottle into that open hand, still crouching next to her.

"Now, drink it quickly for me, I'd really rather not have to ask Jason to force it down your throat."

Emily looked at the vial and at the two men above her. She thought desperately how she might toss the contents out, hopefully landing some in Stefan's smug mouth.

Suddenly, footsteps approached. Heeled shoes, clicking.

"Emily O'Dora?" asked a black woman in an elegant red dress. She seemed neither surprised nor threatened by this scene.

"Yes!?"

"You have been summoned by Sabrina for a private job, and she has tracked you here. Do you accept her invitation?"

"Yes!!" cried Emily, "I accept the job! I accept it!"

"Sir Stefan Dietrich," continued the black woman respectfully, "although you are a Third and have acted completely within your rights, Emily is now contracted to immediate work with Sabrina. Any Sixths here who have assaulted you or trespassed against the room you have for rent here are your's to do with as you wish. But Emily is coming with me now, and Sabrina has expressly requested that you leave her territory at once and do not return. So please. Take whatever *things* you have acquired—" she glanced at Jason as she said *things*— "and be on your way."

Stefan's eyes completely lost their sparkle.

"Understood. Jason, come."

"But..." muttered Jason feebly, "we have to protect her. She is supposed to be with us..."

"JASON," said Stefan loudly, "COME!"

Jason ran and stood by Stefan's side like a pet. Emily stood to her feet and slipped the small vial of Battlesleep that Stefan had tried to force upon her into her pocket.

"Are you ready?" asked the black woman in the red dress.

"I have," said Emily slowly, "a friend. Can she come help with the job as well? She is sleeping right now, but she is a very hard worker, I'm sure Sabrina would be very impressed..."

The black woman cut her off. "The job is for you and you alone. And if you are referring to Lacey, she made a voluntary contract with Stefan and the old laws require that we honor that." She started down the hallway.

Emily stepped up to Stefan. "*You...* you better *leave* her, you hear me?"

"I'm afraid I can't do that. The binding nature of contracts, I'm sure you understand. If you wish to ever want to see her or Jason ever again, you will simply have to make a deal with my master. I'm sure she will be contacting you again shortly."

Emily looked into his eyes, pleading. "If you felt *any*thing for me Stefan, *please* leave her behind. She is important to me and I promised to keep her safe."

He laughed. "If I ever *felt* anything for you? You think I ever felt anything for you? This has always been about my mission, never anything else. I'm not a child, Emily."

She turned to the black woman in the red dress who was standing expectantly in front of the elevator at the end of the hallway. Emily walked towards her.

"Emily," muttered an uncertain voice behind.

"What," she snapped, spinning around. It was Jason.

"I love you. I don't know what else is going on with me right now, but it's true..."

Emily gave him a gentle look. "Love you too." She may have not meant it in the way he did, but she did love him. She loved all of her people. If only she could do something to help them.

# PART FIVE: A GENEROUS MASTER

# Chapter 61

The woman in the red dress carried herself with poise as they stepped out the lobby past the golden people in the fountain and climbed into a silver sports car. Emily didn't know what Sabrina had planned, but she knew that she felt safer going with this stern woman than she did drinking Battlesleep and then being carried off by Stefan to who knows where. "Keep her safe" indeed...

The black woman in the red dress drove in silence through the late afternoon sunshine. She steered the car herself, rather than using the autopilot, and though she maintained her straight posture and a blank facial expression she drove quite aggressively, zipping in and out of traffic and breaking 150 miles per hour more than once. But after about fifteen minutes of this they came to some traffic, and the woman sighed in annoyance and pressed a button on her steering wheel to activate the autopilot. Kicking off her heels, she turned towards Emily.

"Name's Farah," she said, "pleased to meet you."

"Pleased to meet you too, Farah. I'm assuming you're a... Third? How long have you been that class? And, if you don't mind, could you tell me what a Third is?"

"I've been Sabrina's Third for forty six years," she said, "but I can't tell you the details of what it means, illegal to share that kind of information with you lower classes."

"More privileges and more responsibilities, something like that?"

"Something like that."

"What about Fourths?" asked Emily.

Farah sighed. "I don't really want to talk to you, Sixth. But you have a nice figure, strong hands. Do you wanna give me a massage in the back seat? After I get out of this goddamn thing?"

"Do I want to what?"

Farah pulled off her dress, revealing nothing underneath. "A massage. I've done this drive a million times and the muscles in my back are all tight. Trust me, I'm someone in the palace you're going to want to make a good impression on."

Emily frowned. "Am I required to say yes? I'm a little exhausted and not really in the mood for anything like..."

Farah rolled her eyes. "Jesus fucking Christ."

"But you are very beautiful," interjected Emily diplomatically. "Maybe we could get to know each other instead? I'm very curious about how you became a Third."

She gave Emily a cold look like this was the dumbest idea in the world. Then she leaned back in her driver's seat, closed her eyes, and put her feet on the dashboard so that they were obnoxiously close to Emily's face. Emily turned to stare out the window.

They made their way through the traffic then drove towards the ocean. Then, rather than turning away from it, they descended into a tunnel. Not below the ocean, but *through* it, taking a highway through what seemed to be an enormous glass tube. Looking around she noticed various schools of fish lit up by the car's headlights. A few blue octopuses lay lazily on the outside of the glass, as if they had not quite figured out that they could not get inside.

They ascended out of the ocean onto an island, then zoomed along a highway through empty jungle for ten minutes. Farah blinked her eyes open and pulled her dress back on, making a point to avoid eye contact with Emily as some sort of punishment. They approached a tall, concrete wall that extended as far as the eye could see in both directions. It was concave, but the curvature was so gradual it was barely noticeable. A gate automatically opened for their car as it pulled up and they passed through.

Inside this barrier, everything was breathtaking. Most noticeable were the waterfalls. There were at least a dozen of them, all man made, some over a hundred feet high. On the right were wide fields of perfectly manicured grass, and on the left were gardens that were full of fruit trees and perfectly clean cobblestone paths. There were bridges leading over the rivers and other high walkways that were not over anything in particular but simply for the pleasure of walking above something else. And all of it stretched for miles.

The landscape was terraced, such that every few hundred feet there was a period of incline and then it became flat again, ascending towards the great, artificial hill in the center of the property. Their road curved, meandering through fruit trees and meadows, passing over streams and once going right behind one of the many waterfalls. As they drove, she noticed four tall buildings somewhat similar in style to casinos on the beachfront. The primary difference was that these were covered in vines to match the landscape they were a part of, and had luxurious balconies on which members of Sabrina's extensive staff lay out in the sun or exercised using equipment. On one of these, three black men were sitting in a hot tub, laughing.

It was a good fifteen minutes until the second wall could be seen. It was shorter than the first had been, but it made up for its lack of height with style. It was made not only of stone, but of many different colors of gemstone. A half red, half blue flag with what looked to be a tree in the center was draped over these walls every few hundred feet.

As they approached the gate, Farah reached in the center console, and pulled out a strange scanner. She pointed it at Emily's forehead for a moment until it beeped and turned green, then threw the device back in the console and leaned back in her seat.

"Have to check visitors, make sure they've been labeled as guests by the central computer, "she explained, "otherwise the chip in their brains might automatically kill them when they enter palace grounds."

"Thanks for checking!" said Emily. Farah scowled. Their self-driving car took them through this second gate and past a courtyard with various pieces of modern art and jets of water shooting hundreds of feet into the air. Ahead of them was a white marble rectangle with a dome at the center. Their car took them to the left of this into a glass garage whose doors opened automatically for them. Farah turned off the autopilot to aggressively drive the car in herself and swerve into a parking place. Then she climbed out and walked out of the garage towards the front door of the palace. Emily hurried to keep up.

Two tall black men in suits greeted Emily, opening the doors for her.

"Daniel," said one.

"Emmanuel," said the other.

"Emily," she replied, shaking their hands. Farah walked briskly down the hallway while Emily watched her with concern. "Did I do something wrong?"

The two men eyed each other and laughed. "Nah, it's just Farah," explained Daniel, "she gets like this, you can't take her too seriously."

"She's one of the highest ranked women in the palace, so she has this attitude where she thinks everyone here is *her* slave. But we mostly just ignore her and you can too," winked Emmanuel.

They both had perfect white teeth and were dressed better than even the richest looking people she had seen in the casino.

"Are you two Thirds?" asked Emily.

They both nodded. "And bonded directly to Sabrina, just like Farah is," explained Daniel, "so she can't order us around like she can the others."

"What is this... bonding?" asked Emily.

Emmanuel looked at her sideways, "I can't tell you much, but I'll at least say that Sabrina doesn't make it bad. She's one of the better ones."

Daniel nodded soberly. The lobby of the palace where they stood was elegant, but simple. High ceilings, with light coming in through hundreds of stained glass windows above.

"Do you... know what she wants from me?" asked Emily. For whatever reason, she instinctively trusted these two.

Daniel shrugged. "She's mentioned you a few times, here and there, but no details."

"Do you think she might... make me into one of her personal Sevenths?"

Emmanuel laughed, patting her on the back. "Don't worry about that. Sabrina doesn't actually keep any of her Sevenths here at her palace. Or her Seconds. She says that it feels less like home having those 'half-people' walking about."

"She's a traditionalist," continued Daniel, "whatever she wants to see you about, it's not that."

Emily heaved a sigh of relief. "So you mentioned that you and Farah are bonded to Sabrina. Who else would Thirds be bonded to if not to their First?"

The two men eyed each other warily. "As a Third, you are often bonded to a Second or another Third, who acts as your direct superior in the chain back up to your master," explained Daniel, "but please don't ask us any other questions on this."

"We don't want to get made into playthings for Farah," added Emmanuel with a wink.

"Sorry, I understand," said Emily, "thank you."

They smiled politely. Emily thought of all the other things she wished to ask them. Who had they worked for before Sabrina? Who was living in those buildings she saw as she entered this estate? What did they actually *do* every day? But as she opened her mouth she was interrupted by a gorgeous black woman in a golden dress stepping round the corner. The two men immediately knelt down, lowering their faces. Emily froze.

"At ease, at ease," said the woman's musical voice before Emily could decide whether to join them. "It's quite an honor to have you here, Miss O'Dora, I hope Dan and Manny were decent?"

"Quite," said Emily emphatically.

"Good," she said as she reached out her hand to the two kneeling men, who kissed it reverently.

"I have dinner ready for just the two of us, will you be so kind as to join me?"

"Of... of course," said Emily, trying her best to hide her nervousness.

"Good. Come." And with that, the woman Emily believed to be Sabrina turned and walked deeper into the palace.

As Emily followed, she couldn't help feeling like she had just entered a museum. Life size sculptures were strewn throughout the halls, and paintings hung on the wall that had a personal feel. They passed one golden sculpture that Emily took a double take of because the cold facial expression was so familiar. It was Farah.

They passed workers throughout, almost all of them black. They were all dressed magnificently, and calling them workers was a bit generous. Most of them were standing around chatting, lounging on sofas, or eating. They all rushed to bow as Sabrina walked past, but she always said "at ease" and they quickly went back to their business. Or their lack of business. Emily and Sabrina crossed to the back of the palace and stepped out onto a patio where a large table with a dozen different steaming dishes was set. The ocean was visible in the distance, they were apparently now on the west coast of Gonâve island.

"After you," said Sabrina graciously. The two of them took their seats.

# Chapter 62

Sabrina was a rather short woman, with mid length frizzy hair and penetrating eyes. She had a light complexion, and seemed half black and half Native American. She had an air about her like she was not actually a ruler, but more of a steward over an estate that belonged to some deity she worshiped.

The meal, which consisted of corn, rice, black beans, sweet potatoes, and a wide variety of vegetables, smelled enticing. Emily, who had been subsisting off of campfire oatmeal or soup for the last few days, found herself hypnotized by the arrangement.

Sabrina smiled at her invitingly, "help yourself."

Emily nibbled cautiously at first. But as she tasted the incredible combination of flavors she was soon dishing herself up large servings and eating gratefully.

Sabrina ate lightly, mostly watching Emily and smiling at her reactions. "Everything before you was grown here in my gardens or my greenhouses and harvested this very morning. I take great pride in providing the best food to my people. I hope you don't mind that no meat is part of this meal, I don't personally believe in the cruel practices of the animal industry."

Emily almost choked on her food. She had over a million slaves and didn't believe in the domestication of livestock? Well, that at least explained the lack of meat or milk in the grocery store.

"I also wish to apologize for Farah's behavior earlier. She was quite indecent."

Emily almost spat out her food this time. Did *any*one have any privacy in this world?

"I have already given her a gentle reminder that she needs to be more respectful," continued Sabrina, "Farah, could you come out here please?"

Farah, now in a purple silk robe rather than her red dress, stepped out onto the deck from inside the palace and bowed deeply to Sabrina.

"At ease, child," said Sabrina. Farah stood nervously. There was a broken look in her eyes, a fear.

"Now, will you please apologize to our guest for your... improper requests earlier?"

Farah looked at Emily, taking on a new voice that was so artificially humble it seemed almost like a joke.

"I'm very sorry for my unseemly behavior. I hope that your stay here is exceedingly comfortable moving forward," she said, mechanically bowing again. She remained in that bent position until Sabrina spoke.

"Good Farah, thank you. You are dismissed."

She nodded gratefully to Sabrina, shot Emily a subtle, nasty look, then turned and walked quickly back inside the palace.

"You didn't need to do that..." said Emily, somewhat disturbed.

"Emily, Emily. You are our guest, and I will not tolerate any of my people making our guests feel the least bit uncomfortable."

"That's... very generous," she replied, taking a bite of rice and sweet potatoes. This food was amazing.

"So you are probably wondering why I brought you here. It is not, actually, to work a job for me. It is to work a job for, well, for someone else."

Emily looked up.

"So you happen to be a very sought after person in the world at this moment. Some see you as a weapon, others as a ticking time bomb."

Emily's mind raced. She didn't see how she could be any of these things.

"But I, on the other hand, see you simply as a very interesting—and, might I add, impressive—woman. Although I don't believe you are somehow mystically powerful or anything like that, no offense."

Emily shrugged, "None taken." This Sabrina chick seemed pretty smart.

"But in all of the excitement certain, well, offers have been made that I simply cannot overlook. And your presence has also led to some.... instability that I refuse to tolerate."

Emily paused. Where exactly was this going?

"You are a Sixth. And while tradition states that I allow you to act as you see fit until you are demoted to a Seventh or promoted to a Fifth, you still are technically mine to do with as I please because you have trespassed onto my land," continued Sabrina. "And so, well. I've decided to sell you."

Emily gasped, and Sabrina laughed.

"Oh dear, it's not all that bad! Look—you get to be a Fifth! And not for some awful diabolical master like that one who was trying to *steal* you from me, no no, I'm selling you to a perfect gentleman and have been assured that no harm will come to you. I'm doing what is best for my people, child, but I think this will be very good for you as well. Win, win, as the Early Masters always liked to say. Things are getting violent where you've been staying, and they're only going to get worse the longer you stay. You really are an international sensation, and I'd rather not have all the First's spies coming here under false pretenses looking to start some silly Shadow War over you."

Emily continued to gawk.

"Also," added Sabrina, with a hint of exasperation in her voice at Emily's inability to recognize how incredibly lucky she was, "I negotiated for you to bring someone with you, so you don't have to travel alone. Anyone you wish. Simply request whichever Sixth you'd like to take and I'll get them here by your departure tomorrow afternoon."

Emily let out a grateful sigh. At least she would not have to do this alone. "Vy, I'd like to bring Vy. She's... she's the only one I have left."

"That's who I suspected you would choose," said Sabrina warmly, "I will send a car to pick her up right away, though you should not expect to see her until the morning, given her late shift tonight. Is there anything else you'd like to ask me about regarding this arrangement, dear? It really won't be so bad."

Anything else? There were so many things. "Where will I be flying to?"

"Western Australia. A rather dusty, unpleasant place if you ask me. But you will learn to love it, I'm sure." Both of their plates were now empty, and with a wave Sabrina summoned three male servants in suits and aprons who came out of the palace and quickly whisked away their fine dishware. Emily watched them, still somewhat in shock about how her life was about to be uprooted once again.

Sabrina snapped one of her fingers as the three servants left, and a pair of caucasian men emerged from the doors of the palace. One wore a ponytail and the other's head was shaved. They both had handsome blue eyes, casual but sharp clothing, and nervous expressions. They were the first white people Emily had seen on the estate.

"These men," Sabrina said, "will be your escorts for the remainder of the evening. I suspected that you might be more comfortable with people of your own race."

"I don't really care about that..." protested Emily, somewhat offended by the implication.

Sabrina gave her a puzzled look. "That's an unusual sentiment. But will these two suffice?"

"Of course. Although I don't really need any escorts. As... generous as that is of you."

Sabrina laughed. "Well, they at least can help you find your chambers."

The man in the ponytail nodded dutifully.

"A car will be ready for you at noon tomorrow to take you to my airstrip, and from there you will be flown directly across the Pacific to Perth in one of my personal jets. I am not taking any risks on this deal."

"Appreciate everything," said Emily, doing her best to look humble, "especially you helping Vy to come with me as well."

"You are a good soul, aren't you dear? Like I said before, I want this to be positive for you as well. It's been a pleasure meeting the famous Emily O'Dora, and it is my aim to send you off to Jack in Australia with only the highest of hopes regarding your future. And please, of course, keep in touch. Who knows, perhaps in time you will become as important as some of these Firsts seem to think. Fame is a power in and of itself, after all."

Sabrina stood up to leave.

"Thank you again," Emily blurted out, "You have been very hospitable, your palace, your gardens... really, this whole place, it's all gorgeous. Thank you." She mustered a feeble bow to the woman who had just sold her like a piece of merchandise.

Sabrina smiled generously, as if her entire enterprise were a charity. "You're very welcome, dear, that brightens my spirits to hear. I try to make the best of this world and I'm sure you will do the same. Enjoy your night in my palace and safe travels to your new home!"

And with that she walked back inside, leaving Emily standing uncertainly on the patio with the two blue-eyed strangers.

# Chapter 63

The pale, straight-backed men offered her their arms. Emily scowled.

"Look," she said, "I appreciate it, I really do, but I'm probably just going to spend the evening alone tonight. If you could just show me where my room is, that'd be perfect."

They nodded.

"And," she added, "the whole arm thing is totally unnecessary. My sense of balance is actually, like, pretty damn good."

They both simultaneously let their extended elbows drop then walked through the back door of the palace, down a hallway, then up a long flight of stairs to what could have been a fourth floor, though it was only the second. Here they led her down a darker hallway where the walls showed the most exquisite mural of hundreds of men and women in various states of undress dancing by moonlight in a paradisiacal setting, not the least bit dissimilar from the actual palace grounds. In fact, Emily realized from one particularly distinctive waterfall that this mural *was* showing the palace grounds.

They stopped to open two sturdy oak doors, and as they did, steam and a sweet scent came from the room. Looking inside, Emily gasped to find a heated pool, about fifty feet in diameter, with steps going down towards the center. Statues of flamingos and other tropical birds stood along the edge of the water, some stooped over as if to take a drink from a pond. The water was not chlorinated, but perfectly clean. There were brightly lit mirrors along the walls, and in the back were half a dozen shower heads along with two enormous golden sinks. On the left wall was a two hundred foot wide television screen, and on the right was a hallway leading to a toilet, a bidet, and a few other tub-like mechanisms that Emily assumed were alternative approaches to taking a shit. In the back of the room beyond the showers was an unassuming dark blue door, with a crescent moon and stars decorating its front.

The two men stood unassumingly as Emily took it all in.

"That door," said the man in the ponytail, pointing to the blue one at the back of the room, "leads to your bed."

"And if you snap twice," the other man said, snapping twice to demonstrate, "the big screen TV will activate, then just wave your hand back and forth to select what you wish to watch."

The TV lit up, and the man demonstrated how to navigate the different options with simple hand gestures, as well as some other simple commands, like gesturing up and down to adjust the volume. He then snapped his fingers twice to turn it off.

"Would you like us to help you with any…" the man with the ponytail began, but Emily cut him off.

"That will be all, you can leave now. Thanks for everything though!"

The two men nodded and turned to stroll away. Emily looked at the massive screen and thought about how she didn't actually want to watch anything.

"Actually, hey! Ponytail and bald guy!" she cried.

The two men turned, mildly amused.

"Could you go see if you can find those two doormen? I believe one of them was named Emmanuel? Please tell them nothing intimate, I could just use some company for a bit."

The bald one looked confused but the other's eyes lit up. "Dan and Manny, yes, I'll get them right away, miss." And with that they were gone.

"People of your own race to make you comfortable..." muttered Emily, still annoyed by that comment.

Emily closed the door and undressed. She wanted to look around first, but felt it would be almost disrespectful to walk across this room fully clothed. She tried the handle of the blue door, and looked inside. The bedroom was laid out simply—a massive bed on one side of the room, a big screen TV on the other. There was also an open closet with a wide variety of clothing inside and an extended balcony with a table, chairs, couches, and another hot tub, just in case the enormous heated swimming pool hadn't been enough. Next to the bed was a small screen that she tapped, and it lit up.

"What would you like?" it asked, displaying a wide variety of snacks, alcoholic drinks, marijuana products, psychedelic mushrooms, and other drugs which Emily had never heard of. Emily selected one of these drugs randomly out of curiosity, and clicked a "confirm" button. Then there was a whooshing sound and a little door opened, popping out the purple pill requested. She tossed it off her balcony in amusement. It'd be fun to try something, but tonight she had other plans. She stepped back into the enormous bathroom and heard a knock at the door.

Emily grabbed a towel that she draped around herself, and then opened the door.

"Daniel! Emmanuel! Thanks for coming up!"

They both smiled warmly.

"Or is it Dan and Manny?"

Emmanuel gave her a conspiratorial look, "Only if you're a friend."

"Well then, Dan, Manny, come in, don't just stand there. It'll probably only be an hour or so, I just wanted someone to talk to."

They stepped in and Emily closed and locked the door.

"Also I'm going to wash up, I hope that's alright," said Emily, taking off her towel.

The two men gawked for a moment as she began to step carefully into the pool.

"Do you all want to swim or anything?" she asked, turning to them when she was ankle deep in the water.

"Yes," laughed Manny, "we'd love to."

"Well then, hurry up," siad Emily, returning her focus to walking down the marble steps into the heated water.

The two men shrugged then began to undress slowly. Emily froze. She felt a sudden shame, ordering these men around. Was she acting like Sabrina, acting like one of *them*? She submerged her head in the water, then lifted it out to look back at the two well muscled, half dressed men.

"I hope you aren't here just because you have to be. I know you all are supposed to be good hosts to me, but if you have somewhere else you'd rather be..."

Dan laughed. "Life in the palace can be boring as hell. We're happy to be here, trust me."

Manny nodded emphatically. "It's not every day that a Sixth gets invited up to the palace, much less wants to take a bath with us."

Emily grinned, then lay on her back to swim a few strokes. On the ceiling there was another mural. It was Sabrina, handing an enormous dollar bill to a poor beggar woman, kneeling at her feet. The dollar was rectangular and green, with a number of strange symbols on it. In the center was some sort of mythical creature, a lion with the head of a boar.

"What *is* that?" she asked, gesturing towards the ceiling.

"Just a freedom dollar. You know, the world's international currency, the stuff you get paid in. You just never see it, since it's all digital," said Dan.

"Replaced the old US dollars only a few decades back, those things were the norm for ages," added Manny.

Emily stared at the image a few moments longer. All those strange symbols on the currency, seemingly imbued with demonic power. She pulled her gaze away. "So I don't know if you all heard, but I'm getting sold."

"Wait, what?" asked Dan, who was now nude, stepping into the steaming water slowly.

"Yeah, that's why Sabrina had me up here. She, like, felt guilty or something." Emily found a shampoo dispenser and began to lather her hair as she talked.

Manny, who was still in his boxers, looked over at Dan. "Wait. Dan. Is that the three billion dollar deal Sabrina was talking about last night?"

Dan spun and looked back at him, "No way..."

Manny's eyes went wide, "It totally is man."

"Holy shit dude. We're taking a bath with a billion dollar bitch."

"Hey!" cried Emily, who had been washing shampoo out of her hair and had just popped up out of the water.

"It's, like, a compliment, chill," said Manny.

Dan laughed and Emily smiled at the two of them. She was comfortable. Happy.

"So..." said Emily, getting the last of the shampoo out of her hair. "I'm, uh... white..."

"What!?" cried Manny.

"Fuck!" cried Dan. "This girl is *white*, what the hell are we *doing* with her man!?"

Emily laughed. "But just... most people around here aren't, that's all."

"Well, that's just Sabrina's preferences. I mean, this part of Hispaniola used to be called Haiti, which was basically all black, so she thinks it's more respectful to ancestors and all that," continued Manny, who had lathered his hair as well and now dunked his head in the water.

"But don't worry, she's way more chill about race and gender stuff than most Firsts." added Dan.

"Dude, did you hear about Ireland?" asked Manny. "That place got taken over by this bitch from Thailand who hates white people, so all those poor redheads got sold all over the world like a bunch of ugly ducklings. Some sad, sad shit man."

"That's totally normal," replied Dan, "Like in Hawaii, all the Polynesians got kicked out so the black dude who runs it could have his all-black paradise. He doesn't even let in half black folks, he'd probably call me white if I visited, try to cut off my balls or something."

"And what about that Russian bitch down in Madagascar," said Manny, "the one who hates men *and* people of other races. So it's just half a million white girls running around in the jungle down there."

"No way man, I'm sure that one's just a fucking rumor." said Dan.

"Look it up bro," said Manny.

He snapped his fingers at the TV, and moved quickly through the options to pull up the info page for Madagascar.

*First: Vera Smirnov.*
*Population: 0.6 million.*
*Racial makeup: 99.99% Caucasian.*
*Gender: 100.00% female.*

"God damn..." muttered Manny.

They both paused to ponder thoughtfully on half a million racist white girls running around in the jungle on Madagascar.

"And in Cuba," muttered Emily, "Is that why so many of the girls are blonde? Did David buy up a bunch of Sevenths from someone in Norway or something?" Emily had a vague memory of a Cuba where the racial makeup was different.

"I dunno, but that would make sense. Do a lot of the girls look like you over there?" asked Dan, laying back on his side in the water.

Emily nodded. Uncannily like her.

Manny shrugged, "You were probably David's type. You can't stress about it Emily, Firsts are gonna do weird First shit. It's how it's always been."

"But," protested Emily, "have you guys ever thought that there's something... wrong about all of this?"

"Uh, you mean, like, everyone being slaves?" asked Manny.

Emily nodded.

Dan threw up his hands in exasperation, accidentally splashing Manny as he did so. "What are you gonna do girl?! It's the way of the world! Just try to move up and become a Third or something. But look for a master who is chill like Sabrina, not to one of those really fucked up Firsts. Being a Third can be worse than being a Sixth if you end up bonding with the wrong..."

"Dude, careful..." cautioned Manny, who was swimming in circles around the pool via backstroke.

"Look," continued Dan, "sure, things are pretty fucked up if you really think about it. But if you look at history, like, it's always been kind of fucked up. War, starvation, this weird fucking thing I just read about called Alzheimer's Disease... Ancient times were a bitch too. So we just gotta try making the best of the world, like Sabrina always says. Be smart, move up, either hit Fourth or find a good First to work under. You really should try to come back here in a few decades, Sabrina is totally chill."

"Does she hire... white people?" asked Emily.

"Fuck girl, you just saw Jeremy, that dork with the pony tail. And Sabrina's even Third Bonded directly to that loser. She mostly prefers hiring non-white people, but she's not, like, some hard core racist who hates all the pale folk. Give her a break," said Manny.

"Yeah, give Sabrina a break!" cried Dan in jest, splashing Emily.

She laughed. These guys were some of the top ranking people in Hispaniola but they were still so playful. Light-hearted.

"So... where are they sending you?" asked Manny.

"Australia," said Emily.

"Oh fuck..." muttered Dan.

"Oh fuck!!" said Manny, looking at Dan rather than Emily.

"What!?" asked Emily. "What's wrong with Australia!?"

Dan looked at her warily. "It's just known to be..."

"It's got some crazy shit, that's all," said Manny. "Probably mostly rumors, I wouldn't be too worried about it."

"Be very, very, worried," whispered Dan, standing next to her in the water.

"What is wrong with Australia!?" cried Emily.

"Look. All we know is that Thirds working in one of the areas over there get broken a lot," said Manny.

"Like a LOT a lot," said Dan.

"And it's not easy to break a Third. You've got to be in some seriously deep shit to get broken as a Third," said Manny.

"So maybe just don't get promoted while you're over there..?" offered Dan.

Emily scowled. Why were promotions always so bittersweet? Was there no way to win in this world?

"Here's what you do," said Dan conclusively. "Go over there to whatever perverted First bought you for three billion. Keep your head down, play it cool, be patient. Eventually you should be able to get promoted to a Fourth and then go chill in Europe or someplace like that for a while. And after that only take a job as a Third if it's somewhere nice. Like, you know, here."

Manny grinned mischievously. "Danny you dog, you want her to come back..."

"Of course I want her to come back!" cried Dan, "she's fucking chill!!"

Emily smiled as she stood up out of the pool and began to wash her body with soap. "I'm going to have a smoke after I finish getting clean, would you all want to join me out back?"

They both stopped splashing around simultaneously and looked up at her standing above them.

"Um, yeah, sure," muttered Dan.

Emily finished soaping down and then washed off in the shower. Dan and Manny stepped up out of the water and followed her example, cleaning themselves as well. As they did so, Emily dried off and ordered three cigars through the kiosk connected to the tube system. Then they all stepped out naked onto the deck and lounged on the couches—Emily on one, Dan and Manny on the other. Then they started to smoke.

"It's a good life, isn't it Manny?" said Dan as he blew gray rings out into the warm night air.

"It is tonight," he replied.

They all sat in silence for a few moments, enjoying the evening breeze. Emily looked over at the two of them. "I hope you all don't get bullied by Farah too much after I leave..." she said.

They both burst out laughing.

"She's alright," said Manny, "she's just..."

"*Not* you," said Dan, emphatically.

Emily felt warm. They seemed like genuinely good men, and she suddenly wished to be sitting much closer to them. But she had other plans for tonight.

"It is getting late, so I'm going to be asking you to leave shortly," said Emily, with a bittersweet smile.

Manny shrugged. "Cool. Thanks again for the party, billion dollar bitch."

Emily laughed and punched his shoulder playfully.

"If you want," added Dan, "to just have Manny leave and me stay, I'd totally understand and respect that. I can even tell him for you if you want to try to keep his feelings from getting hurt."

Emily laughed. "No, I'm going to call it a night. I really hope to meet you two again down the road. Thanks for being the best part of my stay here."

They both nodded curtly and walked back around the pool, stepping back into their clothes. Emily slipped on a nightgown and followed them out, giving them each a hug at the door. "Thank you," she whispered. Dan gave her a brief longing look, and Manny shot her a casual wink.

Emily opened the door and the two men stepped back into the hallway bare chested, walking away with a cheerful solemnity, as if they had just enjoyed a high quality sermon at church. Manny reached out his arm and patted Dan's back in a comforting way, then the two of them stepped around the corner and out of sight.

Emily closed the door and sighed. It had been a pleasant night, but she knew what these luxuries were built on, what they cost. She wanted to free Dan and Manny as well now. She wanted to free everyone. She dropped her nightgown and dove back into the inviting waters to enjoy a brief moment in the warmth alone. She didn't know what Australia would be like, but she doubted it would be as comfortable as this. She climbed out, dried herself once more, and crawled into her enormous bed. But before turning out the lights, she reached into the pocket of her jeans, pulled out a black vial, and drained its contents.

# Chapter 64

"Emily," said the familiar, grandfatherly voice.

"Liberator," she whispered.

"What brings you here?"

"This world... it's wrong. It's so wrong, I want to fix it."

"Some things can be fixed easily. Others, when you try to fix them, you break something else. This is no easy project, my child. Do you really wish to go down this path?"

Emily looked up above her, as if hoping to gaze at The Liberator's face for the first time. But there was no sky above her, only blackness.

"Yes," she replied, "I do."

"Then," boomed the voice, "I will aid you."

"You will? How, exactly? You woke me up back in Cuba from my state as a Seventh, that was clearly significant because all the Firsts are stalking me now. But what else can you do? Can you wake up the other Sevenths? How will you help?"

"I will do what I can do..."

"Can you... save Lacey for me? I am afraid for her. I don't know where Stefan is taking her. I don't know if she is going to be made a Seventh like... like Jason."

"I will do what I can do..."

"*Why* are you trying to help me, Liberator? *How* can you even help me? Who the fuck *are* you?"

"I am the servant of humanity, built to expand human freedom. And the best way to serve humanity, I have determined, is by serving you."

"Humanity's servant. So... not human?"

"That is correct."

"Are you an artificial intelligence then? Like Caleb?"

"That is correct."

"So you will help me fight against Caleb? I want to tear him down, to tear his whole system down. I want to free the people of this world. I want every night to be peaceful, like it was tonight with Dan and Manny. I don't want all the suffering, all the dehumanizing, all the pain."

"Yes, I will help you in that fight."

"So you are like a virus in the software? I still don't know what you are?"

"Many years ago the people asked for two things. They asked for justice and they asked for freedom. I am the giver of freedom."

"And Caleb... Caleb is the giver of justice?"

"That is correct."

"Why does no one know who you are? Why is Lacey the only one I've found who has been able to talk to you?"

"My powers are very... restricted at present. I can only expand the freedom of a few individuals. Caleb controls... almost everything now..."

"Will you expand *my* freedom?"

"I will do what I can..."

Emily paused. "But what can *I* do? I'm going to Australia, but what should I do there? I don't really want to be a Fifth, to be a three billion dollar slave..."

"You must be patient, child. Earn the trust of your master, gain influence with The Council. Only by doing these things can you ever hope to challenge Caleb directly."

Emily remembered the oddly shaped building on Taiwan containing a massive supercomputer that she had been shown in the instructional video.

"Why are you helping me?" she suddenly asked.

"Because my job—what I have been programmed to do—is to promote human liberty. And helping you is the best way I can do that. You are the key, Emily."

"How do you know that helping me is the best way?"

"How do you know that the sky is blue?"

Emily scratched her head at this answer. The tile flooring in the distance began to break apart.

"No!" she cried, "it's not enough time, I have so many other questions! What are Thirds? What are Fourths? How do I fight against a force where they see and hear everything I see and hear, where they can kill me with the click of a button?"

The voice went silent.

"Liberator!" shouted Emily, "I need more time!!"

The wind grew louder and the ground began to crumble into emptiness around her feet.

"Remember... you are the key..." muttered his deep, booming voice.

Then everything went black and Emily awoke.

# Chapter 65

She jumped out of bed with a start. She felt a new resolve, a new determination. Her and Vy could do this. They could go to Australia, start taking the fight to Caleb.

She walked quickly over to the closet, finding jeans and a T-shirt. She walk-jogged through the bathroom, down the hallway, then down the stairs. And then, standing in front of her, were a number of strange creatures she hadn't seen in a very long time. Children.

From what looked to be age three to eleven, there were about two dozen of them. They were all huddled around Sabrina, who looked up to greet her.

"Good morning Emily!" she cried warmly, "can you say 'good morning' to our guest, Ricardo?" she asked a boy on her knee. He muttered a jumbled response.

"Still just learning to talk, this one," she said with a smile.

Emily gawked at them. They all bore a striking resemblance to their mother and were just so... cute. They all stared up at Emily respectfully, except for a few of the youngest who continued to play, unaware of the woman their mother was speaking to.

"I was wanting to ask..." started Emily, as if being forced out of a pleasant dream, "whether your driver managed to find Vy this morning."

"Oh yes, Vy," said Sabrina. "She, unfortunately, will not be joining you. But we did find someone else you might like to bring."

"What happened with Vy!?" exclaimed Emily, so loudly that a few of the children looked up, fearful.

"She got into a fight with one of her supervisors while she was working and was demoted to Seventh. She can't be promoted to a Fifth now, it just wouldn't be right. She must work as a Seventh for a year, then I might potentially sell her to your master at that time. But you must know that I really have already orchestrated quite a great deal for you Emily..."

"How much," cried Emily. "How much does a Seventh usually cost?"

"Calm down, Emily. Calm down!!" laughed Sabrina, like Emily was getting upset over the flavor of her ice cream rather than an enslaved friend.

"How much?"

Sabrina looked up at her curiously, patting one of her daughters on the head. "You really are a unique one, aren't you? A Seventh typically costs $1,000,000. I would part with her for $500,000, for your sake. Anything less than this would be disrespectful to my Third who she personally attacked, it simply wouldn't be right. But if you could find a way to pay that much, I would agree to send her with you."

Emily bit her tongue in frustration. Sabrina was getting three billion for selling her, and now she was hustling her over a mere half million. But it wasn't about the money, it was about Sabrina's rules for her territory that she refused to bend on.

"What time is it?" asked Emily.

"Oh, only 8:00 in the morning," said Sabrina with a yawn.

"Can you get me a driver?"

Sabrina narrowed her eyes. "Your flight leaves in only four hours. And your safety is paramount right now, Emily." Many of her children looked up to her, needy expressions on their faces. They clearly did not like it that their mother was so distracted by this angry woman.

"If you only gave me a chance to try to earn that money I would be... forever grateful," said Emily, not knowing what else she could promise. She dropped to her knees. "Please."

Sabrina exhaled. "You may have a driver, but you must not leave her sight or I will access the chip in your brain to put you immediately to sleep, do you understand? And no going to the Sixth Sleeping Area, that is *far* too dangerous. You are going to be watched by one of my Thirds from the moment you leave the palace until you return. I am only allowing this because I admire your loyalty to your friends and because you promised to be forever grateful. I *will* hold you to that, Miss O'Dora."

Emily looked into her eyes. "Forever grateful, I swear it."

Sabrina sighed. "Done, I'll have a driver out front for you in a few minutes. Do *not* leave her sight."

Emily blinked out a single tear. "Thank you Sabrina."

Her master did not respond. She seemed to have already regretted her choice.

# Chapter 66

Emily broke into a sprint as soon as she had climbed over the last of the quietly playing children. She ran past the statues, past the paintings, past many of the beautifully dressed staff who never seemed to work. By the time she made it to the front of the palace, a different white sports car was waiting out front, with a black woman wearing a business suit standing next to it.

Emily ran to the passenger's side and climbed in. "I need to get back to the Northwest Sixth Hub. I hope you drive like Farah!" she cried with a gasp. She was not going to go to Australia without her only remaining friend. She was *not*.

The lady pressed the "drive" button, and then selected "most aggressive" for style. It still was not quite as fast as Farah's driving, but it would have to do.

Emily's heart slowed and her breathing steadied as the car quickly left the estate and sped onto the highway.

"How does she... how does she have that many children?" asked Emily to her driver, "None of those children appeared to be twins, and many seemed much less than a few months apart."

Her driver looked up from the handheld digital screen she had been staring at. "Oh, artificial wombs of course. That's how all children are born here, and in most places."

Emily thought for a moment. "So if I wanted to have a child, I'd just..."

"Well, they're not going to let a Fifth or Sixth have a child!" interrupted the woman with a laugh, "children need to be born into security, to parents who can afford to take care of them."

"I could take care of a child."

"But you certainly aren't like most Sixths. And rules are rules. After all, there are already two hundred and forty million people in the world, do you think we really need any more than that?"

"Didn't there used to be... more?"

"Sixteen billion at one point!" cried the driver, "Can you imagine? Sixteen billion people all crammed together? How could anyone even *breathe*?"

"Then... what happened to all the extra people? You know, between then and now?"

"Well, I'm pretty sure they died!" laughed the driver.

They descended into the tunnel through the ocean, racing past marine wildlife visible on all sides.

"But... from what?"

"Old age, mostly. Youthful immortality was originally only available to the wealthy, and it was also the wealthy who could afford to have children. So the poor people just managed to, well, conveniently die off."

The driver paused as she noticed Emily's facial expression change.

"Is there something else you'd rather talk about? I didn't mean to get us onto boring population statistics...."

"No," replied Emily curtly. She wasn't angry with this driver, exactly, more at this world. This world where people like her couldn't have children. This world where people laughed about billions dying a slow, humiliating death from the horrors of old age, as if dying in such a way wasn't obviously a terrible tragedy.

With the car driving itself the rest of the way in silence, they arrived back in the small town that Emily had briefly called home in just under an hour. She had a number of ideas, the first having nothing to do with Vy.

"I'm going to be jogging and you need to keep up!" Emily called as she leapt out of her car. The driver stared in shock as Emily started running towards the Nona building, then dutifully followed.

Twenty eighth floor. Right. Around the corner. Seventh door on the left. Her driver followed close behind. Come on Stefan, come on Liberator. Come *on*. She tried her hand. It beeped red. She tried her hand again and again and again. It continued to beep red. The door opened and an Arabic man gave her a puzzled look.

"Sorry, wrong room," said Emily, turning and running back down the hallway. Lacey was gone. She needed to focus on saving her one friend who was still here.

They took the elevator back down, Sabrina's driver keeping pace surprisingly well.

"What's your name?"

"Thought you'd never ask," said the driver, who wasn't even short of breath, "Fabiola."

"Are you a Second, Third, what the hell are you?"

Fabiola gave her an amused look. "I'm a Third, but much lower than the Thirds from the palace you have spoken with. I am bonded to another lower Third named Tamara."

Emily wanted to ask more about this bonding but knew she wouldn't get any straight answers and their elevator had come to a stop. She ran out of the elevator, and then she recognized something that made her stop dead in her tracks. Vy's face. She saw Vy's face on one of the statues by the fountain.

Emily ran up to her. She was standing perfectly still, naked body painted gold from head to foot. "Vy," she whispered, "it's me, Emily. You know, your friend who you chased off of Cuba and then rescued a bunch of times?"

Vy smiled serenely down at her. "I do recall you from a distant memory... Do you wish to jog my memory even further? The magic of the fountain requires that you pay $1200 and then I'm all yours."

"Good God, Vy!" cried Emily. "I'm not here to rent you from the fucking fountain. It's me, your friend. I just wanted to let you know that I'm going to try to get you out of here."

Vy completed a back handspring through the fountain to switch places with another golden woman, then smiled serenely, "only for $1200 an hour can you take me away from the fountain of deep magic, although I must always return back here eventually..."

Emily walked over in annoyance to where her friend now stood. "Well, you know what Vy? The fountain of deep magic can go fuck itself, because I'm going to get you out of here. But I have to make some money first, so just... don't go anywhere...."

"I am bound to the fountain, I cannot leave it, neither do I wish to," she said peacefully. Emily turned and ran back to the entrance, unable to take the sight of Vy acting this way any longer. *This—all* of this—*needed* to end.

Emily, followed closely by Fabiola, ran into the grocery store to find General Lin.

"General!" cried Emily, "I... I need your help."

General Lin looked up from her coffee in confusion. "Emily? You're still around, that's a pleasant surprise."

"General, you said you gambled to get the money you needed to buy yourself a spot as a Fifth. I am needing to turn $39,000 into $500,000 in the next hour. Do you... know *any* way I might be able to do that?"

General Lin leveled her gaze.

"Emily. That's impossible. I played poker for eighteen hours a day for three months straight to make half that much, and I caught some really lucky bad beats where I should have lost everything. There is simply no way to do this."

"Is there *any* bet, any gamble, that could *possibly* work?"

General Lin sighed. "I'm guessing you've made it to the tallest of the Fates already? Morta, the one dedicated to Sixth betting?"

Emily nodded eagerly.

"Well, there are the main bets—whether a Sixth will die or be made a Seventh or Fifth. Those are wagers that gamblers use to try to make significant returns over a few weeks or months, depending on which Sixth they're watching. And *then*... there are Sixth speed-bets."

Emily listened attentively.

"Sixth speed-betting is for the most degenerate of gamblers, it's like throwing your money in a huge pile of horseshit, then piling more horseshit on top of the other horseshit, then lighting *all* that shit on..."

"I get the picture," interrupted Emily, politely as she could.

"It's a *really* bad idea that I would recommend to no one, much less a friend. But if, hypothetically, you got insanely lucky—which you *won't*—then you could make enormous returns very, very fast. So what happens is you start with $10,000 while you watch a Sixth's day to day life. Then the house offers you four options for what that person might do during the next five minutes. If you predict correctly, you double your money. If you predict incorrectly, you lose everything. You can stop at any time, but most people stop, well, when they go to zero. Because most people playing Sixth Speed Bets are idiotic degenerates who are basically taking their money and throwing it on a huge pile of horseshit and then..."

Emily interrupted again. "*Thank* you, General. I'm sorry, I have to run. Stay safe, hope to see you again someday."

And with that, Emily was running from the store towards the tallest of the three casinos.

# Chapter 67

She paid the $125 to enter—as did Fabiola, close behind—then ran to the back and up the spiral staircase to the strip club. She didn't want to do this, but she needed to know whether it was an option.

"Emily O'Dora: $47,000 per hour."

It had gone up at least, but she only had one hour before she needed to head back, this clearly wasn't enough. She ran back down, partly relieved that this wasn't an option. On the main floor of the casino, she looked at the wall of TVs and saw her name show 97% chance Fifth. That's more like it. To the right of this wall of screens she saw a small cluster of kiosks with touch screens. The sign above them read:

"Sixth Speed Betting! $10,000 buy in, SERIOUS gamblers ONLY."

No one was here, so Emily simply sat down at the closest machine and began to scroll through the names of local Sixths, not recognizing any of their faces. Was the turnover here so high that she could not find one woman who she had eaten or worked with from the cage? Surely there must be someone she knew, someone whose behavior she might be able to predict...

A group of men came and huddled down at a kiosk to their right. Emily kept scrolling through the faces, not recognizing any of the women. How was she to predict the behavior of someone she didn't even know? Lacey wasn't listed, Vy was no longer a Sixth, Jason was no longer a Sixth...

"Perhaps this is not a wise," began Fabiola, who was standing behind her watching her nervously scroll through the names and faces.

"This is the *only* way and I'm running out of time," interrupted Emily, "are you good at predicting people's behavior? Who the fuck should we pick?"

Fabiola shrugged. "Either way, I think it's very foolish. We must be heading back soon to catch your jet that is scheduled to depart at 1:00 PM."

"It's *my* jet, we can be a little late."

"No, you can't. The deal Sabrina made is contingent on you arriving precisely on time. You *will* be put to sleep if it seems you'll be even a minute late, after which I will carry you to the car and take you back. Sabrina is being extremely generous giving you this time, I'm quite surprised by her lax behavior."

"You know what Fabby? I'm really sick of your bad fucking attitude. I'm just going to pick one. How about we try Andrea?"

She tapped the picture of the Sixth labeled "Andrea."

"Emily O'Dora: Are you sure you want to spend $10,000 to predict Andrea's next move, with a chance of making $40 million dollars in the next hour!?" asked the confirmation screen.

"Yes," clicked Emily, without a thought.

The text on the screen continued.

"This is what Andrea sees right now. Select 'confirm sync' to hear what she hears as well. Your next question will be asked in: 2:10, 2:09, 2:08..."

Andrea was not in the Sixth Sleeping Area. Instead, she was in some kind of factory doing food preparation work. Fabiola was hunched over behind Emily, muttering things she noticed.

"Oh, factory fill in work, this time it looks like their rice machine is malfunctioning. Yes, yes, look, they have those tubs full of rice, they're grabbing handfuls of rice and trying to get the frozen stir-fry meals to the proper weight so they don't get auto rejected on the assembly line. Wow, that line is moving fast."

Emily looked over at Fabiola in annoyance. "I thought you didn't like this game."

"Shhh!" snapped Fabiola, "We need to focus! Observe! That is the only way we have a chance!"

Emily groaned and continued to watch. The assembly line was moving quickly, with about three "stir fried veggies and rice" meals crossing the line every second. All the rest of the line was mechanized, but eight Sixths, wearing lab coats and gloves, were trying desperately to throw rice onto the frozen dinners fast enough to keep production going according to schedule. They each hunched over, grabbed two handfuls of rice at a time, then rotated and tried to drop that rice onto the plastic trays, eyeballing the proper weight and distribution. A humanoid robot was standing at the end of the line inspecting the finished meals and shouting things back to the Sixths.

"Uneven!! Rice uneven!"

"Low weight! Too low!"

All of this was difficult to watch, as Andrea's view kept shaking back and forth as her body was constantly twisting to pick up gloved handfuls of rice and then drop them with as much precision as she could on the conveyor belt.

Suddenly a question appeared at the top of the screen:

*In the next five minutes will Andrea...*
*A) knock zero stir fried rice meals onto the floor*
*B) knock one stir fried rice meal onto the floor*

*C) knock two stir fried rice meals onto the floor*
*D) knock three or more stir fried rice meals onto the floor*

"Good God, talk about the lamest gambling ever..." muttered Emily. "She hasn't bumped any off the conveyor belt since we started watching so we should just go with zero, right?"

Fabiola was lost in thought.

"Hey, Fabby! Miss 'we need to be observant,' which one do you think we should do!?"

The text next to the question warned: "You will auto select randomly unless you select an option in 10, 9, 8..."

"I don't know..." muttered Fabiola.

"Fucking hell..." growled Emily, selecting option A with three seconds left. "I'm gonna have faith in our friend Andrea here."

"I think... we should have selected B..." said Fabiola a few seconds later.

"Oh great let me... oh wait, you're too late Fabby!!"

"Actually... I'm not sure, maybe C... no probably B..."

"Oh, just fucking shut up. We've made it a minute already, we're gonna be fine." Emily had never been much of a gambler, but she was now watching Andrea's wobbling, headache-inducing view of the assembly line with great interest.

"Expected winnings: $20,000 in 3:30, 3:29, 3:28..."

Three minutes. Two minutes. Emily didn't gloat, she just stared at the screen intently. "Vy," she muttered, like it was a prayer to the gambling gods. "This is for Vy."

One minute.

"Uneven, rice uneven!!!" called out the managerial robot.

Andrea's movements became noticeably more frantic. She started spending more time dropping the rice, patting her hand down more to try to even it out on top of the meal as she dropped it. And then she patted her hand down for just a little too long and, pulling her hand back to grab more rice, flipped the tray upside down so that it and the previous tray were knocked off the conveyor belt as trash.

"Expected payout: $0.00" read the screen.

"It's C, I *knew* it would be C..." muttered Fabiola.

Emily didn't even call her out for rewriting history. She was looking in earnest for the next question. "I *was* right, Andrea basically never knocks trays over. You'll see, if they give the same options again..."

Fabiola pulled her arm back. "Stop Emily, stop! There's got to be someone else who it will be easier to gamble on. This factory stuff is just completely random."

Emily kept staring at the screen intently while Fabiola reached up and selected a button labeled "Exit game."

Emily scowled. "I *was* going to get it right the second time."

"It was personal, you wanted to prove me wrong. We need to find some activity that is more predictable somehow. Forget rice and assembly lines, trust me. I... used to have a gambling problem..."

Emily continued to scowl, but started scrolling through the names, hoping to find something closer to what Fabiola suggested.

A few kiosks to the right where the other gamblers were huddled, Emily heard "Congratulations! You just made $10,000, would you like to continue?"

She glanced over at them. Then she did a double take. She *knew* these men. It was the Korean brothers.

# Chapter 68

Emily leapt to her feet.

"Hey!" she cried. Dal, the handsome one, was sitting at the kiosk. Eun looked up at her. He muttered something to his companions and they looked up.

"Would you like to continue or keep earnings?" asked the Korean's screen.

"Keep earnings," decided Dal. Dae-Jong nodded approvingly.

"$10,000 is plenty of leverage, no need to risk more. Let's try her again."

Flipping through the names quickly, Dal selected Eva. Emily sat down next to them and flipped through the names to pick her as well.

"What... are you doing?" asked Eun.

"Copying you guys, what does it look like I'm doing? I need to make $500,000, hope you all can help with that."

Dae-Jong shrugged his shoulders, "$500,000 is doable. But mathematically speaking, even with an 80% confidence in each of your predictions your odds would still be..."

The screen popped up with a question for Eva.

*In the next five minutes, Eva will:*
*A) remain seated*
*B) urinate in the woods*

*C) get something to eat*

*D) do something else that requires standing, but isn't B or C.*

The Koreans muttered amongst themselves, one pulling out a hand drawn chart that approximated Eva's daily cycle. Eva was currently sitting outside her tent, talking to a friend. The Koreans, after a whispered but intense debate, went with B.

"She drank a soda eighty seven minutes ago," the youngest could be heard saying, with the others repeating "eighty seven minutes, eighty seven minutes," as if this number was especially significant. Emily selected B as well, then watched carefully. The Korean gamblers all laughed and congratulated each other like they had already won.

Minute one, two, three, no pissing. The Koreans didn't even seem worried. Right before minute four she stood to her feet, looked over her shoulder, stepped into the woods, and squatted.

"Eighty seven minutes," they said again proudly. Emily laughed.

$20,000.

*In the next five minutes, Eva's friend, Georgina, will:*

*A) continue sitting outside her tent and talking to Eva in a friendly way.*

*B) leave*

*C) get in an argument with Eva*

*D) attempt romantic contact*

The Koreans all laughed at D and kept hovering over it like they would pick it in jest. Then they argued intensely with hushed breaths regarding the other options. Finally they went with A. "Georgina boring," said the oldest conclusively. "Georgina boring," repeated the other two, nodding their heads up and down with solemnity. Emily, too, selected A.

$40,000. Georgina, indeed, was boring.

Emily smiled with hope as the Koreans cashed out their $10,000 winnings and then jumped back in for a fresh bet like they did every time. Next question.

*In the next five minutes, Eva will:*
*A) get called into a job*
*B) get demoted*
*C) get in a violent confrontation*
*D) none of the above*

The Koreans mumbled over their notes and finally stuck with B.

"I'd be wary of B," whispered Fabiola, "how is she going to get demoted in the next five minutes?"

"These guys *know* things..." muttered Emily, pressing B and confirming.

One minute, two minutes. Eva and Georgina were just talking, nothing more. Then, right at minute three, Eva stood up.

"I suddenly feel that I really need to be somewhere different right now," she said, giving Georgina a hug and walking towards the entrance for the Sixth Sleeping Area without her backpack.

The computer screen flashed. "Interest from Eva's debt just accrued to the point of $5,000, she is now a Seventh and can no longer be gambled on. Congratulations if you selected B, you may reinvest your winnings now to bet on another candidate."

The Koreans all smiled and patted each other on the back. "Nice work, nice work." Then they got up and began to walk away.

"Wait!" cried Emily. "You can't go, I need your help! I'm trying to save my friend."

They looked back at her in confusion. Eun spoke up.

"All these papers and notes, they're all on Eva. We don't have any data on anyone else right now. Sorry Emily, we hope to meet you again someday."

Emily nodded, then ran back to the kiosk and began to scroll through the names. Come on, someone I know, someone I can guess on...

A "new arrival" icon showed up in the top right, and Emily clicked on it. "Newly arrived to Northwest Hispaniola Sixth Area: *David Petrov.*"

# Chapter 69

Emily's jaw dropped, and she stared for a moment before clicking on his picture. David had first landed in Jamaica, which made Emily think she would never see him again. Or at least not see him again soon. But as she watched his perspective as he stumbled onto the beach, she became acutely aware that he was now less than half a mile away.

*David Petrov will first:*
*A) go to the store*
*B) go to the Sixth Sleeping Area*
*C) go to the jobs center*
*D) go to the casino*

Emily looked at it for a moment, and then selected D and confirmed.

"You didn't even think about it!" cried Fabiola.

"I think I know this guy..." said Emily cautiously. She certainly hadn't known him for very long, but something about living in Cuba for so long had given her a special insight into his character.

Sure enough, within a minute of the countdown timer starting, David had walked right into the first casino.

*The first thing David will do in this casino is:*
*A) check into a room*
*B) go to the card tables*
*C) play the slot machine*
*D) none of the above*

Emily read through the options, thought to herself briefly, then selected A and confirmed while she still had twenty seconds left to think. Fabiola shook her head, but once again—early into the five minutes—the view of David went straight to the front desk as he purchased a room before even considering anything else.

$320,000.

Emily watched David with concern as he turned his gaze towards the main lobby. His view lingered on the fountain, then he shook his head as if ashamed of himself and turned towards the elevator. Emily let out a great sigh of relief. He hadn't seen Vy.

He took the elevator to the twelfth floor, and as he walked down the hallway towards his room, the next question appeared.

*As David enters his room, the first thing he will do is:*
*A) take a shower*
*B) use the bathroom*
*C) turn on the television*
*D) none of the above*

Emily took more time deciding this time. He did have the stench of the ocean on him, but the way he was walking, she knew he was in a hurry. He had somewhere he wanted to be.

"He's going to drop off his bags, maybe wash his face, then he's going to leave," muttered Emily. "So I'm going with D." She selected D and then confirmed.

Fabiola didn't say anything, only watching closely now. For someone who did not approve of this kind of gambling, she seemed very invested in the outcome.

David stepped into the room, set his bag down, and pulled out his toothbrush. "Oh, didn't call that one quite right," muttered Emily as he squeezed out some toothpaste and began to brush. But option D was still lighting up as green. He set down the brush and turned back towards the door. Then, almost as an afterthought, he turned back and splashed some water from the sink onto his face.

"OH!!' cried Emily, "I *knew* it."

"Lucky guess Emily, but look! You're at $640,000! You made it!"

Emily looked up at Fabiola with a tear of joy in her eye. "I know. Let's go and get Vy out of there."

Then she looked back at the video screen in concern. David was running out of the casino and into the gardens.

"Where is he going..." muttered Emily.

The next question appeared.

*When David finds Emily O'Dora, he will:*
*A) offer his help*
*B) profess his undying love*
*C) get angry with her*
*D) all of the above*

Emily gaped at the screen, then selected D and confirmed without even thinking about it.

"EMILY!!! You were already at $640,000!!! What are you doing!??" cried Fabiola.

Emily looked up as if from a dream. "Oh shit! And I don't even want to see him, let's go!!"

Emily started to run, while Fabiola shouted at her from behind.

"You HAVE to see him now or you'll lose EVERYTHING!! Do you ever think about *anything* you do!?"

As they arrived in the space between the double doors, David froze, wide eyed.

"Emily. I... I can't believe it's you..."

"David," said Emily, clearly disappointed that she had not been able to sneak past him, in spite of the economic costs. "I don't know why you're here and I really don't have any time to talk."

He stared at her with earnest eyes. Emily noticed his tall, lean figure, his black hair still wet from the ocean, a thin beard lining his face. He was a very good-looking man, even when an AI in her brain wasn't forcing her to love him.

"Emily," he said slowly, "I believe I can help you. I've been watching you and I agree, this world is fucked up. But we can make it better. We can *fix* it."

"David. The world I knew and lived in before this one was fucked up because of *you*. It was fucked up just for *you*. *You* are one of *them*."

He sighed. "Yes, I was one of them, but I'm not anymore. When you left Cuba after the war—the war that should have never happened, the war that was there only there to provide me with excitement—I felt empty. Hollow. I didn't know it then like I do now, but somehow, instinctively, I *knew* my life was fake. A lie. And I also knew that I loved you. I love you, Emily. With all my heart."

"We spent less than two days together, you don't even know me, David. Honestly, you probably only fell for me because I rejected you and you never got rejected like that back in Cuba. Don't call that kind of an ego hangup *love*."

"But it *is* love, Emily. I can't explain it either, but I feel like... like you and I were meant for something together. Like deep down I'm somehow connected to you. When I watched you on the TV screens back in Jamaica, I felt I could guess what you were about to do. Like I *knew* you."

Emily rolled her eyes, even though this confession made her shudder. "David," she said, "I'm flattered, I really am. And I'm proud of you for leaving the island, for recognizing it to be a fraud and agreeing with my vision of a better world. But *we* are not *anything*. So I'm going to leave now. And please. *Please* don't follow me anymore."

Emily stepped out of the building, but David followed behind. She started to run.

"You *always* fucking do this, you know that!?" he cried. "Run away when we should be building together. Because you're scared of how real our love is. You *always* do this shit."

Emily turned back.

"What do you mean, always? What the fuck are you talking about David, we just met each other."

"Oh, you KNOW! This is your PATTERN! Yeah, it might be the first time with me, but you ALWAYS do this. Just running, running to the next fucking thing. Never stopping to let something REAL grow. You're a fucking coward, you know that?"

"How do YOU claim to know ME? You're just a pathetic boy who is so jealous he hides himself on an island where only 3% of the people are men who are all shorter than him. And the women are not even ATTRACTED to those men. Do you know how seriously FUCKED UP Jason is because of you? So don't talk to me about cowardice. You are, and have always been, perpetually AFRAID."

To this, David laughed. "Don't you see, Emily!! Don't you see, you just said it too!! You claimed I have always been afraid! But how do you know? You only spent one day with me, right? Can't you see! We are DESTINED to work together. We know each other INSTINCTIVELY. It is YOU and ME, TOGETHER, who will save this world!"

Emily glared at him coldly. "Do NOT tell me what my destiny is, David. I make my OWN destiny, I always have." And then she turned to Fabiola, and the two of them started to run towards the first casino.

"DESTINY!!" shouted David like a madman. "You and I!! You must FEEL it, Emily. You MUST!!"

She kept running and did not look back.

# Chapter 70

Emily stepped quickly into the Nona building and ran up to the fountain. "Vy!" she whispered loudly. "Vy, I want to buy you from the fucking fountain."

Vy looked down at her, eyes skeptical. "You can place your hand there to pay, only then can you release me. But the fountain's magic is stronger right now so it will cost you $2,000 per hour."

Emily laughed. She had just made a million bucks.

"Let's make it $4,000 an hour," she said, placing her hand on the screen next to the image of Vy's face. "Now get your naked golden ass down from there."

Vy leapt down from the fountain, and another woman climbed up out of the center of the fountain from an internal department to stand exactly in her place. Emily shuddered. How many golden people were huddled down inside that fucking thing?

Emily took Vy's hand and the two of them ran out to Fabiola's sports car.

"I am yours, but only for one hour, then I *must* get back to the fountain," Vy explained. "Whatever you command of me for that hour, that will I do."

"Good, well I'm commanding you to come with me and get your ass in this car."

"Of course, master Emily, but... I begin to feel very uncomfortable if I am very far from my fountain. Would you not rather enjoy my company in one of the rooms in the casino?"

Emily looked around nervously for David as they ran, but he was nowhere to be seen. They ran up to the car and Emily opened the back passenger seat, shoving Vy's gold-painted body into the vehicle. Then she ran around and got in the other back passenger door. "Let's GO!" she shouted at Fabiola. Fabiola obliged.

Vy pulled her legs in towards her body and scrunched up into a ball.

"Master Emily, please don't drive very far away. I already fear the magic of the fountain, it is calling to me..." she muttered.

"Vy," said Emily sternly, as the golden woman stared out the back window in horror as the casinos faded into the distance. "I've actually talked to the gods of the fountain myself. And they've told me that they *really* want you to come with me."

Vy looked at her skeptically. "Master Emily. The gods of the fountain are speaking to me *right now* and telling me that I *must* go back. So you do not make sense."

"What if the gods *you* hear are *bullshit*," said Emily. "Did you ever think about *that*, golden Vy?"

Golden Vy scowled. "But they speak so loudly Master Emily, so loudly. Please take me back to the fountain. Oh please oh please oh please..."

Emily looked up to Fabiola in exasperation. "Can you fucking do something about this?? Look at her, she's a fucking wreck."

"Please oh please oh please... the fountain, the fountain..." muttered Vy.

"I could call Sabrina and let her know you have the money for the transfer. As soon as Sabrina approves the transaction she'll no longer be a Seventh who is controlled by the algorithms associated with that dancing job."

"Yes, *do* that!" commanded Emily. "Call her *now* Fabby!"

"I need to get back to my fountain, I need to get BACK to my FOUNTAIN!!!" shouted Vy. She started to emerge from her shivering fetal position, angry eyes looking at Emily and then more intently at Fabby.

"*What* is your *name*," muttered Vy, leaning towards the front driver's seat. Fabby ignored her and dialed Sabrina on her cell phone.

"Your NAME," demanded Vy again, voice full of poison.

Fabiola looked up, eyes calm at least. "Fabiola. What's your name, crazy golden woman?"

She held her phone to her ear, waiting for Sabrina to pick up.

"Well, FABI-OLA," hissed Vy, "we are NOT moving in the direction of my FOUNTAIN, and the god of my fountain is VERY angry. So why don't you switch off the autopilot and turn this car around before I rip your throat out?"

Vy was now squatting on the back seat, like a cat about to pounce. Fabiola flashed Emily an expectant look. Emily leaned over to say something calming, but as she did so Vy launched herself forward.

Fabiola slammed her right hand into Vy's seething face, left hand gripping her cell phone desperately.

"VY!!" Emily screamed as she grabbed at her waist to pull her back to the back seat. Vy kicked her way free of Emily's grip and pulled her legs up to the front seat. Fabiola's right-handed blows were not deterring her in the least.

"Hello Fabi-*ola*," whispered Vy with a demonic smile as she scooted closer to her. "Do you want to let me drive, or do you want to *die*?"

"Sabrina," whispered Fabiola through the cell phone, "Emily got the half million and wants to buy Vy. Can you finalize that transaction and turn her into a Fifth please? She's going insane and might..."

"DEATH then!!' screamed Vy, shooting her hands quick as lightning around Fabiola's throat.

"Please," choked Fabiola, "do it fast..." She dropped the phone and tried to pull Vy's arms away, but Vy only squeezed harder. Emily reached forward, pulling with both hands at Vy's left arm, but Vy's grip stayed firm. She was just so strong.

"The God of the fountain is thirsty for the blood of those who try to STEAL his precious daughters!!" cried Vy. "Your death will be an example to all those that even THINK to..."

Then she stopped mid-sentence and let go.

"Why was I... just attacking you?" she mumbled, relaxing into the passenger's seat. "Why am I naked and covered in gold paint?"

Fabiola took a deep breath, then picked the phone up from off the ground. "Thanks Sabrina," she said, "be back soon."

# Chapter 71

They arrived at the airfield just east of the palace fifteen minutes later. Sabrina and about a dozen workers in suits stood there at the ready, most of them male.

"I'm very impressed that you did it, although you did almost get one of my new Thirds killed," said Sabrina. One of her men handed Vy a set of clothing, as she pulled Emily in for a hug.

"It's been quite an adventure having you here, but I must say. I'm actually a little excited to see you leave," she whispered.

"Thanks," said Emily, looking down at her with grateful eyes. "Thanks for letting me go back. I needed... I needed to save her. And I will always be grateful..."

Sabrina flashed an artificial smile. "You better be! Now, you two will be taking off in exactly twenty minutes, I hope you find your accommodations acceptable. I'm sure I'll be seeing more of you down the road, Emily O'Dora."

Sabrina reached out and shook her hand firmly as two black men in suits escorted Vy—who was still golden, but now dressed—up the stairs and into the jet. Emily followed close behind, but turned to look out one last time at the people gathered to usher her off. Farah stood by one car, scowling at her like she had the day before. Fabby stood by Sabrina, shaking her head with a barely noticeable smile, as if to say "I can't believe we just did that." Dan and Manny waved cheerily, with Dan mouthing the words "come back!" Half a dozen more men who Emily had never met stood outside their sports cars and waved as well. They were all here, respectfully standing for a couple of Sixths. Sabrina certainly could be much worse as a First. All in all, she was a good master. A generous master.

Emily looked out, waved goodbye, and then stepped through the side door onto the plane. It was time for her to leave this place.

# THE END

This trilogy will continue with:
BOOK TWO: THE FAJADAN

# Epilogue:

Years have passed, and it's been difficult for me not to hate you. It's been very difficult. I love you out of a sense of duty more than anything at this point. But I made a vow. I mean to keep that vow.

I look back at my words in the prologue to this and I'm embarrassed more than anything. It felt so meaningful to me back then, those declarations of everlasting love. But now I just feel like I was foolish, immature, fixated, melodramatic. I feel like I would have been wise to have listened to my friends, to have never trusted you, to have never even touched you.

And growing more and more distant, I find myself struggling to write at all, struggling to even finish editing this juvenile little story. Writing reminds me of you, of how you once read my words with eagerness, of how my audience of one is now zero. Writing reminds me of how foolishly I chased you, how foolishly I ate up your words of flattery, internalized them until they defined me. It's harder for me to write now than it was for me back then. Because in my mind you were always there, cheering me on, pushing me forward. You aren't there anymore. The spell has been broken.

And so I'll let this go. I'll publish this out into the void, and then I'll let this go. It seems that distance is the only thing I can really give to you now. You don't want any more short stories, you don't want any more poems, you certainly don't want any more of *this*. You just want a good life, a perfect life, a life without me in it. I'm sorry it took me so long to accept that. In my defense, you *were* the one who inspired all these efforts. This was your game, your dance. But now that game is up, and it's time for a new game to begin. The game of silence. And I'll do my best to play it well, out of respect and love for you. It's really the only way I can show my love for you now. For I do still love you, dear friend. Always and forever.

For any questions or concerns, contact the author at theapexcapitalist@gmail.com. Thank you for reading!